DEATH'S NEW PET

LOVE AFTER
LIFE SERIES.

BLURB

What do you get when you mix a revenge-driven mortal with an evil God of Death and an opportunity of a lifetime? An erotic fantasy novel filled with angst and trigger warnings.

Death:

I want her dead.

Everything within me howls to destroy that pretty little mortal so that I can claim her deliciously tarnished soul. When I'm done with her, she will be writhing underneath me, sinning like a bad little mortal should.

But no matter how much I long to kill her now, I must wait until she completes the Death Trials my father, The Devil, challenged her to win. Only then will she claim the title of 'Deaths New Pet', and I become free to do whatever the hell I want with her. And trust me, I plan on ruining my little mortal until she realises the true meaning of hate.

Perhaps that will be the day when the evil God of Death finally cracks a smile.

DEDICATION

To all you horny sluts that get
off to deranged & obsessive
dark romance stories.

Welcome to: *The 'Love after Life' series.*

This novel is about an evil God
repeatedly fucking a helpless mortal.

Enjoy!

TRIGGER WARNINGS

This is an **incredibly dark novel** with a main focus on the blurred line of consent. The female main character is seriously abused by her husband and his brother. There are chapters which discuss this in some detail. In the final chapters, there are scenes of heavy torture and disturbing smut.

Throughout the novel, there are many dark romance scenes with these tropes:

- Orgasm denial & forced orgasm
- Power play
- Evil God taking advantage of helpless mortal
- Praise & degradation
- Spanking & pain play
- Breath play
- Primal play & hunting
- Blood play
- Weapon play
- Necrophilia play
- Restraints
- Clear consent
- Heavy BDSM
- Anal play
- Consensual-Non-consensual (CNC) scenes

If any of these scenes seriously disturb you, please do **NOT** read the book. This novel is designed to push the boundaries of dark romance. It is intended to be disturbing but enjoyable.

Still here? Fantastic!

CONTENTS

GLOSSARY & KEY CHARACTERS

Original Beings: Immortal, indestructible Beings that have existed since the beginning of time. The Original family are The Devil, Longing, Death, Pain, Rage, Misery, Power and a couple more (but are not mentioned in this novel).

Hellish Beings: Immortal Beings that live in Hell.

Beta beings: Immortal Beings that were born *after* the original beings.

Realms of Hell: Different places in Hell, separated by a variety of punishments.

Temporary death: A death that lasts only temporarily. Length lasts depending on the punishment of their crime. Only Death can put someone into a temporary death.

Death: The God of dying and removing life from all Beings.

Pain: The Goddess of pain and suffering. (Death's ex-wife).

Longing: The Goddess of longing and desire. (Death's mum, The Devil's wife).

The Devil: Satan, the man who rules over all of Hell. (Death's dad, Longing's husband).

Misery: The Goddess of misery and depression. (Death's sister).

Rage: The God of rage and anger. (Death's brother).

Scarlet Gownes: Female main character (Prey Ten).

Maximo Gownes: Scarlet's evil, abusive husband.

Leonardo Gownes: Maximo's twin brother.

CONTESTANTS IN THE DEATH TRIALS

Prey One:

Crime: Discrimination & assault

Appearance: White man in his forties, bald-headed, covered in tattoos and piercings, large biceps but look artificially made.

Prey Two:

Crime: Murdered six babies whilst working as a nurse.

Appearance: A timid, plump lady in her thirties with beady little eyes and scared of everything.

Prey Three: *(Important)*

Crime: Arson & Pyromania

Appearance: A skinny man in his twenties with a buzz cut. He has severe burns and scar marks on his body from where he died in a house fire which killed many others.

Prey Four:

Crime: Aggravated assault

Appearance: Large, handsome black man with anger issues.

Prey Five:

Crime: Paedophile

Appearance: Skinny thirty-year-old man with a pop belly and a disgusting crooked smile.

Prey Six:

Crime: Murder

Appearance: Teenage girl who killed her parents with her boyfriend after she was convinced to murder. All because they disagreed with her relationship with Prey Seven.

Prey Seven:

Crime: murder and grooming and paedophile

Appearance: A stocky man in his late twenties, groomed Prey Six and convinced her to murder her parents.

Prey Eight:

Crime: A nun that enabled her priest to engage in inappropriate behaviour with minors.

Appearance: In her late fifties, fairly short and round with wrinkly skin and grey hair.

Prey Nine:

Crime: school shooter

Appearance: Teenage man with spots and wonky teeth, very uncertain in himself.

Prey Ten: *(Important)*

Scarlet. Female main character.

CHAPTER ONE

Six months ago.

Y ou need to escape, Scarlet. Escape before the beast gets his claws on you again!

Drenched in dried blood and a thick layer of sweat, my shivering body freezes as I strain to listen for any movement around me. It's a futile task; the pounding of my erratic heartbeat makes it near impossible to listen out for any potential footsteps belonging to the predators I'm running from.

Unwittingly, I resort back to sight and stick my head out from behind the tree trunk, fully expecting a bullet with my name on it to burst through the bushes. I wait for it to send my body soaring backwards to join the rest of the souls murdered on this plot of land. Thankfully, nothing attacks me... *yet.*

Turning white, my knuckles strain as I grip the rough tree bark which crumbles in my fingers. Dust and mud stain under my nails and a sharp object cuts me until I feel the blood seep from the skin. The sensation is so much stickier than what I've read about in the library books but now isn't the time for marvelling at my new discovery, I must keep pushing.

Whilst desperately trying to catch my breath, I scan the surroundings like my life depends on it— *because it fucking does.* Lifeless trees and wilted flowers thrash around in the howling storm that's ripping apart this small town.

Decaying leaves join the dancefloor of misery and the brown stems of grass leap side to side as if dancing to the haunting song of the wind's agonising howls. Everything is either dead or dying. Nothing can flourish in a place where *he* reigns.

Fuck. The storm wasn't supposed to hit us so soon and now I'm caught up in it.

Protectively, I wrap my arms around my shivering body, but it is a useless, thin and skimpy nightdress; it stands very little chance against the storm's attack. My eyes feel painted, as though they've been iced over. I can't remember the last time I blinked. If only the snot dribbling below my nose could be used as a lubricant to wet my achy eyes I might get out of here alive. I can't even cry to bring my tense body some relief.

But is it because of the arctic weather, or because my husband beat it out of me?

My only saving grace is that my wicked, tormented husband has not realised that I'm gone. *This*, I know for sure. If he had, there would be hounds at my heels, flashlights burning into the back of my head, and bullets piercing through my skin. He's probably drunkenly slumped in his office chair, whisky in his rough left hand and a cigar decaying between his lips. He's probably grinning as he conjures up evil thoughts in that disgusting mind of his. Or perhaps he's already stumbling up the stairs, heavily intoxicated, but focused on getting his dirty fucking hands on my should-be-unconscious body.

Not today, Maximo. Not today and not ever again.

A sick part of me wishes I could see the look on his face when it sinks in. *His most valuable property vanished from the fortified prison walls.* I long to watch his horror when he realises that twenty-two years of beating, threatening, and torture will not defy nature. I was built to survive. To fight. To win.

And all it took was one quick slip of the wrist to pop the drug meant for my drink in his unsuspecting guard's tea, for his entire fantasy to come crashing down. My fantasy is short-lived as another awful gale of wind has me losing my balance, and I stumble forward, the wind behind me like a shove in the right direction.

I push further through the treeline until a slight glisten of the metal gates, two hundred metres from me, shines through like a beacon in the light.

Yes, there it is!

It's exactly how it's been described to me — well, not *to me*. More like just in my presence when they thought that I was unconscious, bitching about how long the walk was from the parking to the house gates. It doesn't take a genius to look out of the window and guess the rough location of the road in comparison to the house, even if I have never been allowed to step foot in this forest.

I misjudge how far the gate is through the blur of torrential rain which now pours down on me, and suddenly, I feel ten times heavier as though there are weights tied to my ankles. Not only that but my stomach shrieks in hunger and the ache in my bones begs me to stop pushing so hard. Running off zero sleep and no food for the last two days is really taking a toll on my strength. Fatigue cackles as it works against me, but I don't stop. I *can't* stop.

Better fatigue kills me than my husband.

Finally, my body falls limply against the gate as my breathless pants tear through my body. The sharp talons on a particular design pattern on the gate snags my skin. The sharp pain wakes my foggy mind. An involuntary sob tears past my lips as the blood stains my skin. The agony forces a new stream of adrenaline through me, and it gives me the energy to snatch at the gate lock. Desperately, I try every four-digit code I can think of.

My husband's birthday. My birthday. Our wedding date.

Nothing works and my numb fingers freeze in their clenched position.

Fuck sake, Scarlet, why didn't you plan for a fucking code?

Desperately, my head snaps backwards as I stare up at the two-metre-long fence with spikes and barbed wire circling the top.

There is no fucking way I can climb this.

And the storm frustratingly decimates everything except the gate.

I'm next. The plaguing self-doubt harasses me. *Fuck, I should have waited a week!*

Reason fights back. *No! I wouldn't have survived another week...*

Horrified by the reality of the situation, I grab at the metal bars to see if I can get any friction. Dying through impalement or electrocution would still be kinder than what that monster would do if he found me out here. But my grip is futile as the rain makes it impossible to grab.

A horrifying howl throws fear through me like no other. *I know those snarls.* The bastard has set the wolves on me, and those beasts take no pity on anyone! They've torn more people apart than I've had meals.

Using every inch of energy left, I force myself alongside the fence, desperately searching for a weakness in the defence. The rain slashes at my body like iced knives in the winter and only now do the tears pour down my face. More howling swarms but I'm unsure whether it's from the wind, or the bloodthirsty monsters hunting me down.

The world is swallowed by despair as my bare feet sink into the disgustingly thick mud. It causes a mighty squelch and offers the sick torment of my position away. Not only is it the most uncomfortable sensation between my naked toes, but it *fucking stinks*. I feel as though the fumes intoxicate me and muddy my thoughts. My knee threatens to give way as I leap across a particularly wet sloshy patch of God-knows-what.

In the distance, I finally hear human voices. The wind disguises their words, but it's at this moment I know I'm fucking done for. They shriek at the dogs to find me. To tear me apart. To make me regret ever leaving the home.

Bang!

Suddenly, I fly through the air as my foot catches on a loose tree root hidden in the slosh. I slam against the ground ungracefully. Instant agony shoots through me and I muffle my scream into my arm. My ankle throbs and the swelling is almost instant.

Fuck!

I refuse to look at it, knowing that it's not going to be pretty and will only slow me down. Instead, I use my arms to desperately scoop at the wet ground. I resort to my last choice. *Digging my way out of this Hell hole!*

The process gets quicker and more frantic, and frustratingly clumsier, as the growls roar closer. As though mourning my pending death, the wind shrieks agonisingly, and the puddles of water threaten to drown my face. I struggle to stay above the slosh.

The hole under the fence is tight but I don't have any other choice. I frantically wriggle around in the mud to slip under the fence. However, as I do so, a metal spike slashes me down the spine, catching at my lower back. Trying to kick myself forward, I come to an immediate impasse. Between the weapon pressed against my back and my swollen ankle refusing to cooperate with my escape, I am unable to do much except propel my arms desperately around. The mud gives away far too easily, and I can't get a grip. My fingertips are so fucking close to the tarmacked road and yet so far away.

If I could just grab—

In the distance, the light from a car beam almost blinds me. With a shriek of despair, I try to wave down the car. It feels futile because it's pitch black out and they are hurtling down with no intention of stopping. They'll be past me in a blink of an eye.

Again, I kick on my painful ankle, and it slightly pushes me forward until the fence catches on my ass. I slide my hands under my body and desperately dig to give myself more room, but the rainwater fills up the gap, making it tough to move the muddied clay-like substance. For a moment, I consider throwing my face into the puddle in front of me and praying that drowning kills me before the dogs do. However, looking back was a mistake and I can now see the pack of dogs with their beady evil eyes locked on me.

Terrified, I squeal like a squeaky toy. The only word I can fathom is *"Fuck!"* and it leaves my lips as I scramble as hard as I can.

Suddenly, I feel the weight of one of the beasts on my thigh and it's crushing.

I'm done for!

I cry out in despair and wait for the all-too-familiar pain to assault me. However, just as the enormous beast lands, the sound of shrieking car-breaks rings out, completely overriding the storm. His gnarly fangs barely scrape my skin, but I'm wild now, kicking at the beast with all my might. The beast snarls and pounces again as if finally ready to devour me.

I spoke too soon.

Those devilish jaws widen as if to clamp on my thigh. At the same time, a high-pitched whistle tears through the woods.

To my absolute surprise, no pain scorches my leg, and suddenly, the weight of the beast disappears. Casting a frightened look over my shoulder, I can just about make out the wolf suddenly backing away. His large tail shoots between his legs, his head low and submissive. The rest of the pack copy him, whimpering as though they are in agony.

What the actual fuck?

And then I feel it, the absolute fucking *misery*. Tears spring to my eyes and my heart drops in my chest. It feels as though the world around me is ending. A ridiculous string of sobs and cries leave my lips and suddenly, I'm scrambling at the mud with a newfound sense of desperation. The mud finally breaks free so I can pull the rest of my body under the gate.

Breathlessly, I stumble to my feet, but the pain is agonising on my ankle, and I quickly tumble back down. Before I can connect with the floor, a hand shoots out and grabs me. I'm quickly greeted with expensive musky perfume that snakes up my nose and makes my head feel dizzy. The feeling of misery quickly disappears as though someone has flipped a switch, and a sudden humiliation flows through me. I wipe my eyes with the back of my arm but all I do is smear mud across my face and dirty my eyesight.

The stranger secures their grip around me and before I know it, I'm falling into the front seat of a carelessly parked car. All the while, my hero says nothing.

"Thank you! Thank you! Oh, thank God, thank you so much!" The relief hits me in an instant as soon as the door slams in my face. My heart races one hundred miles an hour and everything aches as though I've been hit by a train. I hear the stranger slide into the car beside me and I frantically try to grab a look at my saviour, but I'm stunned by what I see.

In the frantic haze of escaping, I never stopped to realise my hero was a ridiculously tall, fiery-haired woman with stoically calm composure. Her gloved hands rest at ten-and-two on the wheel, and she pulls away with ease as though we are pulling out of a road and not speeding from the scene of multiple crimes. A large raven-coloured hat shields her face, blocking her appearance from me.

The black lacy dress hides the pedals of the car and snakes around her slim body. And her sleeves are tight around her arms, draping majestically when they get to her gloved fingers.

Do all normal women dress like they've come from a Halloween party in the real world?

Her head turns to me slowly. Instantly, it's as though all the air in the car is sucked out. She exposes her ridiculously pale complexion, thin pointed nose, and blood-red lips. Large sunglasses hide most of her face but it's the way she smiles at me which makes my stomach flip

No. Not a smile, a grimace.

What kind of person wears sunglasses at three in the morning? Who the fuck is this woman? Come to think of it, what the hell is she doing driving around at—

Her head snaps away from me just as quickly as the horror sinks in and the questions run riot. Her frantic movements have me startled in my seat until the whites of my knuckles pop from gripping the seatbelt so viciously.

"You can drop me off here." Even my voice is shaky with fear. She simply ignores me as though I never said a word. "Really, I appreciate what you've done for me, but—"

"You need a hospital," she speaks in a deep, husky tone. There isn't an ounce of concern or shock in her voice; it's almost as though she expected me to be gravely wounded. And what's more nerve-wracking, she asks no questions. It's almost like this is another day in the office for her.

"There isn't a hospital for another twenty miles. Rest, girl." She tips her head back to check her lipstick in the mirror. When she bares her teeth, for a split second, I swear her teeth come to a point, just like Dracula has in the comics. My breath hitches. However, just as quickly as I see them, she snaps her attention back to the road.

It's just delirium. Reason tries to comfort me, but my instincts are on high alert, recognising her as a threat. I will my body to move. It refuses the instruction, pain being its sovereign master.

"Nobody is going to hurt you today, so you might as well relax." Her fingers curl tighter around the wheel, and she barely casts me another glance.

Today.

The word lingers around the car like a bad smell, and I can't stop it repeating in my head. Yet, despite everything within me begging me to stay alert, exhaustion from the day swarms through me until my eyes are too heavy to keep open. I've always found comfort in the unconsciousness. And as much as I long for today to be different, routine is a bitch.

CHAPTER TWO

Present day.
(Six months after escaping the Prison)

If looks could kill, the person in front of me would be dead.

Trust me, I've been trying for a solid twenty minutes, burning daggers into that matted mud-coloured hair which looks like a twisted heaven for lice. I can even feel the little creatures crawling over my own head as I stare at the rivers of grease on her scalp.

She shakes her head and hits it a couple of times with her bony hand. As she turns her head, she flashes her pale skin with blotches of red spots burning her skin. Her eyes dart around in paranoia as she frantically scans her surroundings. They bulge out of the veiny sockets but a washed-out, distant look in her pupils makes it very clear that her frantic movements are the only thing alert about her.

In simple terms, *she is off her fucking head on drugs.* And to make matters worse, I am three bus seats behind her and can still smell her. *Rotting. Decaying. About to die.*

I don't know *Miss Skanky.* She got on the bus a couple of stops after me. At first, she provided a good distraction from the concealed weapon in my lap and the impatient bouncing of my leg. It was something interesting to look. It made a nice change from staring at each of the corners the bus hits, and impatiently counting them down until I reach my destination. But I'm fucking jealous that she gets to be high, and I haven't been able to find the sweet drugs that used to be fed to me. I don't miss the irony that I used to fear those little white pills but now I dream of them. It's been six months but it feels like an eternity. Everything longs to taste mummy's little helpers again.

Apart from her, nobody sits near me. It's like they are too afraid. Perhaps, if they creep closer to the dark-haired lady with swollen red eyes and puffy lips— lips that have forgotten how to smile, skin paler than ice, icy expression stained onto her broken face— they might grow miserable too. Even the way I'm hunched over is unnatural. My back throbs a dull ache and I know I should just straighten my posture, and keep my gaze high and firmly ahead, but *he's* so close; I can almost smell him.

I cannot risk lifting my chin from my chest in case he spots me when he boards the bus. I must be incognito; nothing more than a twisted shadow sticking to the bus walls.

I catch my reflection in the bus window and cringe. Underneath all the dark, baggy clothes which hide my identity, is still the same woman he touched, tasted, and owned. It's been months since I last saw him and yet I haven't been able to look at myself in the mirror without seeing a dark cast behind me. It's like he's always there, leering in every reflective glass, waiting for me to acknowledge him. Only then, can he lurch out and drag me back to that horrifying prison, kicking and screaming, but ultimately, unable to escape. Nobody ever truly escapes from Maximo.

Even his wife's days are numbered.

Maximo used to describe me as *deer coloured* to mock my ridiculously pale skin. A colour only the most imprisoned person could get to. A colour that screams endless nights of dreaming what the sun actually feels like on your skin. That whispers the promise of blending into the icy snow during your rare trips outside of the house. I never remained wholly pale though, much to his amusement. Maximo would paint me in a harsh variety of blacks, blues and reds and I'd look more like the leopard that kills the deer. Beautifully ironic that I'm both the predator and prey.

"Deer-coloured skin, raven locks of hair, lips redder than fire," he would croak as his rough hand clawed at my cheek, pulling my soft skin between his oily fingers. *"Cheekbones sharper than stone, a body carved from sin's wet dreams..."*

Maximo was all types of twisted, cruel and perverse. No matter how hard I try, I can never find the words to fully describe that pathetic excuse of a man. The kind of beast to roar with laughter when he made you bleed. Cackles when the tears pricked your eyes. Smirks when you are being held down and even then, those statements don't fully describe his wickedness. The fucking irony of it is that I bet he would be able to describe himself perfectly.

If nothing else, Maximo had a way with words. I fucking despise that man but deep down, I was always strangely mesmerised by his secret poetic nature. At least he'd give you something mournfully beautiful to listen to before ripping your heart out. Whilst chained to the bed, I'd spend hours at a time trying to recreate poetry as stunning as his. There is a certain attractiveness to how words can be chained together to create such awful beauty, full of meaning and yet drowning with nonsense.

The bus lurches to a halt to allow more passengers to file on. I don't need to look up to know that *he* is climbing on board. Well, not exactly my husband, but his cunt of a twin brother, Leonardo Gownes.

I've counted the minutes down and rehearsed this exact bus journey more times than I care to admit. It's been a twisted fantasy that has gotten me through the sleepless, tormented nights. Burnt into the back of my mind, is my husband's insane brother, in all his fucked-up glory. An ugly motherfucker who would stain the house with that awful pang of ammonia at least once a week.

Despite his near-clean-shaven head, he let a short mohawk grow out in the middle. It's crisp and too damaged beyond repair from bleaching it regularly. One of his fucked-up habits was to rub the blood of his victims on that pale streak to get the most vibrant red. It was difficult for him to wash it all out before his next kill. There was always a faint stain of murder latched onto him.

Just thinking about it reminds me of a particularly haunting line Maximo sang to me one night as he forced my feet into the restraints.

"Beware of the pale-haired man with a landing strip of crimson, for he will sell your soul to the devil for a taste of your sweet demise."

Beautiful, fucked-up words.

I hear the beep of the ticket machine and feel him move closer to me. My heart thumps in my chest, and everything around me drowns out into a low hum. I risk a peek at him— *I can't help it.* Endless months of planning are finally proving worth it.

The huge man stalks his way to the closest seat to the front of the bus, fed-up eyes glued to his phone. His thumbs move fast as he frantically types something, a deep frown etched on his face. It steals my breath away. *Fuck* does he look a lot like Maximo with the same papery skin, crinkled with wrinkles, small beady eyes and thin cracked lips. Even though his eyes are firmly locked on the device in his hands, I can still remember the icy blue orbs that see *through* things. Hauntingly blue, almost white, eyes that I aptly named *cameras* for they see fucking everything. Nothing gets past Leonardo nor his brother, Maximo.

He *never* takes the bus. He would rather walk the two hours than take a twenty-minute bus journey, but this morning something unusual happened: *his car tires were sliced ahead of a big meeting.*

I wonder who did that? A dirty, knowing smile paints my face.

The gun in my lap suddenly feels heavy. A dull throb vibrates around my body, and I can't tell if it's painful or pleasurable. Despite the endless planning, I never truly thought this day would come. The day when my abusive husband's brother died. One step closer to avenging the broken women they skilfully created.

The drugged-up lady in front of me bristles and then shoves her hand into her pocket before digging around. Eventually, she finds a little white pill wrapped in clingfilm. My eyes latch onto it as she tries to unwrap it discreetly, but it doesn't matter, my eyes are firmly fixed upon it. My mouth waters and my fingers twitch. *What is it? Paracetamol? Ecstasy? Ketamine? Something better? Something worse?*

And then the usual spike of chaos pushes through me, making me hold my breath to avoid throwing up everywhere.

No! No! Not now! Fuck!

Around me, the world blurs and I'm forced to grab the seat in front of me to stop myself from tumbling to the floor. My heart races faster and the sweat clings to my skin. Even my eyes feel hazy, and my breaths are too shallow.

Deep breaths. Ride it out. It will fade soon.

The irritability of my mood increases and my skin screams for me to scratch at it until it bleeds. I muffle the yawn in my sleeve. It makes my head hurt worse and it takes everything in me not to groan out as if that will relieve the pain.

I count to ten, and then to twenty, waiting for the withdrawal symptoms to leave but the image of that white little pill never leaves my mind. It's so fucking close that I could quite easily leap across the bus and steal it from her.

The episodes come less frequently nowadays but it doesn't

stop the overwhelming hunger and need that rocks through my world too regularly for my liking. I sink my nails into my thigh until the pain is too much. This usually drags me from a withdrawal episode. It slowly reduces the feeling of attacking the lady in front of me.

Once my eyes stop watering and my jaw unclenches from its yawning position, I frantically cast my gaze back to Leonardo to check that he hasn't noticed me. Like before, he remains fixated on his phone.

With a bitter reminder about what he created, I grind my teeth together.

That's it. The fucker dies now!

My heartbeat spikes for a different reason, adrenaline for what I'm about to do. I lick my lips in anticipation. My fingers curl around the fully loaded weapon and I try to regulate my breathing like I do every time before I make a kill. This time, though, it feels different. This isn't just some dirty man that touched me or hurt me once or twice that I could put a bullet in the back of his head and be done with it. *No.* This one I *need* to see the recognition on his face when he realises that he's going to die at the hands of someone he swore to tear apart.

Cautious not to alert him, I shuffle over to the next seat to get a better aim. He never once looks up from his phone and I almost laugh. The man is a trained assassin and used to preach to me the skill of danger awareness as he dragged knives down my body. Whatever has him hooked to that phone must really be something of value. I almost want to take credit for the distraction. But, this just happens to be a happy coincidence to help me avenge the broken woman inside.

Holding my breath, I wipe my sweaty hands on my leggings before switching the safety button off. I scan the bus one last time to make sure nobody is looking who could perhaps alert him before my first bullet tears through his disgusting body. I gulp down the lump in my throat and then aim at his thigh. I want to demobilise him before showing my face. I might be much stronger since leaving the prison six months ago, but this man was born to kill. He could still easily overpower me. A shiver wracks through me at the thought of being dragged back to that prison.

I force a deep breath to clear the horrifying thoughts. I aim again before pulling the trigger.

Bang—

Crash!

Suddenly, I'm flying left. My entire world is disorientated as the bus spins and the shrieks of tires on the tarmac tear through the bus. A terrible pain slams into my back and I realise I'm pressed up against the ceiling of the bus before gravity slams me back into the floor. It completely snatches my breath, taking me by absolute surprise.

Cries of horror and agony ring out around me from the other crash victims but it's the high-pitched noise haunting my ears which pulls me back into the moment. Gasping and spluttering, I clumsily stumble to my feet, falling into the bus window as I do so. I reach up to the ceiling where the bus seats are hanging in the air to steady myself.

Slowly, my vision restores, and I see the utter chaos of where a truck has slammed into the side of the bus, completely tearing it in two.

My heart drops as I realise Leonardo is nowhere to be seen. Panickily, I race over to the shattered window which gives me my only exit. As I climb out, I catch sight of the lady from earlier. *Or what's left of her anyway.* I don't bother making sense of the body parts. It looks as though she has exploded on impact. As does the old man who sat opposite her. And the man in his forties who spoke on the phone a little too loudly for my liking for the majority of the bus journey.

For a split second, it strikes me as weird that I'm able to stand when the other victims have been fucking obliterated. But I'm quickly distracted by what remains in a pale hand next to my feet. The little white pill wrapped in cling film seems to have made it in one piece.

I know I shouldn't, but instinct is a bitch. I swipe it up and slip it into my pocket before climbing out of the mutilated bus. As fast as I can force my stinging body to move, I charge around the huge lorry which sticks outside of the bus. I hurry to the other side where Leonardo will be, praying that he is still alive.

However, as I stumble around, the heat hits me. The front half of the bus is alight with wild flames and only growing larger.

My heart drops in my chest. *Fuck. Leonardo! He is dead and it's not by me. My revenge! It's gone! Fuck!*

The bubbling sense of fury slams through me, and I release a blood-curdling cry. Half a dozen people leap out of their vehicles to try and search for survivors but it all blurs around me. Strangely, nobody checks on me despite the steady stream of blood pouring down my leg and a loose shard of glass firmly wedged in my chest. They don't even react to the gun in my hand. I should care for why, but the feeling of helplessness and misery pulls around me and I scream again. It's agonising—twenty-two years of pent-up rage and suffering without suitable vengeance.

"Actions have consequences." A sudden female voice cries out amongst the chaos of the crash.

Startled, I tear around, gun at the ready-to-attack in my adrenaline-filled state. A shadowy figure emerges from behind a parked car, wearing a crimson cloak which floats majestically around her. She stands far too close to the fiery wreckage as if she cannot feel the heat.

"What?" I splutter. "Who are you? What the fuck are you saying?"

My whole body trembles as I raise the gun to the oddly dressed lady with a dress that seems to defy the laws of gravity. Yet, I'm not brave enough to make the shot. After what feels like an eternity, she lifts her large red hood. I recognised her instantly.

The woman who saved me that night.

"*You!*" I cry out in horror. The questions blurt out of my mouth just as quickly as they plague my mind. "What the fuck? Who are you? How do you keep finding me? Why are you always here when something bad happens—"

"I won't answer your questions, so don't bother asking."

Frightened, I try to put more distance between us, but she effortlessly closes the gap as if she's floating towards me.

"Don't run from me, Scarlet," the velvety voice coos. It's as if the whole world collapses around me and I choke on a breath. Her stern face suddenly melts into the weirdest smile I've ever seen — her lips curve downwards and yet it's clear that she's trying to look happy.

"How do you know my name?"

"I know everyone's name, silly." She almost giggles before turning her attention to the bus. "Rossa Minta, Miles Glen, Alisha Treng, Thomas Isabel, Maxie DeGeneres, Amy Macdonald, Christopher Jeng —"

"What? Who are they?" I cut her off. "Why are you listing—"

"Taylor Green, Charlie Catch, Amanda Miles, Katie Miles, John Carlise, and of course, Leonardo Gownes. The victims of the crash." She smiles happily as if it's the best news in the world. The feeling of nausea races through me and I vibrate with adrenaline.

"What? How did you—"

"It's funny how one bullet cost thirteen lives."

"What!" my eyes pop out of my head. "What the fuck are you saying?"

"Was it worth it?" She takes a swift step toward me, and I take one back, but I'm suddenly trapped by a carelessly parked car behind me. "Was it worth it? Thirteen lives for justice? Did you enjoy it?"

Frightened, I tear my gaze around to the large crowd gathering around the atrocity. I desperately search for someone to help me but it's as though I'm completely invisible. Defensively, I hold my weapon up and point it at the strange lady, more inclined to use the weapon now.

"Leave me alone! I swear to God I'll—"

"Leave him out of this." She suddenly hisses, that happy demeanour suddenly vanishing. An overwhelming sense of misery fills me and my body collapses to the floor as though it can't hold its own weight any further. It completely takes me by surprise, and I will myself jump up again, but I'm stuck. A frightened cry leaves at the realisation I can't escape.

"What do you want from me? Leave me alone! Who are you? How are you doing this?"

"I don't want anything from you," she says, almost matter-of-factly. Then, she twists slightly to watch the horrified screams and cries of people as they desperately try to put out the fire behind us. A noise nothing short of a chuckle escapes her. "It's actually what *I* can do for *you*."

"What?"

"I'm here to help you."

"I don't need your help! You're crazy!" I shriek. I will myself to move, but again, my body feels too full of misery to move. Even tears start to burn my eyes.

"Yes, you do. You are dead. You killed yourself and other

innocent people trying to get some feeble little revenge."

"What?" I choke on a breath. "I'm de—"

"Oh, come on now, nobody could survive that."

Horrified, I stare over at the mangled bus which is now fully alight in flames. Absolute terror rocks through me. "But I'm still breathing, I'm still conscious—"

"Your body has died, but your soul lives on. And trust me, you're not going to like where you're about to end up because of how many lives you've claimed."

My voice is small and timid, "You mean Hell?"

"Yes, I mean Hell. Oh, come on, don't look so sad, it's not the *worst* place in the world— oh, my bad, of course, it is!" She takes delight in my despair.

"But if I'm dead that means that I can't get my revenge on Maximo." I don't know why the words tumble from my lips. I must be insane. My main priority is still extracting torture on my husband rather than fearing for my safety in Hell, but then again, my whole life has been one long, never-ending hellish event of torture and pain.

What could possibly be worse than that?

Living through it all for nothing.

"Now, we are going to agree," she grins, turning to face me fully. "Come with me and there will be no repercussions for your slaughter of thirteen lives."

"I didn't kill them, I didn't mean to, I jus—"

She frowns. "Yes, you did."

"I didn't! I only shot—"

"Actions have consequences." She suddenly snaps. "The quicker you get that in your head, the easier this will be. Shooting Leonardo caused a bang, which in turn startled the lorry driver in the lane next to you, he lost control of the vehicle and now thirteen people are dead. It's quite simple actually."

"That's not true!" I scream out.

Disbelief fills me and then anger. I throw myself up furiously and suddenly all the sadness dissipates and turns to blind rage. I lunge at the woman and her mouth falls open in shock and fear. She visibly recoils, for the first time, looking taken aback. Before I can connect my fist with her, the sadness returns, and my heavy body falls back to the floor. The rage leaves me and a lump in my throat chokes the violent words I was about to spit.

"How do you know all of that? Who the hell are you? What are you— why are you doing this?" Sobs escape me until I'm fully hunched over, shaking with sadness. My entire body aches and feels heavy, and my eyes sting as the tears merge with the snot pooling out of my nose.

Her frown twitches. "That's better."

I can feel her watching me intently as if she's trying to suss me out. After a long period of silence, she finally answers a question.

"My name is Misery. By the looks of things, I have a bad feeling we are going to get to know each other *very* well."

CHAPTER THREE

"No," the growl rumbles around the room so deeply it almost vanishes as if the word was never uttered from my lips. "I will not take a new fucking pet."

Opposite me in my office, the Devil snarls. "You will accept a new pet because I fucking said so."

"I will not."

His thick eyebrow twitches disapprovingly and he swirls his glass of absinth in one hand, never taking his eyes off me. I maintain eye contact and jut my chin up defensively.

It's not going to fucking happen.

"Son," he tries to reason with me, but he should know better by now. You can't reason with Death, but the daft cunt tries anyway. "You must be *so* lonely down here. I just—" he shakes his head as the frown seeps into his ugly grimace. For a second, it looks as though he's anxious, but it disappears just as quickly as it appears. Getting a better look at the deepening wrinkles in his skin, I rock forward in my chair.

"I don't get it. Why can't you be like your siblings? They get so excited about having pets. It keeps them entertained and gives them something to do. You know this family has had a long history with pets and—"

I drown out the shitty lecture I've been receiving since my last pet died. At least the previous lectures were via telepathy rather than him burdening me with his actual presence in my realm. But here he is, wasting my time and using up far too much oxygen. Subconsciously, my fingers curl into fists until the white balls are threatening to leap out of my knuckles. I just about contain the anger coursing through me.

Kill the daft cunt. Make him explode into thousands of shards of glass and then use them to murder the rest of the family. The evil beast within me craves his demise. It takes everything within me to keep a lid on his untameable fury.

With a clenched jaw, I try to find something else in my office to entertain myself with whilst the devil lists all the benefits of inviting a mortal back into my realm. It's futile. What my father fails to remember is that this realm of Hell sustains no life. The living souls never stay living for long near me. If anything, they get in the way, waste my oxygen, waste my limited resources. And quite frankly, they require too much attention to ensure the other beasts in my realm don't get to them when my back is turned. I've lost millions of pets to one dog alone. They are weak, pathetic, blubbering— and not even in a good way, in a self-wallowing way.

I silently curse only having two armchairs and a dim light in this office. It would be quite easy to conjure up something to join us in the room.

Perhaps I can watch the newly-discovered torture technique I've been perfecting? I think I've now gotten it to the point where I might as well click a button to get the soul to scream for me. It's so fucking delicious. I was up all night playing around with my test subjects. I've never been so erect as when I'm listening to those tortured cries for mercy. Even now I'm starting to get excited about my plans this afternoon of bringing those fantasies to life.

"Are you fucking listening to me?" My father snaps, pulling my attention back to him.

I wave my hand around dismissively. "Don't waste your time, father. I will not get a new pet."

In response, his coal-coloured hair seems to turn darker when those tar-stained eyes harden. His jaw flexes when he grinds his teeth together, making the muscles pop in his face. I instantly recognise the muscle that leaps out of his cheeks as the same one that permanently throbs in my own face, and I unwittingly see the resemblance between father and son when he's angry.

We are similar sizes in our human appearance with large square shoulders, towering a seven-foot height but whereas my father is lean, I am almost entirely muscle from the centuries of torturous labour I have been cursed to endure. The main difference between us though is that my father's tanned skin is relatively free from marks, mine flushes with black inky patterns when I'm angry. Each minuscule, tattooed dot represents a recent death, instructing me that I must transport their soul to whichever part of hell they deserve. If I ignore the souls, they burn and devour into my flesh until the agony is too much to withstand. *A constantly updating, inescapable fucking to-do list,* if you will.

My hand burns as a fresh new set of souls pass into the afterlife and into my realm. One dot stings worse than the others and I find myself rubbing at it absent mindlessly to soothe the never-ending pain.

"I don't want humans in my home," I growl. "They just keep dying. They are fucking useless."

"Don't—" my father pinches his eyebrows together with a frustrated sigh. "They die because you kill them. Stop killing them and then you won't have that problem."

Like a beast that's heard injured prey in the distance, my head snaps to the side. For a moment, the devil hesitates but the moment is so brief it could be mistaken as a breath. The *only* thing he fears is his uncontrollable, unreasonable, erratic eldest son who thirsts for murder. With a click of my fingers, I can remove the life forces from most of the Beings in Hell. The only thing stopping me is that I cannot be bothered to pick up the slack of their laborious tasks as well as rule the underworld.

I am many things: evil, perverse, sinful... but I'm not fucking stupid. Nonetheless, my father has royally pissed me off to the point I consider ending his life.

My eyes darken. "What's the point of the pet if not to kill it?"

Desperately, he tries another avenue. "Are you not lonely?"

"I'm perfectly happy being alone."

"Nobody is happy being alone!" he roars, spilling the alcohol on my marble floors as he throws his arms around. "Ever since Pain was put to death—"

My whole body triples in size and the furious black mist makes my rage evident. "You dare mention that dirty little cunt's name in my home?"

"Woah!" He lurches backwards, hands defensively high. "Calm down, Death, what I meant to say was the last time you let someone into this realm was seven centuries ago with your wife and—"

"*Ex*-wife."

"Whatever. All I'm saying is that you haven't responded to any of our telepathy calls in at least five. You can't keep shutting us out."

"Careful, Father," I warn maliciously. "You're starting to sound *good*."

He bristles. To ease the building anger, I gulp down the remainder of my alcoholic concoction and refill it with a snap of my fingers.

"Death, you will need to forgive us sooner or later. A divided royal family is bad for—"

"Not my problem."

"You're alone here. You *must* get lonely—"

"If I remember correctly, you cursed me down here alone, did you not, dearest father? Perhaps you should have thought about it all those aeons ago... That your eldest son might become unwilling to play happy families after you cursed him to serve *your* punishment. Not to mention recent affairs, right? I didn't cut you all off for no reason, and you fucking know it. You chose that little bitch over your own son. Remember that? Me cutting you all out is kinder than what I would *actually* like to do."

His face twists guiltily and it makes me feel sick. He pushes forward in his chair and the light casts an awful shadow across his face, revealing what I thought I saw earlier— *more wrinkle marks.* My head cocks to the left, confused. *Why is the devil ageing? Hellish Beings never age.*

"Is that—" Before I can finish my question, a ridiculous feeling of sadness fills my chest, slithering into my lungs and tightening until I choke on the breath. The pain stings like thousands of knives being plunged into my heart and my eyes prick with tears. Flashes of blonde hair haunt my mind and an ugly cry leaves my lips as I desperately try to force the image out of my head. I will not think about *her.* As soon as the image enters my mind, I leap to my feet and ready myself for an ugly fight. The realisation dawns on me about who has entered my realm.

"Misery," I snarl my little sister's name. On cue, she steps into the light, revealing those dark red eyes, twinkling with mischief. She smiles up at me and stops her devilish charms, letting my lungs return to normal. That usual mocking look licks her face.

"Is it nice seeing Pain again?"

Even the mention of my ex-wife makes me gag.

"I will torture you like you've never been tortured before," I growl deeply. My fingers curl into fists and I feel the scars on my skin flash darker and darker until they stain my skin permanently.

"Don't torment your brother." The devil scolds my sister, much to her amusement. She sends me a wicked smile and flicks her crimson-coloured cloak out behind her. She juts out her bottom lip. "You are no fun."

"What are you doing here, Misery?" I seethe. "You are not welcome in my Realm."

"Relax, you know I can't stay long anyways." She rolls her eyes and flexes her hand out to check the intensity of her skin colour. A slight grey tinge starts to stain her body.

"Good to see your curse still stands," she says bitterly, but I don't respond to her. Any Being that enters my realm without permission will slowly perish an agonising death. Even though Original Beings may not die permanently through this curse, the process is excruciating after a certain time and will certainly knock them into a temporary deep sleep. If the curse works, they will be knocked out for a couple of millennia.

She turns to our father, "Have you told him the good news yet?"

He shakes his head.

"What news?" I grit my teeth together.

What is it that they'd risk the torturous pain and impending temporary death over?

The two share a knowing look. Dark tendrils of smoke seep from my body as I start to tremble with rage. "Fucking tell me."

My father breaks first. "Your sister is hosting a huge event, the biggest one we've had in aeons, in fact."

"Why?"

"Let's just say there's been some trouble in Hell," Misery scoffs. "Some of the Beta Beings are getting a little restless and bored, they've started turning on each other, starting wars, whispering rumours to the angels." She checks her viciously long fingernails as if the news bores her. "You know, the usual."

This makes me furious.

"You dare come to my realm to tell me you're worried about rumours. Are you not part of the Original Hellish family?" I glare at my father "The fucking founder of the family? And you're scared of some rumours? What has this place turned into? Grow up, we're not humans, rumours do not scare us. *Nothing* scares us." The dark tendrils of smoke hang heavy around the room, almost blocking my view of my wicked family. "You two seem to have turned fucking soft! Where is the anger? The hatred? The torture? Deal with those beta cunts yourselves and leave me out of it."

"Not just any rumours." Misery quickly corrects herself. "*Political* rumours."

My patience thins as my hand stings again in the same spot as before. I glare down at the abnormally large, tattooed blob throbbing. *Must be a pretty awful fucking person for that size of a punishment.* I scratch it. "I don't care for politics, you know this, sister. You are really testing my fucking patience. You have thirty seconds to leave my realm before I put you both to your death bed."

"You might want to care. Give me five minutes and I will be out of your hair," Misery says cryptically, looking between me and my hand almost as if she knows something I don't. "Don't worry about the details, brother, I'm handling that. You just need to be aware of the little game I'm hosting." Her eyes twinkle mischievously as she paces around the room. "You don't want a human because they are weak and pathetic and don't last down here, right? But our dearest daddy needs you to have a human pet to keep up appearances of this powerful, ruling family with subordinates and blah blah blah—"

My jaw tenses. "Where are you going with this, Misery?"

"How about a series of trials to whittle down ten mortals to one to get you one that isn't weak or pathetic? One that might last. The winner will be your new pet."

"I don't want another pet. When will you fuckers get that in your head?"

"Okay, fine, I don't care," she hisses. "You can kill the thing after my trials are done. You can feed it to your dogs, I really don't give two fucks about what you do with the mortal. These trials are how we remind the Beta Beings who are really in charge. We show them the *real* beasts that will rip them apart if they dare consider revolting against us. Besides, who doesn't love a bit of human torture as entertainment? It's been so long since there's been something interesting to watch."

I glare at her pouty face and resist the urge to strangle her. "What's in it for me?"

"The security of Hell," my father says much to my amusement.

I release a dark chuckle. "You really don't know me if you think that bothers me. Hell might fall, Father, but nobody would ever dare take my Realm. The curse of constant agonising labour isn't worth the location and so I'm right as rain whether Hell stands or falls." I stalk closer to him. "Actually, Hell falling works in my favour, remember. You traitorous cunts that call yourself family will be put in restraints, and I won't have to deal with unwanted visits and constant nagging and favour begging. I'll be free to get on with my job."

"If you agree to this, I won't bother you about having another pet," my father suddenly confesses. "I will never enter your realm again."

My ears prick. "So, I can kill the pet after the trials are done? And you guys will be gone for good?"

"Yes," he says reluctantly. "And that is a promise, Death."

He presents me with his bare wrist, forcing his veins to the surface, showing me that he is willing to make a deal. I cock my eyebrow suspiciously. A deal with the devil is never something to refuse, they are some of the most agonisingly delicious acts.

Instinctually, my fangs jump out but common sense screams at me to run away. *What the fuck is going on to make both my sister and father visit me in person and require my appearance in their political games?*

"Agree to the games. Agree to play your part as a willing host in offering the winning mortal the opportunity to become your new pet, and I promise I will *never* enter your realm again once the trials are finished. You can put me into a temporary death if I do."

"Never?" My voice darkens at the fantastic opportunity.

"Never."

He waves his wrist in front of my face, and instinct drives me forward before I can rationalise the deal. I sink my fangs into the soft flesh before he can change his mind. The bitter dusty taste burns my mouth most deliciously as I scar his skin, proving for the rest of eternity that a deal has been made. I put distance between us as quickly as I can once the deal is finalised, feeling dirty with myself.

"May the Death trials begin," Misery grimaces, the smile on her face stretches from ear to ear until I'm convinced it might fall off her face. My father and her exchange a satisfied look with one another but I cannot bring myself to rejoice in the new deal I've just made. Something tells me this is a deal which will have grievous repercussions. One that even Death incarnate might actually fear.

CHAPTER FOUR

It feels strange.

One minute I'm outside the burning bus, and the next I'm suddenly in a dark room with only a dim light. It all happens so fast that I can't compute it. *Fight* it.

All of the sudden, my chest feels heavy and the heat licks at me, though I'm not sure where it's coming from. Even the stench is terrible. It's like rotting meat and gone-off milk. I gag, momentarily blinded by the stench which chokes up my breathing. And then, my heart explodes in panic as the dim light reveals the dark box that I currently reside in.

I leap into action. My whole body heaves as I yank at the bars, though, of course, it's no use.

"Let me out! Help! Help!" My throat throbs from how loudly I yell the plead, but nothing happens. I try again, and again until I feel sick from how dry my throat becomes. My screams break the sound barrier, bouncing off each wall before caving in on themselves. "Please! Let me out! Help! Help!"

My attempts at gripping the bars prove to be feeble, the slime and grime build up making it almost impossible to get a reasonable grip. I desperately try to peer outside the bars, but it's near pitch-black and the stench out there is somehow worse than in here.

"No one will hear you," a female voice calls out.

Frightened, I spin around in horror. A lady in the far shadows of the cell lunges forward so I can see her under the light. A long grey dress clings to her body, draping down her wrists and flowing behind her. She has long chocolate hair which cascades down her back, with random plaits and jewels making her look like some type of royalty. With a soft button nose, kind warm eyes and a smile that makes you feel welcome, she doesn't ooze the danger I expected of someone who has just appeared out of thin air.

She crosses the cell slowly, as if not to startle me, and gently takes my hand. Everything within me screams to run away, but like a deer startled in the headlights, I'm completely frozen. Despite all my attempts to stop it, I find myself mindlessly gravitating towards her.

Then, suddenly, all signs of motherly instinct vanish, and abrupt flashes of Maximo storm through my mind. His wonky decaying teeth, menacing grimace and terrifying eyes force their way into my head. He leers over me in my mind as though he's going to attack, and it fills me with absolute terror. In his hand, he holds a dagger and he's about to plunge it into my naked skin like he used to do. It feels as though the world around me is going to explode as fear strangles me.

I scream as horror consumes me until my throat aches. I feel helpless, flinging each limb around to get him to stop, but I'm quickly learning I have less power here than I did in the prison.

It's utterly useless. I'm abruptly completely pinned to the bed, staring at his horrible grimace. The same one he'd present just moments before he'd leave irreversible damage to my skin.

Just as the dagger connects with my skin, everything changes. Suddenly, he's the one naked and chained to the bed and it's my dagger connecting with his thigh. Roars of agony fill my mind followed by silence. The vision changes just as quickly. I am no longer stabbing him, but now I have a gun pressed to his forehead as he pleads for his life on his knees.

It changes again.

Maximo is bent over a table, ropes forcing his wriggling body still. In my hand, I clutch onto a broom, ready to fuck him with it, the exact same way he'd force me down and rape me over and over growing up.

Without warning, the visions disappear, and a frightened shriek escapes my lips. My fists leap into a self-defence position after I shove the lady away from me as though she was responsible for the conjured images in my mind.

"What the hell? What the fuck! I swear to God get away from me —"

"Tut, tut," the evil woman's face distorts into an ugly scowl, making my blood turn to ice, "You shouldn't use that name down here."

"Down here?" I cry out in horror.

Fuck, have I been taken to Hell already?

"Mother, don't scare her!" another voice booms.

As if appearing from thin air, Misery makes herself known. My eyes slam shut, and I count down from five, convinced that I'm seeing things. I slowly reopen them, expecting her to disappear.

I must be insane. I must have hit my head on the bus and this is all some fucked-up concussed dream.

But, ultimately, the two women leer over me, intently watching my every reaction. A horrified noise slips from my mouth as nausea leaps into my mouth.

It's not a fucking dream! This is actually happening!

Then, Misery's head rears toward her mother. "I told you not to meet her without me."

"I couldn't resist!" she licks her lips as if eyeing me up for her next meal. "You know I love mortals."

Unwillingly, I ready myself to fight to the death. I have no fucking clue what these things are in front of me, but they are not human, and they are not *good*. My whole body screams to run away but the bars lock me in a cell with these demons.

Misery steps towards me but she no longer wears her sunglasses, revealing her *real* eyes. I shriek in horror. Blood-like orbs glare back at me except for a thick strip of pupil, resembling a snake.

Fuck!

"Oh God! Oh my God! What the fuck are you?"

Both the women flinch. I scream louder. "Where am I? Let me go! Oh my God, let me go! Please!"

Panic floods through me like no other. I cast my gaze around at the prison shackled bars and the dirty floors, and my breathing became irregular. It reminds me far too much of what I escaped from. *Trapped in a prison with a monster.* And yet I don't know what's worse, Maximo or these creatures!

"No, no, no!"

"Scarlet, calm down," Misery tries, holding her hands out to soothe me. I use my whole body to pull at the bars again, but nothing happens. Fear and adrenaline force me to face the women and raise my fists again. Absolute terror makes me jump to awful conclusions.

"Are you working with him? Is that why you are here? Because I killed his brother? Did he send you? Oh Hell!" I ramble incoherently, "Fuck! Please, let me go! I swear, I'll do anything! I won't tell a soul what I've seen!"

"Him?" the lady in black frowns.

"Maximo," Misery notes sourly as if she knows exactly what I'm blabbering on about. A disgusted look crosses her face as she glares at me. "He has nothing to do with this, Scarlet. He's not the one to be afraid of. *We are.*"

Something twisted in my heart knows that these demons are the true enemy and the things to be frightened of, but something far worse tells me Maximo is still the one to watch out for. They might be lying to me. They might lure me towards him. After all, I *know* true evil in the face of my husband. I've lied next to him for twenty-two years and I've never had a pain-free moment. Surely, *that* is evil?

"Who the fuck are you then? How do you know my name? How are you doing all of this—" I holler as the adrenaline gives me a newfound confidence. Then, I remember the gun from earlier, and desperately try to find it, but it's completely gone. The only thing in my pocket is the little white pill, begging to be tasted.

"You want to shoot me?" Misery cocks her eyebrow in amusement.

"How did you know—"

"A feisty one," the other lady says in a velvety voice. It fills me with more dread than if she spat it.

"Let me go!"

"Why would we do that?" Misery sighs, taking a lunge towards me, trapping me against the bars. "We are here to help you."

"Help me?" I boom. "You've imprisoned me! Kidnapped me!" I become uncontrollable. "People will realise that I'm gone! They will find you and they will kill you for doing this to me!"

It's a complete lie, anything to get me out of this prison. Much to my horror, Misery and the other lady look at each other and explode with laughter, to the point Misery wipes a tear from her face.

"Nobody is looking for you, Scarlet, don't kid yourself. You made it so nobody knew where you even were," Misery tuts, grabbing my chin and forcing it in the air. "Silly girl," she taunts. "Silly, silly girl."

Tears prick in my eyes, but surprisingly not from fear but rage now. It's like she's tormenting me, and the injustice of finally escaping a prison just to be thrown into another doesn't escape me. What these women don't know is I have *nothing* to lose. They will not be able to do anything to me that Maximo hasn't done first. Pain all becomes the same once someone slaughters your will to live.

"Let! Me! Go!"

"Ohh, *so* threatening." The other lady squints her eyes as she mocks me. A low growl escapes me. Survival instincts kick in and all my fear switches into desperation.

I will fight and kick and scream and kill my way out of this hell hole!

As if sensing my sudden bravery, her head snaps to the side as though she's trying to read me. It makes the hairs on the back of my arms leap to attention, but I never lower my fists.

"You shouldn't make enemies with us, sweetheart, we aren't here to hurt you. *Yet*, anyway."

"We are actually here to offer you a fantastic deal," Misery beams.

"A deal?" I swallow down the lump in my throat and put another step between me and the woman. Thankfully, they allow me the breathing space I so desperately need.

"Sure," Misery beams, "What if I tell you that we can give you Maximo."

My mouth dries. "What?"

"We can give you all of them. It's up to you what you do with them. Torture, kill, let go…"

"I want to kill them!" The rage floods through me before I can bottle it up.

The other lady's hand shoots out and she cups my cheek. For a moment, another flash of Maximo fills my mind before it disappears quickly. The lady smiles wide, sending shivers through me. "I know, I know, and it's only fair you get your revenge."

"M—My revenge? How— how did you know?"

"Hush, sweet pea." The lady speaks over me, "It doesn't matter how, and it doesn't matter what. What should interest you is *why*."

She nods her head as if to permit me to ask the question. I choke on the words as I spit them out. "Why? Why are you doing this?"

"If you want your prize, you must compete."

"Compete?"

"There will be some *trials,* let's say. If you survive and win, you get all the revenge you could possibly *long* for. And more." She enunciates certain words, and it confuses me. I know whatever is happening is wrong and should be avoided. These women in front of me, though beautiful, ooze a deception. My jaw clenches and my eyes burn from where I haven't blinked in so long, afraid the momentary vulnerability will give them time to strike.

"And if I say no?" I bristle.

Misery's head snaps backwards as she laughs. It's such an ugly sound, one that fills me with dread. When she finishes, her head cocks to the side and her red eyes darken, "If you say no, you die."

Silence haunts the space between us. The lump in my throat burns as I realise I might not have many options. "What kind of trials are these?"

"I won't lie to you, Scarlet, these trials will be unlike anything you've ever heard of or could even possibly dream of. They're dangerous. Your soul might die, and you will be sorted into the punishment hell that fits the crimes you committed whilst physically alive, but the reward is fruitful."

"So, if I say no, I die, and if I say yes, I die," I croak.

Misery's eyes light up happily, "Now you understand!"

The other lady shoves Misery to the side. "It's not just that," she sends daggers at the smaller lady, "Focus on what you gain. If you say yes, and you win, you get your long dreamt of revenge.

Twenty-two years of torture will finally be settled, Scarlet. All you have to do is beat the other contestants."

"How do I know you're not lying to me?"

"We may be evil," she coos, "But we *never* break our deals."

I ponder on the thought for a second, and it's enough for me to realise I might have completely lost my fucking mind. *As if I'm actually considering accepting this deal!* These women are bad, like *very* bad. They are clearly something worse than human, something forged from the depths of Hell. And yet, this doesn't frighten me. What truly horrifies me is the idea that I might die before getting my revenge. Whatever these women have in store for me, Maximo must have done worse.

Right?

It's a gamble with my life, but it's also a game I've been playing for twenty-two years. Surely, that counts for something.

Right?

"Do we have a deal?" Misery thrusts her hand out at me and hurries me for an answer. I eye up the deceptively dainty-looking thing. I feel like I can't breathe as my arm lifts on its own accord.

I must have a fucking death wish.

Before I can say anything else, I clasp my fingers around her hand and shake. "Deal."

CHAPTER FIVE

The four-headed beast with fangs longer than my arms and twenty-three beady eyes rips into a shrieking soul. With one slice, the soul explodes into dozens of red dots, only to reform into the shape of a thin woman with red-raw spots all over her face. My beast attacks again and again until the soul has been murdered and brought back to life numerous times only to die more horrifically.

I can't resist the smirk on my lips as I slump back into my chair and bring the glass of whisky to my lips. The agonised cries ring around the room, like a sensual melody to my ears. I focus on the buzzing feeling within my chest that throbs shallowly. This soul hasn't done *much* wrong to be fair to her. Perhaps a couple of thefts, maybe overindulging in drugs and high levels of selfishness. Not worth being sentenced to Hell for all eternity, but I'll welcome the food in, nonetheless.

With a sigh, I shake my hand slightly to the left, signalling to the beast that she needs to go to hell realm with all the other overindulgent souls.

She will be good food for the gatekeepers of that realm.

"Next!"

My beast bows his head at my command and tears into her skin one last time, sending her into her new realm now that she's been sorted. She explodes into a confetti of red sprinkles and then the new soul takes the form of an old man with a large, bumpy nose and sad-looking eyes. The thumping in my chest is less than the lady before.

My nostrils flare. "Another boring, obvious one, Beast? Why do you bother checking with me about their new assortment? You should fucking know this by now!"

I hurl a tendril of black smoke at the beast, striking him across the scruff of his neck. He shrieks in agony as the pixels leave a fiery trail of scorch marks; it bubbles and eats away at his nerves. His once-orange skin turns grey and black as the mould and decay devour him. Pathetically, he darts around as if running away will stop his punishment. His frantic movements trigger something within me.

"*Tag!*" The word swarms my mind before I can stop it.

Fuck off. I grit my teeth and will the word away as it screams in my mind louder and louder.

"*Tag! Death, Tag!*" The beautiful blonde woman squeals after she smacks me in the arm. Even though I reject the memory, my torturous mind forces me to relive the past. It's instantly as though my wife is in front of me now, slowly backing away from me with the largest grin. Her crystal blue eyes twinkle under the light of our bedroom and I can taste the maliciousness in the room.

"*Tag?*" I hear myself respond despite viciously gritting my teeth together to stop the nightmare.

"*Yes, Tag. It's a game the humans play. Where I hit you, say tag and then run away. You then have to catch me. Duhhh.*"

Everything inside of my body twists and pulls until it feels like I'm one giant knot, ready to explode. Even at the time, I was confused by her knowledge, but now it all makes sense. It wasn't possible for her to know *anything* about the playfulness of humans.

The minute we were forced to marry, she became trapped in the Hellish Realm with me, something she resented me for. She blamed her entrapment on me as though I had a say in who I had to marry. Fate had sworn the God of Death and Goddess of Pain to an eternity of tortuous marriage together. Locked up in this Realm, her only experiences of humans should have been the evil souls being tortured. The pathetic little game of *Tag* should never have crossed her path.

"Catch me, Death. That's the game. The humans love it! Please play with me, I am so bored waiting for you to finish sorting." She hoists her long dress up so that she doesn't trip and puts space between us. Unwillingly, I find myself following her as though a curse forces me to be near the evil bitch. She backs herself closer to the bed which suddenly appears. Then, she sends me the dirtiest look.

"What do you know about the humans, wife?" I frown. At the time, I tried to mask my curiosity with playfulness to not alert her to my caution, but I've never been good at hiding my real emotions.

With a lopsided smile, she invites me closer. *"I know a lot about them."*

"Do tell me how."

"Secret." The word barely slips past her lips before she throws herself at me and kisses me like she hates me. Her kiss feels as though somebody has sliced my lips off. I feel them bleed but the evil taste it so addictive, making me crave more. I don't crave her. I crave the self-punishment and my fucked-up wife could always offer me that.

I need more.

My fingers lose themselves on her body, and our tortured whimpers become one. She locks herself against me by wrapping her thighs around my waist, though she doesn't need to restrain me, the curse forces me to be obsessed. I'm drunk on her kiss, the pain making my eyes prick and a lump in my throat forms.

She drives her long nails into my face and yanks until the blood bubbles to the surface.

She pulls away momentarily to taste the torture she inflicts, and moans in delight. *"Yes, it tastes so good,"*

She is breathless as she pushes my head to the side, exposing my neck. Instinctively, I bare my teeth at her as though to threaten her. The vulnerable position is not one I'm used to. Nonetheless, she holds all the control as she runs her sharp fangs against my sensitive skin. It's fucking torturous.

I hate her so much, I *really* fucking hate her. I want to push her *and* the memory from me, but I can't, she has me locked in. It was always agonising fucking her, but I had no other options, and I needed to shoot my load somehow.

I knew she was bad news, even back then. That awful part of my soul knew that she was always going to betray me. It was within our nature: *nothing ever stays good for long in Hell.*

"Chase me, Death," she whispers. *"Pretend you're hunting me, and I will pretend you are playing my game."*

I want to refuse her, but I'm too far gone to listen to reason. The beast inside of me roars to overpower the hateful little bitch.

My fangs flare menacingly. *"Fine. You better not let me catch you then."*

Finally, I snap out of the nightmare and sink more burning pixels into my creature as though it's his fault my brain is playing tricks on me. I continue until his horrified cries give me a headache. Only now that we've both been suitably punished, do I cease his suffering. With one final whimper, he drops his head low before bringing me the next soul that needs a second checking of their assortment.

This time, it is an older man with a bizarre white stripe of hair on his head. Instantly, this one feels different to the others. The throbbing in my chest is deep and painful, and completely takes me by surprise. Curiosity has me readjusting myself in my seat when the painful dot in my hand, the same one that played up earlier, shoots electricity through me.

With one hand, my beast uses its large claws to completely disembowel the man before it leaps onto him to feast on the organs. The soul bashes as hard as he can into my beast's back but it's futile. Humans barely make a dent when it comes to combat with my Hellish creatures.

Yet another reason why these trials are so fucking stupid.

They will all perish an awful fiery death in the first trial, and it will bring me great pleasure getting the shitty task over and done with. But despite the horrific torture, the new soul doesn't scream as loud as he should. It's as though he was made suffering, and this is just a new day for him. It infuriates me.

With a flick of my finger, I up the torture so the beast tears out the man's eyes, casting them across the floor. With a disgusting thump followed by a squelchy roll, they roll towards me, stopping by my boot. I lift my foot and roll the squishy thing, causing the soul to now sing his beautiful pain to me. Trying to soak up as much sin from this man as possible, I tease his agony and fear for a bit longer. It's been a long fucking time since I've felt evil as much as I do now from this mortal. Plus, there is an awful bitter smell seeping from him too, one that is... *familiar?*

The temperature of the room suddenly becomes unbearably hot, a sharp contrast to the usual freezing depths, and, sensing danger, my fangs leap out menacingly.

"Mother," I growl as it becomes clear to me who has entered my Realm. Out of the corner of my eye, *Longing* strides into my torture chamber, with her usual twisted smile. Her tumbling black dress drags and tugs at the skulls etched into my marble floors, creating a disgusting ripping sound, but she refuses to acknowledge it. That usual intense stare burns into the side of my face but I do not give her the satisfaction of rubbing at it to soothe the ache.

"What do you want?"

"You're late. The games have begun," her deceptively soft voice rings around the room. She reaches out for me, but realising better, she quickly drops her long, spindly fingers before they can connect with my shoulder. "Death, listen to me. Everybody is waiting."

"Let them wait."

"Now, son. Don't be like that. You agreed to your father's deal. Do not break your deal with the Devil." Her soft velvety voice makes me bristle.

It's been centuries since I heard from the wicked, soft-spoken lady with malicious intent disguised as a loving, warm figure. It's perhaps why I am more unnerved by her than my own father. At least he is honest about what he is. *Evil, sinful, spiteful.* My mother is deceitful and malicious, drawing out your deepest desires. She knows everything and anything about what you long for, and then aptly destroys it. A wicked, tormented curse which runs through her hot-blooded veins. I know she can't help it, *Hell*, nobody in my family can resist the pull of their nature, but my mother is more wicked than them all. I've fallen for her motherly charms more times than I care to count and destroyed souls that probably didn't deserve it, simply because she whispered for me to.

With a small smile, she tilts her head to the side, those sharp eyes looking *through* me. Her fiery, invasive pixels tickle my brain, trying to tease out the information she desires. I swiftly block her out. Throwing myself to my feet, I put as much distance as I can between my mother and me, as if that will help.

"Watch it," I warn her darkly.

Her eyes flash, and she pouts. "Come on, Son. Tell me, why are you making us wait? Will you not attend?"

"I had work to do. I'm coming now," I hiss, casting my gaze back to the shrieking soul with the white strip of hair. My heart still thumps loudly with his energy floating around the room. He punches my beast on the snout over and over, and I frown at his perseverance.

Swiftly, I slam my foot down on the soul's eyeball which pops under my weight. Then, he explodes into pixels as I send him to the worst realm of Hell for me to visit later.

He is going to need a lesson in some fucking manners.

"No more sorting," I bark at my beast. "Get back to sorting the newcomers, and I will figure out the more difficult souls when I get back."

He gives me a low bow, still trembling with pain and terror from his torture earlier, before limping away to lick his wounds. Out of the corner of my eye, my mother frowns. "You shouldn't hurt those loyal to you."

"Fucking what?"

"You mustn't cause such damage, it's not right, it's—"

Without warning, I flash across the room and wrap my large hand around her small neck. She splutters and coughs, momentarily startled by the speed and intensity of my movement.

"Rephrase that," I bark. Her eyes widen in fear and her long nails sink into my skin as she tries to scratch me away. My mother might be a malicious, deceitful little bitch, but we both know who is to *really* be feared out of the two of us.

"Let go of me, Death!"

"Don't make me ask again." The dark black of anger seeps from my body.

Her eyes squeeze shut as the panic floods through her. "Death! De — okay, fine! You mustn't hurt the beasts!"

"I mustn't hurt the *Hellish* beasts, you mean? The creatures *I* created? The creatures *made* for torture? What the fuck are you talking about, woman? May I remind you where you are." My grip becomes tighter around my mother's neck until her face is purple. It only adds to the greying of her skin as my curse slowly eats her up. I have two options, I can strangle the evil cunt or I can hold her hostage long enough for the curse I set on my family to work. She'll be a pile of bones in no time. "I've heard the whispers from my beasts. My family have become weak. It's fucking pathetic! Must I wipe out my whole family and rule Hell myself to regain some control over the realm?"

"Hell is changing!" she cries out desperately. "It's not all about torture and killing! There are other methods—"

The cackle which erupts from my lips echoes around the torture chamber, growing louder and louder each time until she winces and throws her hands over her ears. My eyes sparkle with the familiar flame that erupts before I claim a soul. The beast inside of me roars to be released.

"Hell will always be about torture and killing as long as I still breathe. Do you understand, Mother? Or must I remind you about the curse poisoning me? A curse *you* bestowed unto me."

Just as my hot breath kisses her cheek, the room around me suddenly changes and a blinding light catches me by surprise.

"Release her, Death!" The Devil's roar painfully shakes my brain. To my left, he leers over me, clutching his staff in his hand. He visibly shakes and drains the energy from the room, snatching anything he can get to fight his wicked son.

Kill her. The tormented pleas from my heart begs. *Kill the whole family. Get rid of these burdens. Return to your Realm and rule fearlessly.*

My fangs throb and I feel my eyes shifting to their monstrous black as my dark nature bleeds through me. But before I can fully transform into my whole Being, a sharp pain in my left cheek has me eyeing up the demon bone attached to my father's staff. It slides into my skin and the pain spreads out until my whole jaw screams in agony. I grind my teeth together. The intense pain immediately grounds me, stopping the beast from fully taking over.

With a low grunt, I release my mother's black and blue throat. She scrambles away from me in fear. It's such a pathetic sight; I almost punish her again. She hides behind my father, who doesn't release the weapon. He doesn't tremble in front of me nor show any clear signs of fear, but I can smell that slight tinge of uncertainty. He might be the Devil, ruler of Hell, but he still has that terrible angelic side locked up in his chest somewhere.

They all do. *Angels gone rogue* the Heavenly cunts call my family. I'm the only one who doesn't have that weakness. Forged from ultimate sin and evil, Death has no weakness; I consume all.

"Family," I say through gritted teeth as the blinding lights around us fade out. My father pulls the dagger from my cheek and puts distance between us. I feel the skin close around the wound, healing everything but the pain.

And then suddenly, the excited roar from all the Hellish beasts leering from their seats around the room has me snarling. Beasts and monsters of every kind throw their drinks around, rip into one another, shrieking their enthusiasm for the Death trials as soon as they see their mighty murderous leader. *Me.*

The audience perch in seats wrapped around the large, round colosseum, all looking down at a large arena with a dragon glass enclosed to keep the humans in and to keep the Hellish creatures out. The arena must be about three hundred metres wide, and there is currently a foggy smoke hiding what is inside there.

Next to me, Misery appears, rocking back in her seat in delight. She laughs at a joke nobody else hears before her beady eyes fall on me. "You're finally here! Take a seat brother, you're going to be very impressed with my lineup."

With a scowl, I sink into my skull-shaped throne which has small swords sticking out of it. I grit my teeth as the pain scratches at my back, legs and ass. The familiar agony grounds me and keeps me from transforming and sucking the lives of everybody in this fucking Colosseum.

My parents take their seats on their own thrones next to me. They lose themselves in excited chatter, gossiping about what is to come. I don't bother joining in. After what feels like eternity, the announcement begins.

"Welcome to the Death trials!" my father booms, and the crowd roars to life in response. "This is the first-ever event where you get to see the wickedest beasts in action against sinful mortals! As I'm sure you will all know by now, this event is being hosted to provide my son, Death, with a new mortal pet!"

I swallow down the lump in my throat and glare at the currently empty dome directly in front of me.

My sister asked me to donate some of my most wicked creatures to the cause. I agreed, thinking that the worse they were, the quicker these mortals would be killed off and the quicker I could go home. However, now that I'm sitting here, the realisation quickly sinks in.

The beasts I've selected could very easily break through the glass dome if they were so inclined. Then, it's *my* problem to capture them again. Capture *and* punish. My nature drives the desire to hurt and destroy, like an evil voice in my head or a strong pull from my heart, but when I punish my creatures, I punish myself too. *How can I hurt them for instincts I bestowed onto them? How can I punish them for the limitations I forced on them? How can I torture them without torturing myself?* They're my children, and though I don't love or care for them, duty keeps me suffering for their suffering.

Currently, my body aches with the throbbing of unassorted souls that are crying out for a home and that fucking annoying stinging in my cheek. Plus, I have a whole week of these shitty trials so I could *really* do without inflicting more pain on myself.

"The Death trials will whittle ten mortals down to one through a series of deadly challenges!" My father continues. "But participation is required from you hideous lot, too! Before each event, you can bet on who you think will win. And after the event, you can vote for your winner! Of course, there is a huge prize if your mortal goes through to the next round! With that being said, let's meet the contestants!"

Again, the crowd roars to life with excitement as a podium rises in the middle of the dome and the fog clears. I smell the wretched creatures before I see them, and that muggy, salty stench makes my stomach flip. The alluring scent of their blood and pounding heartbeats make me readjust myself in my seat. I sink my fangs into my tongue to resist the urge to take them all to an early grave. There's nothing sweeter than a dead human, but imagining ten dead humans, and a whole room of pissed-off creatures looking for a fight, makes my cock hard.

Delighted, Misery leaps to her feet as the humans are slowly revealed, and a deadly hush falls upon the crowd as everyone intently watches their potential next meal. Each human wears the same tight, black jumpsuit, but each jumpsuit has a different number stitched onto the stomach.

"Prey One," Misery announces as a spotlight shines down on the first human on the left. He has a bald head, and every inch of skin is coated in tattoos or piercings of some type. Shielding his eyes from the light, he lifts his hand to his face and this small movement reveals his large biceps that threaten to burst out of his jumpsuit. The man visibly shakes with fear, making me smile. A man of that size and notable arrogance stained into his soul, trembling in front of the real bad guys. It's a sight for sore eyes.

"Prey Two," Misery continues to the next person. A large woman with pale skin shakes under the blaring lights. Her eyes dart left and right worriedly and she takes shallow breaths trying to steady herself. Her cheeks are flushed red, and I wait for her to hit the floor like a sack of potatoes. *The fat ones always faint first.*

"Prey Three,"

The spotlight assaults a thinner man with a buzz cut. Scars rip into his skin, making his face all distorted, and with a single sniff, I can feel the terror ripping around his body. The stench of smoke and fire stains his soul as if he's come straight from a building fire.

"Prey Four,"

A muscly man with skin the colour of chocolate stares back out at the crowd. For a moment, he's quiet, and then he erupts with anger, screaming and shouting. He won't be able to see the audience even if he can see my family and me in the viewing gallery leering over the top of them. Misery hid the audience from the humans to not distract them in the trials. Nonetheless, he charges forward to the glass dome but as soon as his fist connects with it, he is sent flying backwards. With a satisfying thump, he smacks against the floor. As his lifeline staggers, I smile, but then it steadies and my scowl returns.

Misery talks through the rest of the group, each as frightened and quivering as the last as they stare up at my family and me. Though we are in our human form, every creature will be able to smell the evilness seeping from our beautifully haunted forms. Even humans.

Boring! The beast whines and I can't help agreeing with him. I drown it out, not bothering to take any more notice. With luck, they will all die in this first round, and I will meet them down in whichever realm of hell they are sorted into, and I can have my fun with them then. However, Misery suddenly increases her volume and it's no longer possible to ignore her.

"Last, but never least, *Prey Ten*."

Intrigued, I stare down at the final mortal. Raven-coloured hair curls down the back of a pale woman with dark lips and lightly freckled cheeks. She stands almost numbly at the end of the lineup, her arms hanging limply by her sides. She doesn't tremble, she doesn't cry or sob or scream. It looks as though she is standing in a queue for some mortal shop and not in front of the Original Hellish family.

Bored, her eyes cast over the other contestants and she sighs, before staring back in front of her, lost in her own world. When she blinks, she doesn't let her lashes caress her cheeks for a second longer than they need to. It's so hurried it completely contrasts her calm demeanour, and it has my curiosity peaked.

What are you doing, little mortal? How are you so at ease?

More frustratingly, her heartbeat doesn't even spike, either, nor can I smell sweat from fear. She runs her tongue across her top lip and a thin coating of saliva covers those red pillows.

The beast within me stirs. *'I want to rip them from her face.'*

"And there we have it! Our ten mortals," Misery beams proudly, clasping her hands together. The sharpness of her voice comes as a welcome surprise, and I force my eyes away from the little mortal and reclaim control over the beast inside.

Misery continues her speech. "The first round is a test of physical strength. The Prey will battle it out with a Hellish beast for the chance to progress into the next trial. For our entertainment, the prey will have a weapon. A wishbone—"

"What?" I splutter in anger.

A *wishbone,* also known as the most dangerous weapon against a hellish creature. *My fucking sister is handing out death sentences to my children!*

"Relax," my father hisses so nobody else hears us. "Do you really think any of them will be able to take down a beast?"

Angrily, I rake my eyes over the lineup of humans and sigh as reason takes over. These are creatures I created from the depths of hell, born into places where there is no mercy, only suffering. There is no way a human could overpower my beasts or even get close to them.

With a low growl, I sink further into my seat.

"They must survive six minutes in the arena with the creature or, better yet, kill the beast with the weapon! Now that you've met the contestants and heard about the first trial, please place your bets on which human you think will make it to the next round!"

Stubbornly, I do not vote. Instead, I place silent bets on who will be slaughtered first. By the time my eyes find Prey Ten, I'm bored with wasting the seconds. I expect to look down at a trembling mortal with frantic eye movements now that she's heard her trial. Instead, I'm pleasantly surprised. Staring straight back at me, unwaveringly, two dark eyes with long lashes. She doesn't blink. Her gaze is strong and heavy as though she is looking directly into my eyes. For a brief moment, I consider whether she is blind or deaf or maybe just stupid.

Does she know what is going on around her? Why isn't she trembling in fear or crying with despair?

But those dark orbs are the eyes of a woman so full of hatred and pain, *and clarity*. Malicious excitement rushes through me before I can register what's happening. Something familiar twists in my stomach when I smell the anger oozing from her body, mixed with a hint of cherries. She is intoxicating with her confidence and the beast inside of me roars. It longs to see if her oddly beautiful skin is as delicate as it looks or whether it would burn and bubble under my fingertips. It begs to taste her anger and confidence on the tip of my forked tongue. I want to make her writhe in pain below me, to teach her true fear, to remove her life. My face must make clear all the evil plans I have for her, and yet, she is *still* staring at me.

Slightly amused, my head cocks to the side and I lick my lips. Only then does she avert her eyes but it's not in a frightened way that I long for. *Oh no*, the little bitch looks away as if I bore her! The growl bubbles up in my throat and my fingers curl into fists.

"Has everyone voted?" Misery's voice echoes around the

Colosseum, and a wave of noise responds to her. She lifts her arms sharply to silence the room before turning to Longing.

"Mother," she says expectantly. Longing slowly rises to her feet before turning her hands, so her palms are facing upwards. Then, her eyes roll back in her head. The grey orbs with swimming snakes inside her irises appear. My mother's fingers dance around in the air as she counts the votes in her mind. Within seconds, she has her answer. She turns to Misery with a twisted smile, and they silently communicate the answer.

"Interesting," Misery nods her head slowly before addressing the audience again. "You have voted that Prey One will win the physical strength trial!"

A celebratory roar from the audience confirms the results. I don't bother looking at the tattooed man who is most likely feigning confidence. Instead, I look at the little mortal at the end of the line, eyeing up the potential winner. Her lips tighten and she looks almost pissed off that she wasn't selected. My cock throbs in anticipation. *What a confident little thing.*

'I can't wait to see her die! The beast cries out in excitement. *She's going to be delicious spread against the floor and then we can fuck whatever is left of her!'* My Beast cries out excitedly.

'Shut the fuck up'. I spit back, but he doesn't calm down. I feel his heartbeat pick up and he momentarily takes control of our body to wet our fangs. Despite my restraint, the beast manages to plant the perverse thoughts in my head, and I find myself readjusting in my seat. I fucking hope she has done some heinous crime and is forced to suffer for all eternity in my Realm. That way, I can have my way with her repeatedly until I grow bored and find some new toy to fuck.

I pray repeatedly for this dirty, fucked up fantasy to become real, but then again, God's never been one to grant prayers to sinners.

CHAPTER SIX

Sin. Torture. Anguish. *Death.*

The words leap into my head as soon as I feel the beast's ineffable gaze on me. My stomach twists angrily and the hairs on the back of my neck stand to attention. *Prey recognises Predator.*

I've never been looked at like *that* before. A look that promises so much pain, anguish, hatred and *death*. Human words can't even describe the awful look that was just fixed on me, and yet, despite the mortifying sight in front of me, no fear coursed through my veins. When you've lived a life of fear and suffering, it becomes your normal. Your body will adjust itself and spare the adrenaline for when it's necessary, not when it's normal. It's only the spark within my heart that screams danger when everything else is numb.

His head cocks to the side and the light bounces off his chiselled face, casting shadows on the rest of his body. He doesn't look different from a human, but the aura he gives off couldn't be more parallel. If anything, he's very handsome. Tar-coloured hair, dark red eyes, pale skin, and round, full lips. Inky patterns kiss his pale, exposed skin on his fingers and hands, on his neck and face and down to his chest. He wears an unfamiliar material on his torso and legs, and his huge muscular arms threaten to burst out of a raven-coloured long-sleeved top.

Beside him, he has a large, deranged weapon, shaped like a large talon with a stunning red jewel at the top. I watch carefully as he twiddles it around menacingly. I can only liken his outfit to war armour. He looks utterly breathtaking in it, oozing anger and deadly promises. A coal-coloured mist seeps out of him when he glares down at me, and I'm momentarily stunned. It reminds me that he is not human. He is something I should stay away from, I should fear, but I've never been one to fear the unknown. In my experience, the known is always far more dangerous.

Something in those shadowy eyes twinkles maliciously. It makes my mouth dry and my fingers curl into fists as I recognise him as a threat. My tongue darts out to wet my bottom lip, and his bleeding eyes seem to catch every movement.

I force myself to look away and inspect the other creatures in the viewing gallery too.

My gaze drifts to the oldest-looking man there who announced himself as the handsome man's father. He seems cold and calculated, with beady little eyes darting everywhere, as though he can hear everyone's thoughts. Slicked back hair, and paler-than-pale skin. So white that it could almost be transparent. He has a slight shadow of wrinkles which kiss his exposed skin and a hairy chest that sticks out the top of his dark suit.

He looks skittish as he rocks forward in his chair and whispers something to the lady next to him. The same older woman from the cell. Her innocent, alluring, motherly-tone has me almost drifting towards her. I have to physically remind myself to stay still as I watch the beautiful woman who seems to attract people towards her. She makes me want to spill my secrets; tell her everything she wants to know. There's something weirdly irresistible yet terrifying about that woman.

Beside her, is Misery. She is no longer covered by large sunglasses and her fiery hair hovers beside her perfectly sculpted face. The bottom ends of her hair slither out as though they are snakes. For a split second, I see little tongues shoot out of the tendrils of hair, and I stiffen. She's too far away to see for certain, but from here, it's almost as if the balls of her eyes are completely white. It is difficult to see where she is focusing her attention if it were not for her little snake hairs that stare at the row of seats lower. Her beautiful face twists into a scowl as she sees something she dislikes in the audience. I wonder what *things* are in the arena with us that the mere human cannot see or hear.

When I look back at the handsome beast on the end, I feel his gaze trail down my body slowly. He still observes me, analyses me, and looks *through* me. Before he can get the satisfaction of seeing me tremble for him, I look away again and force my face to be inscrutable.

Someone sobs beside me, and for the first time, I turn my attention to the other contestants. Six men, three women. The person crying is an old lady in her mid-sixties, hands pressed together in a prayer sign as she chants.

No use down here, I want to tell her, but instead, my lips stay firmly pressed together.

The other lady must be in her late thirties, a rather round lady with a sweaty, rashy face. She cries softly to herself, but the sound is almost haunted. Snot drips from under her nose and she wipes it away with the back of her arm.

The last woman is— well, a *girl*. She is barely a woman with spotty skin, greasy black hair and sad, mournful eyes filled with unshed tears. Shakily, she clings to the man next to her who must be ten years her senior. He wraps her in a half-hearted hug and presses a kiss to her head, eyes scanning the surroundings for threats. When he catches me staring, he sends me the dirtiest look and bares his teeth. I do not give him the satisfaction of a reaction.

"Mortals," a deep raspy boom brings my attention back to the viewing gallery. The father stands from his throne. "Which of you would like to go first?"

His thin papery lips stretch across his face in a disgusting way that has my stomach churning. Absolute silence prevails. All eyes fall on me when my hand shoots up in the air.

The quicker I win; the quicker Maximo suffers.

"Prey Ten wishes to start us off," he bellows, his voice laced with amusement. "Remove the other contestants."

Suddenly, the most overwhelming roar of an audience shrieks to life that even I flinch, and my fists raise instinctively. A single glimmer within the empty seats reveals the most grotesque wave of green, grey and black slimy, scaley, fiery bleeding creatures with huge menacing jaws and thousands of eyes. It looks like something from my nightmares as the flicker quickly reveals the thousands of beasts leering down at us in the audience. Just as quickly as they appear, they disappear, revealing the sea of empty seats around the arena.

My heart thumps one hundred miles an hour in my chest and the nausea rises as the weight of the situation seeps in. I don't have a moment to gather my thoughts before the world suddenly changes around me.

Within the arena, the other mortals suddenly disappear, and the ground turns to dust and rocks. It shakes and trembles, knocking me onto my knees. I hiss as the harsh ground already tears through the pathetically weak jumpsuit supposedly designed to protect me.

"And so, we begin! You have three minutes without a weapon and then three minutes with a weapon. If you survive the whole six minutes, you pass the trial."

My head snaps up furiously at the man howling his delight, but my anger is short-lived as the floor begins shaking again and a furious, demonic howl in the distance sends a shiver shooting through me.

As if it only just hits me, it finally sinks in that what I'm about to do isn't normal and the dread replaces any confidence I once mustered.

HOLLY GUY

What the fuck have I signed up to?

CHAPTER SEVEN

Suddenly, the floor gives way, tilting ninety degrees. I scramble, desperately reaching for the rocks, but my attempts prove to be futile. With very little time to prepare myself, I'm falling through the air.

Fear swarms through me as I realise this arena is about three hundred metres in circumference and if I fall, I'm going to explode on impact. Frightened, I scramble around for something to grab onto. The vicious wind rushes through my hair and clothes, however, before I can fall any further, the ground connects with my shoulder without warning and forcefully drives me upward. Tilting anticlockwise, I fall again. Just like before, before I can hurl down to my inevitable death, the floor changes again, smashing back into me. A scream of agony rips through me as the ground keeps tilting and changing direction, throwing itself into me. My whole body pounds with bruising but the awful attack from the moving ground is too fast and irregular to figure out. It disorientates me and sends me spinning each time, making it impossible to fight. I'm thrown around like a rag doll two more times before I realise the floor is starting to slow down and not tilt as much. My head pounds and my vision blots in and out.

They are trying to disorientate you. The little voice in the back of my head screams for me to snap out of it but it's impossible as the nausea rises up in my throat. *Just like how Maximo would strap you on the spinning chair and whirl you around for ten minutes to stop your fight.*

Everything aches beyond belief. My hearing is nothing but a high-pitched scream from where I hit my head against the stone floor. The familiar feeling never gets easier. I force the bile back down my throat, but it doesn't go down without a fight.

Abruptly, the floor tilts in the other direction and my legs scramble around to get some contact with a rock to steady myself. Finally, I manage to get to my feet and run up the slope to avoid falling into the other side of the glass dome again.

Much to my relief, the steepness of the slope isn't as severe, and I can just about fight gravity. The floor does this a couple of more times and I find myself finding a good pattern of charging up to whichever side is the highest and remaining there until it changes again. It keeps me steady and gives me the edge if anything joins me in this arena, but I'm utterly exhausted already.

My plan swiftly goes out of the window as the floor throws itself out of balance again and I fall ungracefully to the lowest side of the tilted ground. The left side of my body smashes against the concrete and I roll a couple of times until I hit the glass. I have a couple of moments to regain my breath and my senses, but I almost wish my hearing never returned because the most awful growl echoes around the dome.

Horrified, I stare up at a huge goblin-looking creature, dribbling green slime and spitting out puddles of saliva at the top of the sloped floor. Its teeth are the size of my arms and sharpened like daggers. The creature slams its jaws open and shut and the sound of the slicing weapons is deafening. It completely takes my breath away.

It charges down the slope towards me. Its face is all muddled up with eyes that have a thin film of green over it, and gill-looking slices in its face around that terrifying jaw. He doesn't seem to have a nose or ears, but I don't count either of those senses out without knowing what those gills do. His ridiculously long arms swing by its side, propelling it faster forward up the slope and I don't doubt if they get me, I'm royally fucked: he could bludgeon me to death with a single swipe! His entire being is faster than ever deemed imaginable, and I don't have time to plan my escape. Just in time, the floor lurches in the opposite direction, causing the creature to stumble. Luckily, we are both disorientated and I use this to my advantage.

Without thinking, I throw myself down the slope between the monster's legs, narrowly missing his large arms. I fall fast but manage to twist onto my stomach and scramble to my feet before the awful floor can do much more damage. Thankfully, the monster is disgruntled and confused as it stares around, desperately trying to find me. It gives me time to put some distance between us.

"Three minutes without a weapon is up," Misery's voice fills the dome. Relief consumes me as I suddenly spot a dagger in the middle of the arena floor. I risk a glance at the family on the other side, and now I see the sinfully attractive man from earlier with wide, furious eyes. He rises to his feet and glares down at the scene in front of him. I can't see anyone else, that black mist around him has managed to fully block them all out.

All of the sudden, the roar of the angry beast in front of me pulls my attention back to what's happening. He still stumbles around about a hundred metres from me, but it's only fifty from the weapon. I start to charge towards it as the floor finally levels itself out and stops tilting.

Despite that, my whole body still moves as though I'm still rocking back and forth. The nausea rises up and I have to desperately swallow it down to avoid spewing up everywhere and becoming vulnerable. It takes a moment to steady myself, but that's one moment too many, and now the monster is racing back across the arena. He moves so fucking fast it's blinding.

I only just about manage to roll out of his way before that large body can connect with me. He continues running until he bangs into the glass on the other side of the dome, creating the loudest thud. To my surprise, the dome doesn't shatter. With him momentarily distracted, I lurch for the weapon. However, as I grab it, I skid on the loose stones, sending them flying across the arena as I fall on my ass.

Expectedly, the monster's head snaps in my direction when he hears me. Without hesitation, he charges back over to me again, but curiously enough, he lurches for where I tripped on the stones, not where I ended up. I ready my fighting stance and resist the smile which threatens my lips.

He's blind.

Testing my theory, I grab a pebble from the floor and throw it as far away from me as I can. It smashes into the glass dome and the Goblin charges after it. Pride settles in as I finally feel back in control of the fight.

As the monster throws himself around in confusion, swinging at nothing, desperately trying to find me, I toss the weapon from one hand to the other, getting familiar with the way the ribbed handle kisses my skin. It shines beautifully under the blaring stage lights, the silver tooth-like dagger sparkling as if it's made from thousands of diamonds. I run my finger across the blade and something sticky stains my skin. I rub it between my fingers feeling the slimy and oily texture. Then, my heart jumps out of my chest as I frantically wipe my hand on my jumpsuit.

Poison.

Horrified, the blood drains from my body and I stupidly let the weapon fall to my feet. Everything in the arena dulls into a low thud of my heartbeat and my whole body feels as though it's going to give way. Not from the poison itself, but from my fucking brain which hurls me back into a traumatic memory.

Maximo's face swarms my mind in all his wicked ugliness. Then that fucking awful cackle stings my head and the pain is unlike no other. Fragments of memories of him tying my naked body down. Him pouring two clear liquids into one another until it created a white foggy poison. Him forcing my lips open and putting a tiny pipette of liquid on my gums. I can taste the disgusting plastic taste of his gloves as he rubs it into my gums to ensure I fully digest the poison. And then the pain — *oh fuck, the pain!*

My entire body seizes up as though he's here right now, drugging me. In the distance, I hear the roar of the monster as he hears the thud of the weapon on the ground, giving my position away. His tremendous footsteps shake the ground, and I can *smell* him getting close, rotten eggs and decaying flesh attack me. *But I can't fucking move.* My whole body is frozen still, locked in the curse of post-traumatic stress, and there isn't one fucking thing I can do about it.

CHAPTER EIGHT

Holy fuck. Prey ten knows how to survive.

From the first slam of the ground into her small body, I thought she was done for. The second time, I had myself brushing the dust off my trousers, readying for the next candidate. But she took it like a winner.

With every attack, she bounced back up, beaten and bruised but not ready to give up. And then my Goblin showed up. The nine-foot-tall creature of destruction. Even I found myself on the edge of my seat, eager to see whether she'd figure out that he was blind *and* had no sense of smell. And then Misery gave the little bitch a demon's claw, something that will disintegrate my creature into thousands of dust particles.

"You fucking bitch," I hiss under my breath to Misery when the weapon appears in the dome.

Out of the corner of my eye, Misery laughs and rocks back in her chair happily, but I don't remove my eyes from the scene as Prey Ten spots the weapon in the middle of the room. She leers for it, sliding along the floor, scratching up her jumpsuit until the blood on her knees shines through before throwing herself out of the way. My eyes fix on her blood and images of her giving up the wound for me to taste flash in my mind. My cock throbs approvingly and the monster within me thumps to be released again.

For a second, my fangs flash out and I feel the pull of evil within me, longing to escape. The temptation is too much, and I've never had to control myself as much as I must now in front of my family and thousands of wicked beasts, almost waiting for me to screw up and be punished.

The mysterious little mortal figured out my creature's weaknesses far too quickly for my liking and it vexes me.

She then grabs a rock and throws it across the dome, sending my creature charging like a fucking dog after a ball. The black mist seeps out faster and my fingers curl into fists. Impatiently, I glare up at the countdown on the wall which says she only has two minutes and sixteen seconds left in the dome.

When I turn my gaze back to her, I'm momentarily stunned as she stares down at the weapon in awe, lost in her own world. I expected to see disgust or confusion, but no, she stares at it as if it's the most mesmerising thing she's ever held. Then she throws it from one hand to the other and my heart leaps from my chest.

The Beast within me bristles. *'The bitch knows exactly what to do with it. Fuck!'*

"Kill her." I bark at my Goblin telepathically. *"Kill her or I'll kill you."*

He bristles when he hears the growl in his ears and looks visibly distraught. He charges around, lost and confused, now desperate to get his mighty hands on her. My lips twist into something resembling a smile with his newfound desire to destroy.

Her eyebrows pull together in confusion as she reaches out to feel the poison on the blade. For a short moment, she is curious as she rubs the poison into her fingers. It won't do her any damage unless it pierces her skin, but she won't know that, and her awe makes my cock stir. And then, without warning, her entire demeanour changes. Fear flashes across her face and a haunted cry escapes her lips.

The weapon tumbles from her fingers and she makes no move to grab it. It hits the floor with a thud, and the noise echoes around my head louder and louder until it is painful. Desperate, my goblin rears its ugly head in her direction and without hesitation, charges. Wide-eyed, I watch as she shakes and sweats, staring down at her fingers in absolute horror.

She is completely lost in her own world, a world that clearly brings more fear than the creature hurtling towards her. Petrified, her breathing becomes unsteady, and I hear the ridiculous beating of her heart, loud and fast, as though she has seen her death. My body is tense, and then a bitter smell storms my nose.

"Who is it?" I hiss. "Who is controlling her?"

Nobody answers me. Furiously, I spin on my heel and shoot a violent bolt of fire around the viewing gallery, torturing my family. They are the only ones capable enough of interfering with the trial so one of them *must* be orchestrating the scene. The howls of agony echo around the room as the never-ending burning particles chew away at their flesh. Their screams become a melody that drowns out the anxiety in my chest.

Stressed, I turn back to the little mortal and see my Goblin barely fifty metres from her. She is still locked in whatever it is that is keeping her from defending herself. I don't know why my whole body shrieks in anxiety but I don't have time to question it.

"It's not us!" Misery screams at me. "Let us go, Death! *Fuck!*"

"Death!" my father booms, his grave voice making the hairs on the back of my neck shot up.

Suddenly, the mortal snaps out of her trance. She is no longer petrified, and instead, pure anger settles on her face. With a dismissive hand, I remove the torture from my family and ignore their miserable complaints. Instead, I find myself stumbling towards the glass of the viewing area, eyes fixated on the little mortal with a strong desire to kill my child.

Fuck, who do we want to die?

She's back in action, dagger tightly locked in her fingers. The goblin charges, but she just about manages to slip between his legs, ripping the dagger through his skin. The cry of my beast has me completely changing sides again, and I long for him to squish her in the last twenty-something seconds of the trial.

He's momentarily startled by the sudden pain in his groin and howls. The loud sound vibrates around the arena, shaking the walls and shattering one section of the glass. I hold my breath and ready my fists. *If he tries to escape, I'm fucking ready.*

The little mortal barely flinches. Instead, she skids on her heels before readying her stance again and charging forward, the dagger held high.

My nostrils flare as I check the clock. It's no fucking use, she's about to leap up and plunge the demon claw so far into my baby's heart that he will hit the bottom circle of hell before he can take his next breath. *And what's worse, he will make me a laughingstock of all of Hell for supplying such a weak beast for combat.*

I can't fucking bare it.

Without hesitation, I flash into the dome. I put myself between her and my Goblin and snatch her by the arm using my body as a barrier for her to slam into. I barely move, but she rebounds backwards. Everything happens so quickly; she doesn't register it and the blare of the countdown rings around the Colosseum. Before she can fall on her ass, my arm snaps around her waist and I hold her still.

"What? What the fuck? Huh? What?" she's confused, but what's better. She's *furious.* Her anger is palpable and radiates off of her like the heat of her body. "He was mine. *Move!*"

Pathetically, she tries to wriggle out of my grasp, but she stops when my fingers curl into her soft skin. A yelp escapes her, and she now focuses her attention on escaping me rather than attacking my beast. It's the most delicious fucking sound.

'Do it again! Make her cry for us again!'

The thoughts have me forcing my eyes shut to hide the blackness that now seeps into them as my perverse beast howls to escape.

Just one taste. Just one touch! Wait— what is that?

My eyes shoot back open as I smell her murderous intent shifting around the arena. Without hesitation, she raises the weapon at me and strikes. Before she can take her next breath, I snatch the weapon from her and dispose of it across the room. Her eyes widen in horror as she is left completely defenceless.

As her gaze meets mine, she spots the black spreading through my eyes, forcing her to fight harder. Every wild punch and kick I receive only makes the monster howl louder and more violent. My erection is so fucking obvious that everybody in the room must see it, but I don't fucking care. All her wriggling and reluctance make me that much harder. And then it hits me.

She isn't fighting me out of fear, but because my Goblin bares his teeth at her, almost as if to mock her. Fury flashes through me when I see my Goblin leer over us teasingly. *The little bitch would prefer to fight him than me! Oh no, little mortal, we can't have that now...*

Before I can do anything that I regret to the beast, I click my fingers and he disappears. I don't know why it makes me feel some sort of sick humour. I've had to remove my Goblin from the arena because a *mortal* might kill him. It should be the other way around. I shouldn't be able to keep my goblin away from *her*, and yet here we are.

"Fuck!" she roars. "I almost had him! Get him back!"

She shoves me in the chest and her eyes flash with surprise at the hardness. I don't flinch once. I shake so hard I could shatter her bones if I held on any more tightly. The fury shoots through me and a red mist stains my sight.

Fucking teach her a lesson! Who does she think she is? Embarrassing us in front of everyone—

"Calm down, Prey Ten. You've passed," Misery's voice suddenly appears next to me. "Death, let her go."

I fucking long to have the little mortal on her knees begging for forgiveness. I want her pale skin stained red. I want to fuck her cocky little mouth so she can't throw any more threats out.

"Death," Misery warns me, and I feel pain sting my shoulder as she grips me. The beast shrieks at me to attack and everything within me supports him, but that little slither of reason knows I can't destroy the mortal in front of this whole audience. My father would have to punish me publicly and this will only reveal a weak united front. I fucking hate politics but I despise dealing with the consequences more.

Cold air stings my hands as soon as I let the little mortal go, and something inside of me longs to grab her again. To hold her against my hard body. She should be writhing on the floor in agony, the demon claw plunged so far into her heart that she is sent to the most fearsome circle of hell. She should be pleading for mercy for hurting my monster. For fucking daring to try and attack me, and yet, here she is, hard challenging eyes and murderous intent. She doesn't realise how much danger she's in with that attitude alone and fuck do I want to be the one to teach her.

As if sensing my intentions, Misery steps between me and the mortal.

She turns to face the audience , throwing her arms in the air to make them roar in excitement. "There we have it, Monsters and Monstresses," she quickly regains control of the situation. "We have our first contestant entered into the next trial!"

Behind her, the little mortal doesn't even flinch. Her furious gaze burns into me before darting to the weapon on the other side of the arena. For a brief moment, she schemes about killing me. I feel that pull within her, one very similar to my own. My whole body throbs in anger until the black mist seeps out of me, fogging up the arena.

And honestly? I fucking long for her to try again. Only then can I justify the awful, torturous things I plan to do to her when I get her alone.

CHAPTER NINE

Who the *fuck* does he think he is? I earned that kill! That disgusting Goblin was *mine*! I don't care if the trial was finished, I had something to prove. The fact I even got my dagger near the Goblin was statement enough for my success, but *he* stopped me from fully proving what I could do.

Maybe it is my ego speaking but I need that beast's death on my hands to prove to the gruesome audience to vote for me. Let's not waste any more time playing these childish games. I *am* going to win. Give me my deal with the Devil now.

My fingers curl into fists. The Being in front of me threw the weapon away two hundred metres, and I know he's much faster and stronger than me, but the desire to hurt him floods through me. I want to kill him for neglecting me of my kill.

Just as I lurch towards the dagger, the whole world around me changes. A blinding light flashes and I hold my arms up to protect my eyes from the beam. When it slowly fades, I find myself in a large room smelling of bitter lemons and overwhelming bleach. Trying to regain my balance, I stumble around before falling into something hard and red.

A sofa?

Blinking back my surprise, I glare around the large red room with ten crimson sofas in the middle and the other contestants sitting nervously on the edge of each one. Wide-eyed, they all stare at me in shock as we all try to adjust to the whole idea of *flashing* in and out of places.

My nature kicks in and I quickly scan the room for threats. To the left of the room, there seems to be a kitchen, and around the rest of the room, there are eight doors.

"Bedrooms," a croaky voice tells me. I swallow down the lump in my throat and turn to face the older lady with grey hair. Her hands are still clasped in a prayer sign from earlier, and her eyes are still wet with tears. "Only eight. They must anticipate two people dying in this trial!"

I don't say a single word as I cast my gaze around the room at lots of expectant faces. Just as I step into the room, Misery's voice echoes around the room even though her physical body never appears.

"Prey Nine is next."

Suddenly, the young man in the corner of the sofa disappears, much to the other contestant's horror. It creates a frenzy amongst the group, but I force the buzzing noise out. My head throbs painfully from being thrown around in the trial, and I'm still shaking in anger.

A hand around my arm has me looking at a large black man with crazy eyes, staring at me in fear. "Well? What was it? What was in there with you? What should we expect?"

I ignore him and go to step past, but he doesn't let me leave. "Tell us!"

Realising I'm not going to be able to avoid the question, I keep my answer short. I don't want to get to know any of these people. They are all my enemies. They are in the way of my deal with the devil. "Moving floor. Goblin."

"Moving floor!" the teenage girl screams behind me, before sobbing into the man's shoulder who sits next to her. "Moving floors, Tom! How will we beat that?"

"Hey, love, don't cry," he coos her reassuringly. "Don't worry about it. If she did it, we can do it."

I don't bother biting back a retort. From the sparkle within his beady little eyes, he wants me to fight back. Adrenaline is one hell of a drug. He stares at me and gives me a disgusting grimace. I glare at 'Prey Seven' in his black jumpsuit and silently pray that he dies in the trial.

Warily, I cross the room and stand in front of the contestants to get a better look at them. Instinct tells me to retreat to a room and sleep off the battering I received but reason tells me to stay and gain as much information from these fools as I can. I'm still trying to decide which is better.

"You, how did you defeat the Goblin?" Prey Seven barks at me, shoving a finger dangerously close to my face. I stare at the digit and images of Leonardo biting off fingers fill my mind. He told me chomping through bone was just as easy as biting a carrot, it's just that the human brain wills you not to.

Do it. My perverse mind coos. *Bite his finger off.*

"Go on, don't keep your secrets." His ugliness is both inside and outside.

I glare at him through dark eyes, daring him to keep pressing. He drops his finger and I put some distance between us, for his safety rather than mine. The contestants break into frightened conversations about what-ifs and strategy, but I don't bother joining in. Instead, my mouth dries and I long for water to quench the thirst.

I make my way over to the kitchen counters and run my hand across the granite. Usually, it's smooth with the pattern trapped inside, but here, it's rough and sharp, awful to balance anything on it.

I get to what I assume is the tap. A large hollow bone curls into a bowl-shaped large skull. I click the button next to it and boiling hot water squirts out, steam quickly filling up the room. I click it again and it stops. I hold the button down, but hot water comes out again. Then I click twice quickly, *again hot water*. No matter what I do, I can't get cold water.

Suddenly, on the granite counters stuck to the wall above the counters, a little label appears. *Prey Ten.*

That's me.

My hand warily reaches out to the jagged rock, and I pull it open. The cabinet reveals tinned food with pictures of different meats and vegetables on it, skull-shaped bowls, and cups, and then a singular fork, knife and spoon. Instinctively, I pocket the knife.

"Who you gonna kill?" a male voice startles me, and I jump around to see Prey Three, a thin man with small spikes of hair in the style of a buzzcut, and scars which tear into his skin making his face look all funny. The skin he does have is bumpy, scarred and hairless. I've seen someone like this before... *Leonardo poured gasoline over them and lit a match—*

"Is it me?" He smiles but it's odd and makes my stomach flip. One side is much higher than the other and makes it look more like a lopsided scowl than an actual smile. "Are you going to kill me?"

"Depends on if you attack first," I say bluntly, putting distance between us. He mistakes my words for humour and chuckles. His oceanic eyes flicker back to me once he stops laughing and I'm mesmerised by the way his pupils look exploded.

"Fire does that, apparently." He remarks. I make no effort to apologise for my rudeness; he seems taken aback by my lack of social skills and blinks frantically a couple of times. I learnt in the six months with me on the run that I seem to have a different etiquette to the rest of society.

"What did you do then? Why are you here?" He jumps up onto the counter and sits on the rough granite. Amazed, I watch expectantly for some type of pain to ripple across his face. *Nothing.* I reach out and feel the granite again and the little shard cuts me, and a small stream of blood instantly pours out.

"Does that not hurt?"

"My nerve endings were fried in the fire." His answer creates more questions. He must see the confused expression on my face because he clarifies. "I killed seven people in a house fire. The landlord tried to evict me, so I lit a match. I didn't think the victims would be that slow to react."

He speaks about the murders so casually and even rolls his eyes. My lips curl into disgust and I avert my attention from him. When I glare over at the other contestants, I can't help but wonder what awful things they have done to end up here too. *Am I really stuck in a game with villains? Have I really become one of them?*

"Prey One discriminated and committed assault, Prey Two killed babies in the hospital she worked at," the man starts listing them off as though he has interrogated each of them, "Prey Four was done for domestic assault. Prey Five was a nonce, Six and Seven appear to be lovers and killed her disapproving parents. Prey Eight was a nun who allowed awful things to happen to her choir boys. And Prey Nine was a school shooter." He releases a sharp breath.

Wide-eyed, I stare at the strange man in front of me. He shrugs nonchalantly and that lopsided grin returns. "What? Six minutes is plenty of time to suss out the competition. You're welcome for that information, by the way. You can repay me by telling me how you ended up here. What did you do?"

I remain quiet, trying to figure out how to escape this crazy conversation.

"Theft?" His eyes roam down my body as he desperately tries to figure me out. "Assault? Kidnapping? Arson? Murder?"

My heart heaves in my chest when he mentions murder and it must reveal itself on my face because he releases a sharp breath.

"No wonder you survived the trial then."

Again, despite the harrowing situation, he tries to find some humour in it. I can't bring myself to crack a smile. The man is far too odd and untrustworthy to let my guard down.

"Was it just one person?" He tries again. This time, I shake my head. "Well, how many then?"

Thirteen on the bus and dozens of my abusers before that. I swallow down the lump in my throat.

His eyes twinkle. "How many deserved it?"

"Too many," I finally answer. My hand jumps to the weapon in my pocket instinctively as though the thought alone is triggering my fight or flight. *And since I escaped that prison, I will never use flight again.*

Noticing my sudden change in mood, Prey Three jumps off the side defensively. He raises his hands. "Don't kill me, Prey Ten. We need an alliance."

"An alliance?" I spit.

"Sure. Look around you. This is a competition where we fight to the death. Alliances have already begun." He nods towards the sofas and my heart twists in my ribcage. *He's right.* There are two clear camps in the room. On the far left, there are Prey One, Two, Five and Eight. And on the right, Prey Four, Six and Seven.

I stare at the two camps, and Prey Three's words come back to me about their crimes. There is a clear distance between those who have been killed and those who have not. *Typical, even in Hell humans will judge those who sin differently to them.*

I crinkle my nose. "I don't need any allies."

As if on cue, across the room, Prey Six's eyes latch on me. She spots my open cupboard and wipes excitedly at her sweaty teenage face to push the strands of hair away from her eyes.

"She has access to her cupboard!"

Suddenly, the large skinhead with huge tattoos and 'Prey One' written across his chest, jumps over the sofa and hurries towards me. His eyes are furious, the fear and anxiety of the day now transforming into anger towards me.

"How did you do that?"

I stiffen as a bit of spit hits me on the cheek. It takes everything within me to keep my calm and not strike out at this man. The knife in my pocket burns and throbs, begging me to use it, and an awful thought runs around my brain. *Who would stop me from killing each of these sinners now and getting my deal faster? There are no rules here, right?*

"Relax, bro. She won her trial, so she's moved on to the next trial." Prey Three steps in front of me, putting distance between me and the triggered man who is begging to be stabbed. "When you pass, you'll get one too. Or, I should say, *if* you pass."

"What did you say, asshole?" Prey One seethes but Prey Three doesn't relent.

His fire-scarred face only smiles brighter with the anticipation of a fight. "I said you ain't gonna make it. You might be big and muscly, but answer me this, how many drugs did you take for your build-a-body?"

"You fucking cunt, I was voted most likely to be successful. *You're* the one who isn't going to make it."

"We'll see." His eyes twinkle with the challenge. The cock-measuring-contest bores me. It's all words, and soon, they will all die, if not by my knife, then by whatever those awful trials throw at them. I don't join in the threats, but I do protect myself in case words grow more violent.

With them distracted, I fill up the skull-shaped cup with boiling water and manage to prop it up on the least bumpy part of the counter. I reach for the bowl before filling it up with scolding water and placing it next to the cup. Then, I twist around and face the two men who are so close they could kiss.

"She's got food too!" the teenage girl hollers, pointing to my shelf. My teeth grind together defensively. I know what it is like to fight for food, so she has no fucking chance.

My head cocks to the side maliciously. Adrenaline from the fight still courses through my veins and something evil within me longs to kill her. "Come and get it then. See what happens."

"Are you threatening her?" Prey Seven pushes her behind him before getting inches away from my face. I resist the smile when he steps within striking range. *What is the worst that could happen if I just plunge this knife into his fucking neck?*

"No," my voice doesn't waver even as he towers over me, "I am threatening *you*. Get the fuck out of my face."

"Or what?" He sizes me up, thinking he's safe with his much bigger height and size. My fingers hum in anticipation. *Go on, asshole. One shove. One fucking finger on me. I dare you. I can claim self-defence if there is a rule against killing one another.*

Prey Four comes into vision now, trying to corner me too. He doesn't intimidate me either, and if anything, it makes the delight brim in my chest. I am buzzing with adrenaline from my trial, *and* I have been denied death, so it's only fair I claim my reward now.

Right?

Fuck. Maybe Maximo left a lasting impression on my soul.

Prey Four reaches past me and into the cupboard but as soon as he touches the food, I drive my knee into his stomach.

"Why you little bitch—" he hollers before reaching back to swing at me. Just as he goes to make the connection, I swing around, throwing the boiling cups of water over Prey Seven and Four, to momentarily startle them with the scolding heat. Next to me, Prey Three starts pummelling prey One, to the tune of the screaming old lady and teenager behind us.

And just like that, alliances have been formed.

I move so quickly that my attackers can't function and throw a hard kick into the back of their legs, so they buckle to their knees. I throw another foot into Prey Four's stomach until he falls back on the floor, but Prey Seven will not get such mercy.

He will die today. He will pay for talking to me like that.

I snap his head back and press the knife under his throat. His girlfriend hollers in fear, shrieking for me to stop, but it only pushes me further. I readjust the weapon to press into his skin until I feel the first layer of skin break, followed by another couple of layers. I watch as the slow trickle of blood stains his neck. It brings a perverse smile to my lips. I resist the urge to lick them.

Maybe Maximo had a point. Watching someone bleed is fucking delicious.

All it would take is one swipe and that's one contestant gone from the competition.

Just as I ready myself to make the kill, the room turns ten degrees colder, and the hairs on the back of my neck jump to attention. I don't need to turn around to know that *he* is behind me. The evil beast that hasn't stopped fucking my kills up.

And then, I feel his rough fingers curl around my neck. He applies a little bit of pressure to make me choke on my breath, but I don't relent. I don't do second chances with men who push me too far. I'd rather kill and then be killed than allow the disrespect. Nonetheless, my weapon doesn't sink further into my victim's skin no matter how much I will it to.

"Well, well, well," he coos in that raspy voice. I feel his hot breath caresses my cheek, a stark contrast to his cold presence. "Must you try and kill everything around you, little mortal?"

"He started it." I can't see his face. Hell, I don't even know the man, but I swear I can *feel* him smirk.

"Let him go."

"No."

"No?" He sounds amused. There is a short pause before he applies more pressure around my throat. I splutter as he restricts the oxygen from me. Tears brim in my eyes and my head feels hot, but Prey Seven has started crying in fear and wriggling around. It sets off that fucked up instinct within me that was tortured into my soul. *No mercy, no forgiveness, just revenge.*

"No—" The word doesn't fully get past my lips before the beast behind me snatches at my arms and forcefully removes me from Prey Seven, who scurries away with a cry of pain.

His arms snake around my neck, and he holds me in a tight lock. For a moment, I feel as though I might actually die here. The oxygen comes short and not strong enough and I splutter for air but the beast behind me doesn't give me the satisfaction. I claw at his arms before throwing my body back into him to try and wind him. It makes no difference.

Desperately, my eyes snap over to Prey Three who is on his knees, head snatched up in the air like he's being strangled by an invisible forcefield. Tears stream down his face but he makes no noise of distress, his eyes do all the speaking— popped out from his head, blood-shot and frightened. And, more frighteningly, everybody in the room is in the exact same position. It's as though all time has stopped and frozen them in agony.

"What the fuck?" The words finally slip through as he eases up a little, but not enough to be comfortable. I throw myself back against him again, all my fighting experience flying out the window, so I resort to desperate wiggles and cheap kicks. His spare hand reaches down and claws into my hip so tightly that I gasp in pain.

"Stop wriggling, little mortal." His voice is gruff and pained, and full of desperation as though he is losing control. I ignore him and push my hips outwards before slamming my whole body back into him, trying to wind him. It doesn't work at all.

"Fucking stop it." His voice is incredibly powerful. It completely takes me by surprise and shockingly, my body responds to his commands and I'm stiff to the ground. "You listen to me, little bitch—"

His grip slips from my throat as he drops his hand down to his pants. I feel his large fingers graze my ass as he readjusts himself in his trousers. Instantly, I freak out. I try to escape his tight grip, but his spare hand grabs my hip and forces me to the ground. He holds me fast with nowhere to escape. Panic consumes me at this all too familiar position.

"I never thought I'd say this," he growls, "But stop trying to kill everything. My family require contestants to compete in the trials for the audience. If you kill them, we will have to replace them, and it makes this whole shit show longer. If they die by your hands, I will pull you limb from limb until you're screaming for mercy. Got it?"

"What about the creatures? Can I kill them?" I don't know why I try to test boundaries, but it's instilled into me. *Never take no for an answer when men play by the same rules.*

"No."

"But—"

He cuts me off. "You won't be able to."

"I almost did," I hiss angrily. He stiffens behind me, sinking his claws into my skin. I bite back a hiss, not wanting to give him the satisfaction of crying out.

"That was a one-time thing. I gave you a weak creature to start the trials off. It was pure luck that you managed to fall over and scrape him."

Furiously, I throw my head back into his hard chest, trying to hurt him, and almost give myself a concussion. "You know full well it wasn't an accident! I fought well and almost ripped his fucking guts out, and I would have killed him if it hadn't been for y—"

My answer displeases him. A low, menacing growl falls from his lips as he spins me around so quickly it disorientates me, and I forget where I am going with my sentence.

Instinctively, my hands shoot out to grab his chest to steady myself and I instantly regret it as those stony muscles greet me. I pull away quickly as if I've been burnt. Stumbling backwards, I put some distance between us. He closes the gap effortlessly before snatching my arm. It's as though he can't resist being violent to me, and for some reason, my traitorous stomach twists deliciously at this thought.

"Do you know who I am?" he warns. Slowly, I shake my head when the words suddenly vanish from the top of my tongue. "Death," he coos the word so mesmerizingly. It's only after he says it that I feel the evilness, sin and destruction surrounding him. Thick, heavy and dark, like it weighs the whole room down with all the souls attached to him. It seems to sift into my lungs and choke me. "Now, you listen here, little mortal. I'm just trying to get through these fucking trials so I can return to my realm, but I can't seem to do it quickly because you keep getting in the way and ruining everything."

Something stupid within me has me wanting to poke the beast. I want to see how far I can anger Death. I've never been one to fear the idea of death. *Why would I?* Pain is a much greater master over humans. But now that I'm standing in front of him, I should be afraid, so why am I not? *Has Maximo beaten all fear out of me? Has he turned me crazy?*

"Got it, little girl? Stop getting in my way."

I'm too far gone to let him threaten me like that. With dark, challenging eyes, I rise to my tiptoes. My eyes flicker to his plump lips and the tongue that darts out to wet them when he notices my stare. His pink tongue is forked at the end and flickers out like a snake, a hissing sound slipping out too. My eyes dart back to his bleeding eyes which slowly turn black. And then, I do something no other sane person would do, I threaten death.

"Then stop getting in mine."

CHAPTER TEN

"Then stop getting in mine." The cheeky little bitch spits at me. My fingers hum with the desire to strike her across the face or to wrap around her throat and *squeeze* until she is begging for me to stop. The way she just spluttered and fought me just then is still ringing around my memory. My cock is still throbbing and longing for her small hand to curl around it. *Holy fuck.* She's so close, I can smell her anger, *the lives that she's claimed.* I need her. In the most violent way possible. I want her to fight and scream and hate me. She needs to throw all her madness at me.

My fingers snatch around her arm and I grip it tightly until it turns purple through the gaps in her tracksuit material. She bares her teeth but disappointingly, doesn't make a sound.

"Hand me the knife."

"No, I need it."

The vein in the side of my forehead pops at her blatant disregard for fear and reason. "You've lost that privilege."

"What if I need to cut my food?"

"You should have thought about that before you tried to cut the head off another contestant." I flash my fangs to try and intimidate her. She barely flinches and instead twiddles the knife in her fingers. For a moment, for the briefest second, for the tiniest pause, it looks as though she's going to plunge the weapon into my chest. Again, for the third time today, the little girl thinks she can kill the God of Death.

'Fuck yes, little mortal. Fuck us up. Give us a reason to punish you and release our tormented sexual desires onto you.'

"Fine." Surprisingly, she gives up without a large fight, and disappointment settles in my chest. I wanted to feel her violence and anger. Something twinkles in her eyes as she comes up with another devious plan and I really *really* want to find out what she is planning but I also long to be surprised.

"That's a good little mortal." I resort to teasing to get a reaction out of her. Her nostrils flare angrily, and her eyes darken but she makes no retort. *A shame.* Instead, she shoves the knife flat against my chest and drops it, making me move quickly to stop it from falling.

'She is trying to control us, the little bitch!'

With a snap of my fingers, the room roars to life again before my angry beast can slip out. The commotion explodes with anger and fury as they scutter away from one another. Prey Seven shrieks as he grabs his throat which has a slight trail of blood dripping down. My fangs extend and my tongue shoots between my lips. The overwhelming urge to claim his life and drain him overpowers me. Or even more sinfully, I want to hand her the knife again and fist my cock as she kills him for me.

Startled by the intrusive thought, I put some more distance between us as if that would help.

"She tried to kill me!" he hollers in horror. He makes a whole scene of throwing his arms around, and snapping his head left and around to convince witnesses to advocate for him. His blubbering girlfriend drops to her knees in front of him and tries to scoop up the blood. It makes the corner of my lips twitch.

"If she wanted you dead, you'd be dead,"

All blood drains from his face when he stares at me, leering over them. He stumbles on his words, truly frightened. The others aren't much better at hiding their fear. *What is it with mortals and their pathetic nature?*

My eyes skim the room one last time, absentmindedly searching for that little challenge of a mortal, but she's gone. I see the furthest bedroom door slam behind her as she marches away from me. My fingers curl into fists and the smoke pours out of my body in anger. My nostrils flare and the tips of my fangs begin to ache.

'Punish her. Punish her. Punish her!'

With one snap of my fingers, I'm no longer in the contestant's home but back in the arena. I need to put as much fucking distance as I can between me and that challenge. The beast longs to burst out and hurt her beyond repair before fucking the remaining bits of her.

Prey Nine is splattered against the floor, guts hanging out and brains decorating the arena wall. There is a howl of celebration amongst the audience. Then, suddenly, Prey Eight appears in the arena, mortified and stumbling as she tries to regain her balance. The floor begins to move. Her trial begins and I'm forced to play the part of enthusiastic host, even though my darkest thoughts are imagining the death of the mortal.

"Did you find out what that energy was? What was happening?" My mother's soft voice wraps around my head. She was the one who sent me when the lights started flickering. I felt the anger in the realm before I saw it with my own eyes. I could feel lifelines depleting and heart rates spiking. And they sent *me* like I'm a fucking babysitter. I could have resisted, sure, but that perverse part of me longed to see the little mortal in action.

"A fight."

"Between?"

"What a stupid question, mother!" my sister quips. "It's Prey Ten. I knew she'd be an entertaining contestant. But she must save the killing and entertainment for my audience, I can't have her killing off people behind closed doors. Where is the fun in that?"

"Good luck with that." My mother scoffs. "She's set on killing people."

Misery's face flashes with some dry humour. "Maybe she is the perfect pet for you then, Death."

"There is no *perfect* pet for me. I will kill the winner as soon as these stupid trials are done, that was the deal."

"We'll see," she says cryptically. It makes my skin crawl the way she twists her lips into a sickening grimace.

A horrifying shriek rings around the arena as Prey Eight falls from a height that shatters the bones in her leg. It's a delicious sound and has me readjusting my pants again. For a brief moment, my challenging little mortal flashes into my mind. I pretend it's *her* screams, *her* pain, *her* torture. I want to see blood, sweat, and tears staining her creamy body, to hear her beg for mercy, plead for the torture to stop. And yet, no matter how I picture it, the deranged little mortal has a lazy smile spread across her face as I do all those things to her body. It's as if she *enjoys* the darkness I have to offer. It's unnerving, but at the same time it makes my stomach twist deliciously and my body hum to life.

"I can't believe that you're going to let her do all those things and get away with it unpunished," Misery snaps me from my thoughts. She sinks back into her chair, bringing her martini glass to her lips and sips at it. Not once does she spare a glance at me. I know she's trying to wind me up, get me to snap and act out. That sick and twisted part of her would love it if I killed all the contestants prematurely so that I'd get in trouble and punished. There is nothing more my family loves than watching each other suffer. I bet she will offer her own curse up to punish me.

My fists squeeze shut, and I try to ignore her. "What makes you think I haven't already punished her?"

She completely ignores me. "Maybe you were right brother, maybe we have gotten weak as a family. I mean the old you would have snapped her pretty little head in half for daring to kill your Goblin." Her eyes widen as if she's come to some sort of discovery. "Oh my goodness, and she tried to kill another contestant! I bet you're itching to punish her. She's stealing your job, Death, and she is very good at it. Or have you just gotten bad at it? Hmm..." She ponders on the thought, letting me simmer on the anger that bubbles up in my chest.

"Fuck off, Misery."

She readjusts herself in her chair and frowns into nothingness. "See, if it were me, she'd be so badly punished she wouldn't be able to walk in the next trial. I'd give her something to think about, remind her of her place. She is a lowly mortal and must remain as much—"

"It's not going to work," I hiss between gritted teeth.

She finally spares me a glance, inspecting my reaction, desperate for my anger to slip out and for me to kill everyone. She's always looking for a way to get me punished and banished to my realm. I try my best to look unfazed but the black mist seeps from me, my whole body is tense and ready to pounce. I want to snap my sister's head in half and drain the life out of my parents. And I so fucking desperately long to sneak back into the contestant's home to teach that little mortal a lesson in punching above her station. I desire everybody's suffering and death. The black in my eyes throb as the beast creeps to the surface.

Misery laughs as she sinks back into her throne with a pleased smile. "It already has."

CHAPTER ELEVEN

Awful sniggers ring through the room after my husband makes a distasteful joke about the paleness of my skin. His rough grip sinks into the soft fleshy part of my thighs, and the pain takes a moment to kick in. My head rocks to the left and then right. I blink rapidly and finally recognise that I'm in the drawing room, sprawled across the table for all my husband's men to leer at. I'm not sure what I'm wearing, and I can't even lift my head to check. It's only when someone walks past my face that I feel a brush of wind against my tongue, so I assume it's hanging out of my mouth. It's too dry and I long for water.

As if on cue, a glass of water comes into vision. With all my strength, I try to pluck up the energy to reach for the cup in someone's hands. I play out all the actions in my head. Sitting up, moving my arm, clasping my fingers around the glass, bringing it to my lips, tilting, and making myself swallow. I know exactly what I must do, and yet nothing happens.

My vision blurs as I fade in and out of consciousness. Before I can bring myself back to reality, the roar of laughter that fills the room does it for me. A sharp pain in my arms has them falling back down onto my stomach.

Leonardo's ugly face swarms my view. To make matters worse, he slaps me twice on my cheek, causing an awful ringing noise to shoot through my head. My jaw twitches as I bring it side to side to check whether he's broken it. It moves without too much of a problem.

Thank God.

"She's a beauty, isn't' she?" Leonardo's voice now pierces through the high-pitched shriek of my brain being rattled from the hit. "You did well with this one."

"You should have seen her ten years ago," my husband whistles. "Why must they grow up?"

My head falls to the side, and I can just about see Leonardo in an armchair, clutching his whisky. His huge mohawk is stained red from a fresh kill. I can't even find the fear within me, just numbness. My whole body screams in pain but there is nothing I can do about it. When he notices my gaze on him, he grins wider. "Morning, princess! You seem to be coming around nicely."

"W-wha —"

"Hush now, little deer." My husband violently slams a finger to my lips. It catches my teeth and makes them throb. "We are not done with you yet. Go back to sleep."

"Please—" My voice is nothing more than a pleading mess and I instantly hate myself for it. There is nothing I hate more than the sound of me begging for mercy, especially under his hands.

"Want another?" Leonardo taunts. He holds up a little white pill and I unwillingly lick my lips.

'No. Don't let him drug you. Fight him!' Reason screams at me to protect myself from more harm but it's futile. Turning my head away from the sight does nothing and he quickly moves it to my lips. Again, I throw my head in the opposite direction, my strength slowly seeping back into my body as the previous drug wears off.

I push Leonardo away, smacking the pill to the floor, but before I can drag my legs off the table, five pairs of hands grip me, forcing me back down. A horrifying and twisted scream leaves my lips, drowning the atmosphere in my terror. The wretched hands belong to faceless men who wear red masks with green-painted facial features. They touch me in all the places I don't want them to.

"Let go of me!" The tears pour freely now down my face as I choke on my pleads. I feel so fucking useless and helpless. I refuse to cry in their presence. It's my biggest rule— show no fear and never beg for mercy. But here I am, utterly exhausted, in agony, and utterly terrified. I want to scream the house down.

"You fucking bitch!" Leonardo's hand strikes me across the face again, sending my head snapping to the left. The sting stuns me. He takes the opportunity to force the pill into my mouth, sticking his fat fucking fingers down my throat to force the pill down. Then, he reaches for the glass of water and pours the whole thing on my face. I splutter and cry out in horror but it's too late, that single motion forces the little pill back into my system. All my fight and anger melt into numbness as that familiar feeling of helplessness takes hold of me.

And then suddenly the room drops in temperature and the chill assaults my shivering body as I slowly drift into unconsciousness. However, just before my eyes flutter shut, I feel another person enter the room. No, not a person. A Being. And a very fucking bad one at that.

Suddenly, Death leers over everybody, baring his huge fangs and bleeding eyes. He holds his hands out and sucks the energy from the room until even I find myself choking to death. I scream and scream for help but it's no use. Absolute terror makes my lungs throb but suddenly, I'm no longer dying, but I feel an enormous sense of power thrash through my body. And without warning, I'm no longer tied to the bed, but I'm free.

My hand shoots out and I grab Leonardo by the shirt. His eyes momentarily flare with fear, and I soak it all up. However, before I can do anything else, my entire body seizes up. The pill storms through my body and forces me back into submission.

Spluttering awake, I shoot upwards and scratch at my throat. It's almost as if I can physically feel the pill travelling down. My body unwillingly collapses to my knees in horror, but I fall a measly foot from the make-shift bed I've been given. A strangled noise escapes my lips and I fall forward, back arched, and heave. Anything to get the vicious sensation from my throat.

It takes me a few minutes to calm down, and even when my breathing grows less erratic, the fear still haunts me. Trembling as my cheeks are soaked with tears, I bring my shaky hand to wipe them away. Instinct forces me to hide them as though I'll be punished for showing this emotion.

Though I've been free from Maximo and his gang of assholes for six months now, he still visits me every night. I feel just as frightened as I did when I was enslaved there.

But that was the first time Death had visited. Why the *fuck* has my brain brought him into my fucked-up memory?

A dim beam of light from the ceiling pulls me back into reality. I try my anxiety-reducing techniques to calm the racing thoughts. *Five things you can see.* My head snaps left and right as I take in the room again, but it quickly becomes apparent this exercise is going to be useless. The only things in this barren, beige-coloured room are a small wardrobe that I haven't dared to look into yet, and a thin, plastic mat on the floor that I've been using as a bed. It's boiling in here which doesn't help the sweat which clings to my body and the dehydration grows too much. Beneath the pillow, I feel the little white pill from the lady I killed on the bus. It burns and pleads for me to taste it.

Just take a little bit to help you sleep, my dear.

My mouth salivates and I suppress the yawn that rocks through me. It would be so easy to slip it into my system and knock myself out for the night. I need it, *right?* I need the energy to make it through the trials. And yet, reason prevails.

Unconscious around mythical creatures that can flash in and out without warning? No thanks!

As though I don't trust myself near the pill any more, I leave the safety of my room and peer into the communal area. Much to my delight, nobody is awake yet and I have the whole room to myself. I stare at the cupboard which now has eight names plastered onto it.

Prey One, Prey Two, Prey Three, Prey Four, Prey Six, Prey Seven, Prey Eight, Prey Ten.

Prey Five and Nine are dead. This thought should fill me with more horror than relief, yet it does the opposite. I find some fucked-up comfort in knowing there are only seven more people between me and my revenge.

I grab my cup and fill it with the boiling water. Part of me wants to wait for it to cool down but the other half it's too thirsty and after a couple of blows, I start to gulp down the water. It burns my throat but in a delicious stinging way that grounds me out of my nightmares.

"Can't sleep?" A voice startles me from my loneliness. Horrified, I turn to face Prey Three who leans cockily on the granite counter on the other side of the kitchen.

"How? What? How are you so quiet?"

"I learnt to be quiet growing up, I guess," he shrugs as if it's no big deal. "Anyways, back to you. Do you scream the house down every night or is it just since you've come here?"

"What?" My cheeks flush red and my thoughts race frantically around in my head, trying to figure out how I should play this conversation.

"You sounded terrified. I thought you were being murdered so I tried to get into your room but there must be some type of spell preventing us into other contestants' rooms. You didn't hear me yelling for you?" His eyes bare into mine in such an intense way that it has me stiff and uneasy. *What is this guy's problem? Why is he so hell-bent on trying to help me?*

"I can handle myself," I say quietly before turning my attention back to the hot water.

"I saw."

A long silence drifts between us, it's tense and miserable. I refuse to be the one to break it. I want him to go away and let me enjoy my scalding water in peace.

Not sensing this, he takes control of the conversation. "Have you decided on what your deal with the devil is going to be if you win?"

I don't know why it rubs me up the wrong way. "You mean *when* I win."

His eyes light up with humour, "Sure. Tell me about it."

"I will get revenge against a very bad man."

"Your dad?" he assumes.

I shake my head slowly. "My husband."

"Husband?" he flinches and visibly recoils. "You're married? But you're so young? What are you twenty-two?"

"It's none of your business."

"I have time—"

"No," I suddenly spit, "Stop trying to be my friend! We are enemies. We are competing against each other."

His hands jump up defensively, and he looks genuinely hurt. "Woah, woah! I'm sorry, I didn't mean to upset you, I was just trying—" he visibly tips over his words as he fumbles around. "I mean, I guess I just wanted to make one last friend before I die here."

Pathetic.

My eyes home in on him. Everything within me searches for some sinister act to be glistening around his eyes, or some perverse double meaning in his words, but I can't seem to find anything. Prey Three stares at me, his lips slightly parted, and cheeks flushed in humiliation.

Reluctantly, I realise he might be telling the truth.

Fuck sake.

"I mean, come on," he says so quietly I almost don't hear it. "I barely made it through that last trial. It was only the luck of the timer that stopped the beast from crushing my head with his arm. I thought I was a goner."

"You made it through so clearly you did something right." I don't know why I try and reassure a stranger, but there is something vulnerable in his behaviour, something stained with pain, something so alike a child I once knew—

"Barely."

"You fought Prey One well too." I point out again. His head cocks to the side and a small smile licks his lips. "That was different. Humans are easy targets."

And with that one sentence alone, I'm instantly reminded of why he is here. *He murdered a flat of people. He's evil. He has sinned. He's now being punished.*

"Don't look so judgmental, killer," he gently pushes my shoulder in a friendly way, but I'm left staring at the place where he touched. I'm still wearing yesterday's-stained clothes, too afraid to dig down the wardrobe or shower in the room opposite the kitchen. *Who knows what will happen when I'm naked and alone? With all the flashing of people in and out—*

The trauma in my heart burns as memories resurface. My breath hitches in my chest and my eyes sting. As per usual, the familiar pull of withdrawal and my PTSD consumes me.

"Woah there, girl," I hear his voice as faint as a whisper. "You okay? What's happening?"

My whole body stumbles left and then right as my vision blurs. Nausea rises in my chest and no matter how much I try to swallow it down, my body refuses to get rid of the bile. My traitorous body plunges me back into a fucked-up nightmare as though I'm still dreaming.

"Touch her there, she hates it." Leonardo's voice vibrates through my mind, much to my desperate attempts to block him out. I grab my head as though that's going to help, and I feel the burning of my skin.

"Prey Ten," I hear his voice in the distance, desperate and worried. "What should I do? Are you okay? Should I get help—"

"No!"

Desperately, I put distance between us, stumbling back towards my room, but it's futile and I fall to my knees. The quick movement only makes me that much dizzier, and I cry out as everything becomes too much. And then, suddenly, arms are wrapped around me. I try to fight but with all the distortion, I'm far too weak to protect myself.

"Prey Ten," he tries again. "It's okay. I'm here. Deep breaths, okay? Do it with me now." He sharply inhales and his body expands around me.

"Fuck, I love it like that. When her arms are tied up and her legs sprea —" another voice shrieks in my mind.

Without thinking, my arms snap around Prey Three and I desperately squeeze, looking for anything to keep me grounded in reality. Leonardo and Maximo's awful words desperately try to pull me back into the nightmare, but I fight harder.

I feel Prey Three's body grow and constrict with every breath and I focus on it. With all my might, I try to copy his breathing, but it takes a lot longer than I want. I feel his hand run shapes down my back and I should be mortified by another man touching me, but it oddly soothes me. He holds me firmly; I nuzzle my head into his shoulder, squeezing my eyes shut as the nightmares still swarm my mind. I never had a brother, but I read about them in stories. The word jumps into my mind when he embraces me.

"Breathe, Prey Ten." He strokes my hair, "Breathe, Carolina, breathe. It's going to be okay."

Carolina?

My eyes snap open and I try to pull back from the embrace, but his arms are tightly wrapped around me. His whole body is stiff as though reliving his own torment. My breaths are hard and shallow, but at least they are stable now, I don't pull away too quickly. It feels as though centuries go by before his heartbeat stops pounding against my chest and I feel him loosen up his grip around me. We use each other for strength in the oddest way I've ever experienced. He still smells of fire too. The smell is oddly grounding. For the first time in my whole life, I feel at ease in another person's arms and make no effort to pull away.

He finally breaks the silence. "Are you okay?"

"Are you?"

His voice is small, embarrassed. "I'm sorry, I don't know what happened there."

I expect it to be awkward as he pulls away from me, but it feels as though we've known each other for a long time and not complete strangers a day ago. Nonetheless, something has changed. He no longer wears that goofy smile on his face. Instead, his eyes are wide, sad, and misty as though he is going to cry. He looks at me, but I know he doesn't see *me*, he is thinking of someone else.

The question is on my tongue: *who is Carolina?* The noisiness within me longs to find it out, but reason keeps my lips sealed shut. I already feel something less than tolerance for this man, and I really don't want to mourn his death when I eventually claim my reward for winning. Something in his eyes shifts, as though he is realising the same thing.

"I hope you sleep better, Prey Ten." There is pain laced in his voice as he stumbles closer to his room. And then, he disappears without so much as another word, and I'm left, sweat clinging to me, and confusion swarming my stomach.

And unfortunately, I'm not strong enough to resist the sweet calling of that little pill under my pillow. It pulls me into a deep sleep, and I'm finally given some solace in this nightmarish life.

CHAPTER TWELVE

I couldn't sleep.

How could I? There are eight mortals downstairs, each begging for their souls to be claimed. It's not enough that their physical bodies have died. I want their screaming, writhing, begging lifelines in my skin, swimming to a new realm. And there was *so* much distress last night. I felt their rapid heart rates, the sickly sweat clinging to each body, and breathless moans as they each tossed and turned in their nightmares. And it was most strongly within Prey Ten, the other cause of my sleepless night.

How her lips are perfect for sucking our cock, that temper fantastic to rival our own, and her skin a perfect easel for us to smear blood and cum…

A roar of the crowd yanks me back into the present time and I desperately will away my throbbing erection in my pants. I slam my foot against the floor to distract myself as my family pile into the viewing gallery.

Surprisingly, I'm early today, and it doesn't escape Misery. She grins before floating over to her chair with a blood-red cloak engulfing her small frame. For some reason, her face holds a genuine smile today.

She directs towards the bustling crowds of beasts before sparing a glance at me. "Morning, brother! How are you this —"

"Start the trials," I cut her off rudely before she could play whatever sick game she was playing. I don't bother addressing my mother and father even though I feel their intense gaze on the side of my head. Misery's eyes twinkle knowingly and her lip curves up into a twisted smile. "Very well then."

She steps forward and raises her arms, causing absolute chaos within the crowds. Roars of glee and excitement echo around the room and I sink further into my chair disapprovingly. *This* isn't Hell— we don't do celebrating and eagerness, and yet here we are, everything enthusiastically cheering for the next event.

"Monsters and Monstresses," Misery booms. "Welcome to the second day of the Deaths trials! Yesterday, we saw two gruesome deaths as the Prey battled it out against the Goblin in a trial of physical strength. You all voted your favourite contest to be Prey One."

The picture of the large skinhead with superficial muscles pops up on the screen. He roars his delight in the video, but when it pans around to him now, it's almost comical. He's stiff, drained of blood, and bruised. Merely a speck of what he used to be.

De-fucking-licious.

"After the trials were shown, there was also a vote for the most entertaining contestant." Misery shakes her hand and the screen switches to my little challenge of a mortal, weapon in the air, charging at my Goblin with a cry not far from a war cry. The excitement and anger bubble up into one in my chest as I watch the fury in her eyes and the confidence in her stance. *A true warrior.*

A number pops up on the screen, much to Misery's delight. "Eighty-six percent of you voted Prey Ten as the most entertaining contestant!"

Eighty-fucking-six percent. A hiss escapes my lips as I glare around at the jeering crowd. Of course, the evil cunts loved watching a mortal trying to murder one of their own. It's perverse, it's illogical, it's spiteful. It's *exactly* them.

"Now, it's time to vote again! The previous trial was one of physical strength. The next one shall be of psychological strength. Vote which candidate you think will be the most entertaining in this next round. You should all know Longing," Misery points our mother, "she will drag out the desires within the Prey. I will swiftly twist them. Thrilling, isn't it?"

I watch as thousands of creatures flick their hands from side to side when the hologram of each contestant pops up in front of their face. A hologram appears in front of me, and I glare down at the remaining eight contestants staring back at me. My eyes instantly fix on Prey Ten. Her eyes are dark and heavy, with a certain fury laced in them. Purple bags pull at her face as though she hasn't slept all night either and her jaw grinds; I can almost hear the way her teeth scrape together.

Beside me, Misery nudges me to vote.

With a grunt, I thwack the hologram away from me and let my vote be void. The sound of screams rings out and everyone votes for their favourite contestant. After a short pause, Misery turns and grins at the audience. She throws her hand out and dark pixels flood the arena's glass walls, turning it into a huge projector screen.

"Wow! A mixed bag of results for who the most entertaining mortal is going to be," she booms, "Prey Two is just about sneaking up there with fifty-three percent!"

The camera pans around to the fat lady sobbing uncontrollably into her arm, barely holding it together. Her suffering only increases the hunger in the audience. "Well, let us see then, shall we?"

Suddenly, Misery and my mother flash from the spot next to me to inside the arena. Misery's long red cloak spans for metres around her, encompassing her in a sea of red. She makes a whole scene of removing her hood purposefully. Everyone sits on the edge of their seat, excited to watch the incredible Misery in action. She then turns to face the contestants and grins in her disgustingly haunting way. Her eyes swirl those grey orbs with little black snakes that swim through them — truly a sight that will send the contestants to an early grave. Her crimson-coloured hair floats around her and the snakes come out to play, hissing and striking at the roaring audience. My sister, as beautiful as she is, truly oozes terror.

Beside her, my equally stunning mother. She wears her usual black lace dress that floods out just as Misery's dress does. Her jet-black hair clings around her face and to below her hip as if she has been soaked in water and she supports a pitiful smile that has my insides reeling.

My mother stares out at the audience and lifts her hands slightly as she spreads her curse across the room. Even I find myself thinking about torturing souls and I lick my lips hungrily. In my mind, the faceless smoke cloud of a soul shrieks and cries in agony before it bursts and fills me with energy. Then, the soul switches but suddenly, it is no longer face-less. Instead, Prey Ten glares back at me. I find myself stiff in my seat, completely taken aback as my mother unknowingly brings out some type of desire within me. Just as quickly as it appears, I shut it down and push my mother out of my head.

Fuck. Fuck. Fuck.

If she notices my strange desire, she doesn't react and instead twists back around to face the candidates.

"Which of you dears want to go first?" Her sultry voice has each of the mortals unwillingly leaning towards her. Prey Four's hand shoots in the air and before anyone else can respond, my sister flashes him into the arena. With a single flick of her wrist, she forces him on her knees in front of them. His face is full of delight and sleaziness, and I have no doubt he is loving every second of these wicked women staring down at him.

Fucking mortals. So easily manipulated. So easily pleasured.

"You have three minutes to survive the trial. Your body might give up or you might choose to kill yourself." My mother's sultry voice echoes around the domed arena. Prey Four gulps.

Silence sweeps through the audience when my mother's hand shoots up in the air. Then, she twists her wrists and Prey Four gasps as she invades his mind. All of his thoughts and feelings reflect onto the back screen, but I'm not interested in him. Instead, my gaze is firmly fixed on the little mortal who rocks forward in her chair. I watch her with great interest as she scans every inch of the screen, quickly soaking up all the information. I'm not sure what her intention is by studying him, or whether she is studying the trial, but she doesn't miss a single bit of information.

Beside her, Prey Three, with his scarred face, whistles. He rocks back in his seat and talks *to* her. She doesn't respond to him but the way her eyebrow cocks, it's clear that she's listening intently. Some type of feeling twists in my stomach when he touches her on the thigh before pointing at something on the screen. I don't bother checking what it is. Instead, I glare holes into the place his hand just was on her clothed thigh. I want to skin the place he touched.

Her intoxicating cherry smell has already been stained with a slight dusting of smoke from him and makes me inexplicably angry. Unknowingly, my fingers curl into fists and my teeth grind together. It isn't until a thin layer of dark smoke escapes my body that I realise I'm working myself up.

Blinking back the anger, I quickly glance around at my father to see if he's spotted me. Thankfully, he's on the edge of his seat, a large smile clutching to his face as he watches Prey Four squirm around on the floor hollering in agony. Misery now twists all of his desires and longing into the worst possible nightmare for him, pulling out any horrific traumatic event or extreme fear. The sounds which escape his lips are strangled and awful. It makes me so fucking hard.

He scrambles around pathetically on the floor before grabbing at his head. Then, he starts bashing his brain into the concrete floor. I finally crack a smile. A small trail of blood turns into a larger gash and then—

"He's fucked," my father chuckles, falling back in his seat. He grabs his whisky glass and drains the remaining liquid before topping it up again with a flick of his fingers. He turns to me and raises a glass, silently offering me one. I grunt in approval and suddenly, I'm holding a large gauntlet of alcohol. Warily, I bring it to my nose and sniff. I half expect to smell some awful tinge of poison or agonising potion that will be insufferable for the next aeon.

"So untrusting."

My head snaps to my disapproving father and my fingers curl tighter around the glass. "Am I wrong?"

"I would never—"

"Lie to me," I spit. "Lie to me, father. See what happens."

He hangs his head almost sheepishly and holds his hands up in the air defensively. "I can't help it."

With a grunt, I turn back to the screen. Prey Four's brains are spread all over the floor from his suicide, but the show must go on. Prey Three raises up from the chair, offering to go next, and looks down at Prey Ten. He sends her a smile. She doesn't return the gesture but doesn't look away quick enough for my liking. Again, for some unknown reason, my blood boils. I zoom in on them, desperate to hear everything they are saying to one another.

"Good luck," she whispers, and suddenly that jealous feeling returns. *Why is she wishing him luck? Where is the fighter talk that she gave out yesterday?* He's her competition, not a friend. She should be wishing him an awful time, but instead, she offers a polite exchange.

I hope he fucking dies.

He is forced onto his knees in front of my evil family, and despite his brave smile, I see the way his body trembles.

"Are you ready?" My mother asks, but without waiting for an answer, she dives into his head. Images of a ginger cat with one eye pop up on the screen, a pretty young woman with freckles leaning in for a kiss, a DVD game of some sort, and then a match being lit.

My mother searches through everything he holds dear to him or anything he longs for. For a couple of moments, more images flicker through his mind. Most are sexual, as is expected of a young man his age, but some are pure and innocent, and the audience holds their breath for a particularly juicy desire for Misery to destroy.

Growing bored of the endless searching, I look away but something out of the corner of my eyes has my head reeling back to the screen. Prey Ten, in his arms, flashes through his mind. It happens so quickly that I almost missed the sight— *but I fucking didn't.*

Images of my mortal plague his desires.

My nose twitches and my snake-like tongue darts out in a hiss. Furiously, I stare down at the mortal who seems to be plaguing *both* our desires. She is wide-eyed as she watches the next clip. A tanned woman with frizzy hair and a huge pregnant belly embraced a tall pale man dressed all in blue. The blonde-bearded man wears a hard hat, and, on his jumpsuit, there is a mining company logo.

The couple embrace and look lovingly into one another's eyes. And then a little blonde girl with pigtails enters the picture and she runs up to her father. He scoops her up quickly, cuddling her and tickling her to which the squeals of happy laughter echo around the room.

For a couple of seconds, the video is nothing but sweet as Longing pulls out Prey Three's deepest affections: a loving, tight-knit family. *It makes me feel sick.* The man lifts the little girl onto his shoulders before holding his hand out to someone outside of the frame. We don't see the child, but it's clear that its Prey Three as a young teenager. He's throwing a tantrum and yelling something at his parents about not wanting to go down a dirty mine.

"Come on, Carolina is going, so you should too!" His mother and father try to reason with him, telling him it's going to be fun.

I glare down at the trembling man on the floor. *He knows what's coming next.* In horror, he throws his hands over his face and shrieks in agony.

The mother rolls her eyes and waves a hand at him. She tells him in a soft voice to wait there for them and that they will only be a couple of minutes. The clip finishes with the small family stepping onto the climbing elevator before the father slowly lowers them down using a rope. Beaming faces are quickly replaced by the dark cave and nothingness.

And then it completely distorts. Suddenly, a boom echoes around the audience followed by a sickening scraping noise and then the images of a mine collapsing follow. We see the father from earlier being crushed repeatedly by falling debris, unsecured scaffolding, and the poorly constructed mining elevator. The child's skull gets crushed under the weight of her father, and the mother's whole body explodes as she gets thrashed against the wall. It happens so quickly that they don't even get to shriek in agony.

Each time the clip replays, the family members die in a different horrific way, but every time, the whole mine explodes into fiery flames. The clip fast forwards to Prey Three pouring gasoline over himself in the bath. There are wet towels around him as if to contain what is about to happen. He reaches for a match and strikes a light. Another boom explodes as he catches fire, and the awful shrieks of agony rip from the projected video *and* the writhing man on the floor.

Good. Increase his pain. Make him suffer for now and all of eternity for touching what is mine.

Frustratingly, the images stop, and Prey Three is released from the trial. He springs to his feet, absolutely furious and wipes the tears from his eyes with his hands. He is unstable as he staggers around. Once he finds his balance again, he throws a pointed finger towards my mother and sister.

"You bitch!" he hollers. "You fuc— that wasn't three minutes!"

Misery smiles slyly and raises her hand to her lips. "Whoops, did I say three minutes for you? I meant it's three minutes for us. For you, it can be *hours*."

My jaw clenches as my wicked sister tortures the shaking man in the middle of the arena. I don't put it past her to put them in Hell-loops, but I thought she'd at least make a song and dance to scare the contestants prior.

She flashes him out of the room and his cheeks puff in anger. Full of tears, Prey Three's eyes dart between the evil women in front of the arena. For a second, it looks as though he's going to say something. But, deciding against it, he lowers his head and takes a seat, lips firmly pressed together.

I watch carefully for any reaction from Prey Ten, but she keeps her eyes locked firmly forward. Neither of them says a word.

Good.

Delighted, Misery clasps her hands together and twists to the other contestants, raking her eyes over each one slowly. She pulls her lower lip between her teeth as she picks out her next victim.

Not Prey Ten. The words leap into my mind before I can stop them, taking me by absolute surprise. *Not Prey Ten. Not Prey Ten.*

But why? Everything inside of me wants to see what is in that pretty little head of hers; what makes her angry; what causes her pain. I almost *need* to know why she is the way she is.

Since when do they make mortals this strong and so full of rage?

And yet, I want to be the one to pull her traumas from her little head. I want to be the one in control of her as she writhes on the ground and pleads for mercy. *Fuck.*

I readjust myself in my seat and clear my throat, anything to distract myself from the sinful, spiteful fantasies I have about the pretty little mortal with a death-stained soul. It seems that this little bitch isn't just any mortal but the beast longs for her to be *our* mortal. We selfishly want to fucking ruin her ourselves and I have no doubt we will do a fantastic job.

CHAPTER THIRTEEN

I don't tremble when I watch Prey Three's whole body snap in half and convulse as his mind is tortured, nor does my breathing change its tempo. I also don't react as Prey Eight snaps her own neck by forcing her head unnaturally to the left. I simply watch with an inscrutable expression, waiting for my turn.

Two deaths and there have only been three fucking attempts at the trial.

This whole trial is not too dissimilar to what I'm used to. Watching my husband and his brother torture other people— criminals, crooks, thieves, whatever it is that they did to him to warrant such wickedness — before he turned his knife on me. Even then, when I watched Prey Three, gargling on his sobs, my eyes did not water and my lips remained tight. *Never show fear, never give the monster what he is looking for.*

And then the name rang out around the room *"Carolina,"* and the screen panned to the little girl with large blue eyes and a smiley face. She looks nothing like me nor are our auras similar. She's sweet and innocent, whereas I'm stained and murderous. Yet, Prey Three has unknowingly revealed a significant weakness in the game that can be used against him if needs be. He sees me as his little sister.

Fuck sake.

Now that the other Prey is dead, Misery steps closer and those beady eyes settle on me. She quietly decides her next victim. Her lips pull downwards into a scowl but the way her head cocks to the side and her cheeks move upwards has me thinking she might be smiling. Her fingers drum over her stomach. For a long moment, I hold her gaze and she doesn't release me. Her head cocks to the left and her eyebrow twitches. It's as though somebody is whispering into her ear and she's listening intently. Then, the spell breaks.

"Prey Six, you're up," she declares, much to the young girl's horror. The thin thing trembles as she slowly stands up from her seat. Her nails sink into her boyfriend's arm and her eyes widen in horror.

She shakes her head slowly at first before it turns more frantic. "No, please!" she sobs, "Not yet not yet!"

Misery revels in the young girl's fear and with a click of her fingers has the girl in the arena. Horrified, the petite blonde throws herself to the floor. She curls up in a ball and protects her head with her arms as though that will help anything. A sharp laugh escapes Misery but she doesn't say anything.

The trial begins within a blink of an eye. Just like the last three times, the contestant ends up shrieking and howling in pain as the screen reveals everything they've ever longed for and then strips it from them. And then Prey Seven goes up, and then Eight, and then Two, and One. Misery calls upon *everyone* except me. Each time she selects, her eyes glisten with delight and it doesn't take long to realise she's stringing me out. There is a certain torture to waiting, and she revels in it.

Finally, she says those horrific four words, "Prey Ten. You're up."

Without so much as a peep, I rise from the seat and brush off the dust from yesterday's clothes. Misery flashes me into the arena but this time, I make a scene of not stumbling or being disorientated. Instead, I keep my head high, and my expression blank. Her head cocks to the side as she watches me. Then, she looks at her mother, and they exchange frightening smiles.

"Are you ready, dear?" Longing coos. Her velvety words seem to float across the room and into my ear. It feels as though they then seep into my brain and unravel every nerve. The physical pain is blinding, sharp and sore, and it goes on for ages until a high-pitched noise joins it. And then, I feel *it*. Like somebody's ripping my brain open, the agonising memories are torn from me.

Instantly, Leonardo's head launches at me, pounding me straight in the nose. Just as suddenly, the blood gushes out down my face and slips into my mouth, the disgusting and familiar metallic taste filling my mouth.

With an astounding crack, my nose breaks under the pressure, and the pain pours through me. He shrieks like a murderous bird circling its prey and the sound is deafening, reverberating around my brain louder and louder until it almost bursts my eardrums.

Suddenly, he moves with such speed that I don't have time to react. The icy coldness of his disgusting gaze has me wanting to run away in fear, but instinct knows better than to give the monster a reason to chase. He has that crazed look in his eyes, the one he used to support after he killed someone.

Blood stains his blonde mohawk and that bitter stench tells me everything I need to know about what he's just done. Without hesitation, his hands leap around my neck, and on cue, the choking begins. His relentless grip stains my throat in different shades of bruises until my head feels hot, weak, and weightless as the oxygen starves itself from the rest of my body, but my legs never give out. I refuse to fall in front of him ever again.

I can *smell* him too. That disgusting whisky, cigar mixed with bitter decay and piss. The hot stench smacks me across the face and my eyes water. He is screaming things at me, vile insults, disgusting threats, horrifying promises, but I stare back into my brother-in-law's eyes unwaveringly.

Silently, I watch as his lips curl with every cuss word he spits, the way his hand flexes into a fist before he flies it into my stomach, snatching the air from me. I look at everything, inspect everything, analyse everything, a trick I learnt on how to endure the punishment. Focus on everything *but* the pain.

His fist pummels into me until I feel as though my intestines are nothing more than mush, but yet again, my lips stay firmly pressed together. Not a single squeak escapes me even though my entire body shakes in pain.

And then suddenly, the world changes around me. I am no longer in the arena with an audience, but I'm locked back inside my old bedroom. It stinks of bleach in here from where I had to clean up my own blood from my husband's attack, it sits in the yellow bucket at my feet.

My entire body pulses with bruises as if I've only just endured the attack and the overwhelming urge to sit down takes hold of me. I *long* for rest, for a break to recover. I don't give it to myself, though, because I know *exactly* what tortured memory this is.

My wedding day.

Horrified, my gaze tears around the familiar concrete floor, brick walls and single sheet of bin liner on the cold floor. My prison was simply a shed in the beginning. However, that isn't what snatches my attention.

I'm here.

On the black bin liner, eight-year-old me is chained down at the wrists and ankles to stakes in the bricks. She is wearing a ripped and dirty wedding gown, stained with blood and sweat where I was beaten for screaming the altar down. The most horrifying shrieks of pain leave her lips and her whole body shakes in fear.

For the first time in months, my heart shatters and some sort of emotion pulls through me. Absolute and utter agony. Then something awful happens, and the world glitches again. I seem to flicker between *being* the tortured, tied-up girl and being me, observing in the corner. The pain worsens each time I fall between each person and only grows when the sound of seven locks unlocking rings through the room.

Terrified, I spin around, and I involuntarily stumble backwards as Leonardo strides into the room.

Without hesitation, I lurch towards the younger me and desperately tug at the restraints around her ankles. She doesn't budge, nor does she see me. The chains rattle when I tug but they make no impact on her. The overwhelming urge to protect and fight for her consumes me.

Knowing what is coming next, my head snaps between little me and the door.

Fuck! Pull, Scarlet! Get us out of here!

On cue, a huge shadow casts across the room and the surroundings drop several degrees in temperature. The hairs on the back of my neck leap to attention and the sweat pools at the nape of my neck.

He's here.

"Hello, little deer." The words haunt my mind as he coos them to us. When my husband takes a step inside the room, my actions get more frantic. I yank at the chains harder but it's completely futile.

A glisten of light bounces off the object in his hand and as my eyes dart down towards it, a whimper escapes my lips. The first sound of pain, and undoubtedly not the last.

He holds that god-awful dagger as though his life depends on it. The same dagger he used to slice my thighs with; A crimson colour already drips from it, no doubt someone else's blood.

With a cocky grin, he takes a step into the room and sucks all the oxygen out. I freeze in fear as he wipes the dagger against his trousers. It stains the material but barely moves from the weapon. I fail miserably at swallowing the lump in my throat.

"Deer-coloured skin," he begins, reciting the haunting poem as he strides further into the room. His cold touch lingers on my skin as he runs his fingers along younger me's legs.

In absolute terror, I lunge for his hand to push him away, but I fall straight through him and younger me. His touch is everywhere and all at once. My skin crawls at his wretched fingertips and I resort to scratching at my own body as if it will remove the touch. It doesn't work.

"Raven locks of hair, lips redder than fire," he croaks, lost in his own world. That intense gaze admires every inch of my sobbing face, before trailing down my body, following his horrific touch. Then, his hands jump to his zipper. "Cheekbones sharper than stone."

In the background, Leonardo touches himself through his suit trousers. I hear his god-awful groan as he gets off on his brother about to rape his new wife.

"A body carved from sin's wet dreams..." Maximo fists his erection. The absolute terror of that day washes through me until I can't see straight. A high-pitched screaming fills my ears and I almost long for him to stab me instead. I want him to actually physically torture me. Anything is better than him *taking* me. Another whimper leaves my lips as I fall to my knees next to the younger me. I try to grab her hand, but my attempts are futile as I fall through her again. The absolute despair destroys me inside.

It isn't real. This isn't real. He isn't real.

But holy fuck does it feel real. It feels like I'm there again, trapped, strapped down, absolutely terrified of what these men are going to do to me. And then, the vision distorts.

In quick succession, short clips of Leonardo and Maximo beating, torturing, and raping me. I live through each and every one, getting more bruised as time goes on. The only thing that changes in the beatings is that I grow older and weaker and number under their control.

My shrieking and fighting disappear as soon as he introduces his friends to his pretty little wife. Almost in every clip I'm unconscious. Contrary to popular belief, not every rapist wants to see a struggle. My husband's friends clearly did not. It was easier to keep me unconscious than my *'sad little eyes stare at them'* as Leonardo used to put it. The clips go on for what feels like hours and absolute horror fills me. A single tear slips down my face.

Every time he touched me, used me, sold me... were *years* of utter torture. He stole my childhood from me. He stole my innocence. He *tried* to steal my life. My agony and pain turn to rage.

A new clip appears, show casting him plunging the dagger into my thigh, twisting it, and laughing as I howl in agony.

Curling into fists, my fingers now tremble and my lip wobbles.

New clip. Leonardo shoves his fingers down my throat and tugs at my tongue until I feel it tear.

My head pumps with overpowering emotions and my jaw throbs as I grind my teeth together.

New clip. There are five men, one me. They take turns, high-fiving each other, and cheering each other with their sickening whisky glasses as they go.

Slowly, I rise to my feet and blink back the furious tears. I feel the clips get more and more intense and they start to throb in tune with my racing heartbeat.

I can see him in the corner of the room, beating me. He is only an illusion, he doesn't exist right now, but the fury in my body doesn't let me register this. Without warning, I find myself lurching across the room, fists curled, eyes set on the monster who ruined me, and the most agonising war cry leaves me.

My fists pound into him— not *through* him— *into* him! The pain is blinding as I break every finger, but it throws him to the floor as I take him by complete surprise.

Before I can register what has happened, the room vanishes, the smells disappear. More importantly, *Maximo* is gone. The blinding lights of the arena return into view just as quickly. Furiously, I charge around the room, searching for him, as though he is still here. I can still feel his evilness leering around the shadows. I look insane, I must do, but I don't care. The anger vibrates through me, my absolute need for revenge controls every fibre of my being.

"Where is he?" The strangled cry doesn't sound like mine. "Where is he!"

Absolute horrified looks from the contestants greet me, so I spin back around to Misery and Longing. However, I'm startled by their expressions. I almost expect to see them grin and look smug at my torture like they had for everybody else. Instead, Misery's eyes gloss over and she's frozen to the ground. Longing is exactly the same. They both stare at me as though I have just committed the most atrocious sin, and I can't tell if they are terrified or furious about it.

CHAPTER FOURTEEN

DEATH

"Where is he?" The little mortal is *fucking fuming*. Her strides are long and purposeful. Her entire body tense and ready for the fight. I smell that deliciously familiar scent of longing to kill; it oozes through her as if it was stained into her soul when she was born, and I'm startled by the intense power of the desire.

She fought two things in her Hell-Loop, but they were shadows. We never got to see her demons, but I wouldn't be surprised if they were mortal men. It pisses me the fuck off. Everything within me longs to figure out who the fuck haunts my little creature so that I can destroy them and make her fear completely mine.

Beside me, my father raises to his feet slowly, eyes fixed on the little mortal. All the blood is drained from his face, and for good reason too. The little mortal unknowingly just portal-hopped by herself, something that only Original Beings are capable of. That is the strongest possible creature in eternity. Yet here she is, the little five-foot-six mortal, portal hopping, full of murderous intent and ready to bring down Hell to find those fuckers haunting her memories. And I'd be fucking lying if I said it didn't make me fully erect.

"What?" she spits, "Why are you looking at me like that?"

Even in front of the Hellish family, she doesn't tremble or shake or show any type of fear. It's as though those mortal men are her only threat and I fucking hate it. The ridiculous urge to remove them from existence pools inside of me. Greediness has me wanting her to tremble for me, no other man. Only I am allowed to fucking destroy the little mortal. Her body is mine. Her suffering is mine. Her death is mine.

Suddenly, my father flashes into the arena next to her, however, he has completely transformed into his *huge* threatening Being. The fire licks at his feet and the flames dance in his eyes. His fingers are now large claws, his body pulsing with dark throbbing red veins, and his dark hair has turned to snakes, all hissing their poison.

I feel it instantly. *His desire for her death.*

What the fuck?

He is quick, but I'm much fucking quicker, and before he can touch her, I'm there, throwing my fist into his chest. It all happens so quickly; I have no time to stop myself. The black mist seeps out, my eyes bleed in their monstrous way, and my fangs snap out.

Within seconds, I am in my beast form too, and my body screams warning signs at my father with the dark pulsing tattoos that now swim around angrily. My demon dagger flashes in my hand, and I swing it warningly. This is usually enough to deter my father, but something sends him into a frenzy, and he strikes again. At the same time, my sister lurches in Prey Ten's direction.

What the fuck?

With one swipe of my black pixels, I counter my father's attack and throw Misery across the room. She smacks into the arena wall with the loudest thud and sinks onto the floor. However, just as she hits the ground, she is back again in front of my face, thrusting a force field of power at me. Just like my father, a crazed look haunts her as she attacks full force, not giving me a moment to send an attack.

They both fight me in their ghastly forms and I'm stuck playing defence before a weak spot in my sister's field lets me scorch her with never-ending fire. She, and the snakes in her hair, shriek in agony, and with her distracted, I focus on my father.

He shoots a bolt of fire in my direction but before I can defend, electricity zaps past my ear. Startled, I dodge the electricity that has come from my mother, but the fire scorches my cheek. A pained hiss escapes my lips, but I push it away and continue fighting my family, spinning to avoid their cheap shots.

Misery and Longing both team up and work their hardest to take me down with their spiteful curses, but I'm *much* faster and more experienced in fighting. It takes everything within me not to lose control and burn this whole fucking place to a crisp. It would be so easy to click my fingers and murder everybody, but for the first time in my life, restraint holds me back. The little mortal would die too, and I plan on dragging out her death in a more beautiful way.

The anger brims in my chest but instead of torturing my family, I work on disarming them. As much as I would love to bring each of them to their knees and beg for mercy, my father is right about keeping politics within the family. And right now, in front of thousands of spiteful beasts who *want* the downfall of the monarchy, killing my family would not be the smartest move.

However, as I work on knocking Misery and Longing over, I spot my father approaching Prey Ten out of the corner of my eye. Without hesitation, I throw my pixels out and they wrap around her arm and suddenly she is flying towards me with a squeal. She tries to fight the pull but it's no use, and within seconds, I have her safely behind my back. Again, the confusion pulls through me at why I'm defending the little mortal when only last week I would have laughed and enjoyed a mortal's death.

The Devil hisses and I smell the poison on his forked tongue, and I stiffen for a moment. I can feel him conjuring up the power to exile me back to my circle, and I panic. A dark, warning growl leaves my body as I conjure up a deadly fireball, one that would put my family into a deep coma for centuries. *A temporary Death.* The most feared curse bestowed unto me.

Suddenly realising my intentions, Misery howls in fear as the reds and blues throb in my hand. "Death, don't you dare!"

"That's too far—" my mother also tries to reason, abruptly snapping out of her furious frenzy.

'Ignore her. They tried to kill your mortal. They tried to hurt us!' The beast roars as I fix my fighting stance.

"Back off, father." I send him one final warning, praying he takes it rather than forcing me to respond. However, he is the only one who doesn't back down. Instead, he flashes his fangs, declaring war.

'Fuck it.' The beast slips free. *'The cunts had it coming.'*

CHAPTER FIFTEEN

Death's large arm curls around my body as he shields me from the attack. My heart hammers in my chest as he easily hides me behind his monstrous form. Black tattoos throb on his skin and swim around on his body like little snakes, eager to attack.

He's doubled in size from his already huge stance, but I can't see what he looks like yet. I don't dare tilt my head back out of fear of putting myself into the firing zone.

A shiver pulls through me as he dodges a huge fiery stream. The heat licks my skin, and the sweat instantly pricks to the surface. He hisses, correcting his stance and throwing his arm out. All the while, he forces me to stay pressed up against him. *Not that I want to do a fucking runner when there are three Hellish beings eager for my death all of a sudden.*

But the hardness and heat of his body utterly take me by surprise. I feel the way his muscles flex when he throws out a force field to stop whatever is lurching towards us. I don't know what the fuck is happening or why it's happening, but I make no move to leave the strange protection of Death incarnate.

Suddenly, the temperature in the arena goes up and I feel myself sticking to Death with sweat. My head pounds and my mouth feels dry, and there is a roaring sound coming from in front of Death.

"Death, don't you dare!" I hear Misery shriek in horror. I make no move to peek my head out to check what is happening, and instead push my head into Death's back, praying that whatever happens next, that I get out in one piece.

"That's too far!" Longing is next to try and negotiate with him, but he is having none of it. He growls and it rumbles through him and into me, that low and challenging sound making the hairs on the back of my arms prick.

"Back off, Father." Death's voice is ridiculously deep now. The sound has my body responding in a way that I've never experienced before. Something deep in my stomach twists and something flutters down *there*.

What the fuck?

"You had it coming," Death growls as the roaring gets louder. He rears back and I see the blue and red fireball the size of a football bubbling and boiling away. Then, just as he aims, a low clap erupts around the arena.

Startled, I spin around and face the creature that has joined the arena. A short but stocky man walks in, hidden in a large black cloak and red flowers on it. He grins but it makes my stomach flip in the most uneasy way possible, and when his beady little eyes nervously flicker to Death, I instantly realise that he is not welcome here.

His features are just as handsome as the others, but two huge scars starting at his eyebrow and pulling through his eyeballs down to his cheeks, make him much less appealing. His eyes are white except for the bloodshot scar that rips through them, and the only way I can tell he is now looking at me is the mutilated-looking iris that looks me up and down.

"Rage!" Misery's head snaps towards him in horror and then down to her hands. Her large mournful eyes then turn to look over at me. And a wallowing noise escapes her lips. "Rage, how dare you! We could have killed her! Wait, does that mean she didn't do that herself?"

What the fuck is going on? And what the hell does she mean to do it myself? Do what myself?

"Oh *boohoo*, another dead mortal." The man rolls his eyes sarcastically and feigns confidence. I can smell the act a mile off. Even though he makes purposeful strides across the arena, his pacing and nervous tics do all the talking. His voice, on the other hand, is powerful and eery, yet, he completely dodges Misery's question. "What even is this shit show? Is this what it's come to since I've been gone? Watching weak little mortals torture themselves with *thoughts*. How pathetic. Where's the real show?"

"Son," Longing whispers. "*Leave.*"

Son? Is this Death's brother?

"Are you not happy to see me?" He frowns at his mother and then turns to his father. "What about you? Happy to see me or are you still a miserable bastard?"

Nobody responds. I hold my breath and wait for another fight to kick off as they all glare each other down. Death is tenser than earlier, and his grip on my body tightens to the point it becomes painful. I yelp and try to pull back, but he doesn't relent.

Furious, Rage turns to his sister, "Misery, I'll assume my invitation got lost in the mail."

"Get fucked." She spits pure venom at him. "You need to leave."

He finds absolute pleasure in taunting them. "But the party has just begun!"

"Don't do this here, Rage," the Devil hisses under his breath, "What are you doing here? How did you get out?"

"It seems brother dearest forgot to renew the curse. Or did he forget that a temporary death is only *temporary?*" Rage twists and faces Death, and a cocky smile kisses his lips.

Death finally releases me and starts for his brother, but before he can get there, the Devil flashes in front of his face. He barks things at Death but it's far too quiet to hear, but Death stays deadly quiet and oozes a black mist that has me stumbling backwards to avoid getting touched by whatever the *fuck* that is. I still haven't been able to get a good look at him. It's as though he is purposely avoiding turning around to face me.

"We will deal with this later." Longing sends her son a pointed look, but I catch the fearful glance. She visibly trembles and no longer oozes that alluring motherly instinct. She's as pale as anything, as if she knows something awful is going to happen as a result of this untimely meeting.

"I'll put him back into the grave now." Death fires up the same ball as earlier but before he can do anything, the Devil grabs him by the arm.

"You know you can't. *Don't.*" The stern words vibrate all around the arena, making me shudder.

What does that even mean?

An awful silence haunts the room. Death shrinks back into his familiar, smaller form, but his tattoos swim faster on his body until they blur. He takes control over his Being, but the fury never leaves him. I gulp.

Whatever the fuck happened between them, Death surely hasn't forgiven him.

"That will be all today, Monsters and Monstresses. Vote on your favourite candidate and we will see you again tomorrow!" Misery rushes the words. Before she can even take a breath after the last sentence, a light flashes before my eyes and the next thing I know, I'm back in the lounge with the other contestants.

Mortified, nobody says a word.

Not even Prey Three. Every single person trembles, shakes and sobs quietly, completely taken aback by what they've just witnessed. The absolutely unimaginable power of Beings forged from the depths of Hell, fighting one another with a force that

135

the human mind could not even comprehend... and yet, crazily, my mind is locked firmly on one thing.

How fucking good it felt to get that punch on Maximo.

CHAPTER SIXTEEN

Miserably, I peer at the unconscious woman in the open casket. She's pale with rosy cheeks, a slender face, and thin, blue lips. Her tight blonde curls remain in place, shaping around her beautiful face, ignoring the rules of gravity. She's a thin creature, and if her eyes were open, they'd be blood-red like mine. Her scarlet pupils would bleed down onto her pale face, creating a stream of red.

Other immortals find it disturbing, but there was something attractive about the pain she brought herself and others.

Next to her, my brother is also unconscious. He wears his best war armour and clutches at the sword in the casket next to him. Even in a temporary death, Rage looks fucking furious with his permanently stained frown lines.

Killing my brother and wife brings me no joy, and if anything, I feel... sad? Is that the right word? I'm now locked in that fucking Hellish Realm completely alone. All because the dirty little cunts couldn't keep their fingers off one another. They were a liability to our united front and if I didn't put them into a temporary death, I fear I might have wiped them out permanently.

My whole Being feels angry, shaking in a tense manner, and the nausea in my stomach creeps up to my throat. Emotionally, I'm utterly drained, and I don't even have the energy to be mad. I'm disappointed, if anything. In her, in him, in myself.

How did I not figure out my wife was sleeping with my brother? How did I not realise they were plotting her escape from Hell?

Hence, the disgusting fucking mortal saying was born: To cheat Death.

"You did the right thing, Son," my father offers stiffly. His hand reaches out and touches my shoulder in an act of comfort. The Hellish family is constantly surrounded by things dying, and the agony is unbearable. A curse bestowed upon us for all of eternity. However, when it's one of our own, it's more agonising. To make matters worse, with two Original Beings down, we are more open to attack from revolting beasts.

"How long for?" Misery wipes her clammy hands down her black, mourning dress. It's the only thing she's said since arriving at their funeral. She was always fond of my wife, feeding off her sadness, and even though she would not admit it, she would miss the company.

The lump in my throat doubles. "Four millennia."

"It'll go by quickly," Longing lies. She tries to touch me, but I shake her off.

"She never wanted to be in my realm. She admired Rage for roaming Earth and wanted to join him. I should have seen it coming."

"You were busy sorting and—"

"Together, in the space of a day, they murdered thousands of humans," I growl. "And I'm the one paying for their fucking actions."

The Devil slowly pushes the casket over my brother's body before doing the same to Pain. He wastes no more time mourning their deaths.

He releases a shaky breath before turning back to me with a pained look. "We all are."

"Death, are you listening?" Misery punches me in the arm, snapping me back into the present. "What are we going to do about Rage?"

"Nothing," The Devil snaps. "He's served his punishment. He's allowed to be free again."

This answer displeases Misery. "And what about Pain? Where is she?"

"She's still in her sleep, I checked before coming here." Longing sighs before rocking back in her seat. She claws at her dress in an attempt to settle her nerves, but her skittish gaze reveals her true feelings.

I remain silent. There is nothing I can say that will please anyone. Now that I've had a couple of millennia to think about it, I want both those cunts permanently dead. Time doesn't heal, it makes the anger grow.

"Fuck! We can't have him running around, can we? Now he's awake, he will stir up the anger within the masses just like he did before. He's learnt nothing!" Misery cries out. "He will *ruin* my trials!"

"What do you propose?" Longing chews at her lower lip.

"Let him fuck up," I hear my grave voice finally speak. "Because we all know he eventually will and then I will punish him again."

"What if he does something worse this time?"

"He will." I sigh. "You can't control the bastard and you can't have him near these trials, you saw what he did to you guys and what he did to her trial."

'Yeah, she attacked her attackers.' The beast desires more trouble. *'She let the anger consume her and released the beast inside of her longing to kill. Make her do it again. I want her to kill for us and then we can fuck her in their blood.'*

I swallow down the desire bubbling under the surface. It's quickly replaced with fury. My fist slams into the skull-shaped table and it shatters into a million pieces, shrieking in pain as it does so.

"These fucking trials," I growl furiously. "If it hadn't been for them, I wouldn't be distracted, and I could have extended his death—"

"You'd risk the punishment?" My father glowers, slowly rising from his seat. He readies himself for the obvious argument pending.

"There is nothing you can do to me that you haven't already done."

"Is that a challenge?" his eyes switch to their monstrous black colour in an attempt to threaten me, but it only excites me. The pixels burn in my fingers, screaming to be let out.

Round two.

"Death!" My mother's harsh hiss echoes across the room. "Stop it, stop being so reckless! You don't know what God will do if you start breaking the rules and—"

"Do you really think the almighty cunt will remove the only Being strong enough to control this realm? The only Being tormented enough to *enjoy* this punishment for the rest of eternity? There is nothing he, or you, or any cunt here can do to control me!"

"He could take what you love," Misery suddenly snaps. My head rears in her direction furiously.

"Love?" The word falls from my lips in the most disgusted spit. "I don't *love* anything. I am not capable of that feeling."

Her whole body seizes up and her eyes grow sad. It's only then I realise she's not on about me. She's on about her ex-girlfriend, Delphi, being snatched from her. The misery in the room increases until I feel it bubbling in my heart, choking up my lungs.

"Everybody is capable of love, Death," my mother whispers. She casts a look at my father whose skin is far greyer than when he first ruled the underworld. His black veins shine through the papery skin. They exchange a look which makes me feel sick.

"You are fallen angels. You feel love, *Eve*." I spit, using my mother's maiden name. "The God of Death cannot love anything because everything fucking dies. I never had such a luxury of being human or even remotely good in my beginning."

"I wouldn't be so sure about that. You never know about your curse; we learn new things every day and—"

"Just shut the fuck up!" I suddenly explode as the beast roars inside of me.

'There is no such thing as love. Only hate, only suffering, only torture. The only love I want is when they completely submit themselves to me, body and soul, ready for me to play with.'

"Are we done here?" The black mist seeps from my body. "I have souls to sort and punish. You deal with Rage because if I do it, everybody in Hell will suffer. Got it?"

Before I get a reply, I find myself flashing out of the boardroom, so I don't take my anger out on the family. But what surprises me is the fact I'm not in my torture room.

Instead, strangely enough, I'm now standing in front of my little mortal, fucking furious and desperate to take my anger out on her trembling body.

CHAPTER SEVENTEEN

One minute I'm perched on the sofa, thoughts churning through the chaos of the day, the next, I'm staring up at the God of Death, towering over me in all of his mighty, sinful glory.

Sweat clings to his skin and his muscles ripple when he flexes his shoulders. Those dark eyes scan the room before settling on me. Unwillingly, I gulp.

"You," he spits the word so spitefully that I almost choke in horror. "Come here. You're going to help me with my anger."

"What?"

Startled, I put as much distance between us. He crosses the room effortlessly and I almost long for someone else to join us in the living room. When it is just us two, I feel as though I can't breathe. His dark eyes glare into mine so deeply that I almost feel as though he could get lost in them. I feel him scrutinise every inch of me, desperately looking for answers to questions he hasn't asked. For a long moment, he is deadly quiet, analysing me.

"Tell me who those men in your trial were."

"I don't know what you're talking about!" I cry out, backing myself into the kitchen. I don't know why I lie, perhaps it's to protect myself from the evil creature leering over me, looking like he could do far more damage than they ever did. My hands outstretch to try and put distance between his chest and me but after the display I saw earlier, I realise how futile it is. "Please, stop—"

Suddenly, I bang into the kitchen counter behind me. His head cocks to the side when he hears the light thump of my ass against the granite. I can feel his warm breath on my skin, and I hate the way my stomach twists again.

Fuck, he looks so undeniably handsome in this light, all ragged, unhinged and angry.

I try to fight the overwhelming thoughts but when his tongue darts out to lick his lips, I find myself transfixed on the movement and my thoughts grow more perverse.

What is he doing to me?

"Must I repeat myself, little mortal?" he snaps. I shake my head in fear and press against his chest to push him away, anything to get the oxygen to return to my lungs. However, his large grip curls around my wrist and he removes me from his chest.

"Leave me alone! What is happening? Why are you here—" The questions flow out of my mouth, but clearly, I've answered him wrong. A menacing growl slips from his lips. That sound should have me trembling in fear and telling him everything he wants to know, but it doesn't. If anything, that feeling between my legs starts again. A dull throbbing in-tune with my heartbeat.

"Tell. Me."

"Why do you want to know?"

I don't know why I poke the beast, perhaps Leonardo and Maximo beat the common sense out of me. His grip sinks into my hips and he yanks me closer to him so that I have to crane my head backwards to maintain eye contact.

"They didn't kill you, but I promise you now, little mortal, I will fucking destroy you. You are mine to kill."

"I'm not afraid of death." The stupid words slip from my lips before I can stop them, and I instantly kick myself. His eyes darken and his eyebrow cocks as if to accept my challenge.

"You're not afraid of me?"

I swallow down the lump in my throat. I can't even bring myself to say the words, so I instead weakly shake my head.

His nostrils flare. "You should be, little mortal. You should be very fucking scared of me."

"And if I'm not?"

"Then I'll fucking make you—" Before he can even finish his sentence, he spins me around and bends me over the granite counter. It presses harshly into my skin, and I feel the resulting pain prick at my body. Yet, much to my horror, my body flutters in the most delicious way.

Feeling his hardness pressing against my back, I gasp. "What are you doing?"

He stiffens and holds me still for a moment. His tight grip on my arms tense and then loosen as though he can't figure out what he wants to do to me. Then, his hand slithers around my neck and I feel his hot breath against me. His sharp fangs scrape against my skin, making me break out in goosebumps. "I've never been one to resist temptation, and unfortunately, little mortal, I am very fucking tempted by you."

"Let me go." I say the words, but I am not sure that I *mean* them. The tingle between my legs is stronger and my breathing becomes ragged. It takes everything within me not to press back up against him. Maybe I am fucking insane because why the hell is my body responding to this creature?

"Fuck, little mortal, I can smell you." He groans deliciously. "I can smell how wet you are for me, and I've hardly touched you yet. You crave your punishment. Don't you?"

A blush stains my cheeks. "What?"

"Oh, that's right, baby, I know *exactly* how well you respond to me."

"Death, let me go," I whisper. He tightens his grip on my neck and pushes my head to the side. His tongue darts out and I feel the forked thing dampen my skin. He leaves a trail of goosebumps where he licks, and I can't help the breathless moan that slips from my lips.

"You don't really want to be let go, though, do you, little mortal? You're desperate for a real fuck with someone who will truly fulfil your dirty little fantasies, and only I can give that to you."

"Please," I beg, but I don't know what for.

Suddenly, he spins me around and forces my head backwards. My lips part on instinct and his gaze fixates on it. He licks his lips hungrily. "I want to fuck you raw, make you cum over and over until you stop hating me."

"I'll never stop hating you."

He ponders on this thought. "Good."

"And I'll never cum for you."

"You don't have to like me to cum, little mortal, and you sure as Hell don't want to challenge me on that topic." He brings his face closer to mine. We are so fucking close that if I lean forward, I'll feel his plump lips against mine.

Everything within me screams to close the gap. *Let him make you feel good. For once, find pleasure in the pain a man will give you.*

The other half of me screams against reason. *Don't relent. Don't give in. You have one mission and one mission only: revenge—*

Suddenly, his lips are against mine and he *inhales* me. *The God of Death fucking kisses me!*

As soon as our lips touch, my whole body explodes with pleasure. He tastes bitter and musky but in the most delicious way possible. He's not slow, gentle, or sweet about it either. He kisses me like he fucking hates me and wants me dead.

His claws sink into the softness of my back as though to control himself. The pain makes me gasp and he forces his tongue in

145

my mouth before I can stop it. His forked tongue explores my mouth, roughly claiming everything as his own. My hands try to push him away, but he forces me to stay intoxicated in his embrace. I whimper but I'm not sure whether it's in fear or pleasure, and he growls. The sound is low, and I feel it vibrate through my chest.

"No," The word is strained as I say it. I'm not even sure I mean it but suddenly, he releases me. Both our bodies heave as we struggle to grab our breath again. He looks so fucking hot with his rippling muscles, swollen lips and black eyes.

He's fighting with himself on whether to fuck the shit out of me or listen to my reluctance. His fingers curl into fists but he doesn't touch me again and I almost cry out at my stupidity for ending the most intense kiss of my life.

"Listen here, little mortal," he growls. "That is the only time you'll ever say no to me, got it?"

Holy fucking shit. My pussy gushes at his words and it takes everything within me not to throw myself at him and continue where we left off. Slowly, he runs his tongue across his lips, tasting me. His eyes flutter closed, and he growls, losing control. When they reopen, they seem darker than before… if that's even possible. The inky tattoos on his body are going wild now too, racing around furiously.

He takes a step closer towards me, snatching what little breath I have left. "I do hope you survive these trials, little mortal. I'll be very disappointed if I don't get to fuck your pretty little brains out before your soul dies. And I'll be furious if someone else gets to kill you. Your death is mine. Got it?"

And with that, he flashes out of the room, leaving me trembling and desperate for more and resounding fear about what the fuck I've just done.

CHAPTER EIGHTEEN

My sorting Beast tears into yet another soul as my tattoos throb and scream for the souls to be sorted. My whole body still trembles, and my erection won't fucking go down no matter how much I try to distract myself. *Why did the little bitch have to be so fucking irresistible?*

"Third circle of Hell," I snap as the soul in front of me explodes into millions of tiny red particles. My beast groans and punches through the particles to send them flying into the right realm. Then, another soul takes place, and I must sort it again.

The new mortal is in his mid-forties and stinks of cigars and cheap whisky. He trembles and cries when he locks eyes on my beast. I slump in my chair, eyeing up the bullet wound in his chest and the knife marks carved into his skin.

My beast plunges a talon through the man until his whole body explodes and his crimes are announced. *Murder and gang wars.* I let the beast torture the mortal for a bit longer, enjoying the way his eyes roll back in his head and he shrieks in agony. It doesn't help my fucking erection either.

My eyes close and I revel in the gurgling and choking of the mortal as his lungs fill with his own blood. It takes me a while to figure out where he needs to be sorted, and even then, I'm stuck between two realms.

Fuck sake.

All I can focus on is that dirty little mortal that plagues my fantasies. I try my fucking hardest to block it all out, but my cock throbs and I'm blinded by lust that I can't pay attention to the task at hand of sorting.

'Fuck yourself, get it out of your system.' **The Beast coos.**

Without even realising it, I unbuckle my trousers and push them down my legs. My large cock springs out and I fist it. It's so wrong but it feels so fucking good. The howls of the tortured soul in front of me only increase my desire and I fuck my hand hard and fast.

My perverted thoughts turn the tortured soul's moans into Prey Ten's whimpers. I imagine it's her being pulled apart and tortured until she's screaming for mercy. However, she's not in pain as I plunge my cock inside of the hole I cut out of her stomach, but in absolute pleasure.

She begs me for more and more until she is a writhing mess, cum staining her thighs, tears melting into her cheeks and eyes wide and frantic. She will take everything I give to her. She will *beg* for me to give her more pain because she knows it will be turned into unimaginable pleasure. I will fuck every part of her body that those cunts touched. She will bathe in my cum until it replaces every other man's juices.

Oh fuck, I need her so bad. I want to fuck her hard until she cries.

I fuck my hand faster until I feel my release around the corner, but the thoughts alone don't feel enough. It's fucking wrong but I can't help myself and before I know it, I find myself in the corner of her bedroom. It's pitch black in here and she is fast asleep, tossing and turning as she is caught up in a nightmare.

My cock swells as I creep closer to her. Her little whimpers and moans have me grabbing my cock again and I'm so grateful for my night vision because her face contorts in fear and anger. Her fury pushes me far too close to the edge already. She is still wearing her jumpsuit, the same one from the last couple of days and she smells of sweat and body odour but it's so fucking delicious. I want to lick it off her and replace it with my cum.

Something primal within me fucking hates that she is trapped in a nightmare where someone else is scaring her, but the pervert within me doesn't wake her up. Instead, I revel in her discomfort, and I pretend that I'm causing it for her. And then suddenly, she tosses around so she's lying on her back. She kicks the covers off as though they are weighing her down and throws her arms around. I'm so fucking close to that pleasurable edge.

And then I smell it... *her desire.* She fights something I cannot see before she grabs her tits as if to pry hands off them.

"Death!" she whimpers. I fucking seize up. *Is she dreaming about me? What the actual fuc—*

Her hand slips lower, down her torso and over her mound. I'm rock solid, frozen to the ground and not blinking. I need to see every fucking thing she is doing to herself.

Another whimper falls from her lips as she rubs her legs together for friction. Her hand tumbles to the side of the bed, forgetting its mission of giving herself pleasure. I can smell her desire increase as her hips slowly start to rock. Her eyes scrunch together, and she holds her breath. I want to scold her and make her gasp and release all the noises her body is desperate to give to me.

My hand jumps back to my cock and with one pump, I'm ready to squirt all over her. I chase my high and sink my fangs into my lower lip to hide the roar as I cum all over myself. I continue fucking myself, eyes burning onto the little mortal whilst she has a wet dream. *No fuck that.* It must be a wet *nightmare* if I'm involved.

My cum stains my hands and my clothes and I know I should leave now that I've shot my load whilst watching the little mortal but how the fuck can I walk away from this sight?

Before I can even register what I'm doing, I find myself scooping up my cum on my fingers and slipping between her legs. I wait for her to stir or wake up, but she doesn't. Instead, my little whore rocks her hips back and forth on my fingers as I play with her clit. The little whimpers grow more frantic as she chases her high.

'Holy fucking shit. She responds so well for us, Death. Fuck her. Now. Wake her up by jamming your cock down her throat and making her choke for us.' The beast loses all sense of control as he howls perverse demands. I just about grip onto my sanity to stop myself from ruining her.

Instead, I begin moving my fingers in tight circles, catching her clit. I then rip at the material right where her hole is and slip a finger inside her sleeping pussy. She's so fucking tight around me, trying to push me out of her.

I slide further in and continue my assault on her clit. Within seconds, I feel her body start to jolt around me as her hips thrust sloppier and more frantically. I force another finger inside of her and curl them, making her explode with her orgasm. The cry tears from her lip as the pleasure storms through her. I fuck her harder and faster, forcing her to ride out the high of her forced orgasm. Her body snaps in half and suddenly, she's wide awake, gasping in shock.

However, before the little mortal can realise who or *what* is happening to her, I flash out of the room. With a dirty evil smirk, I leave her breathless after the most intense orgasm she has probably ever experienced. And I fucking pray that she's feeling dirty and guilty for fantasizing over the man who desires her death.

CHAPTER NINETEEN

My whole body trembles as I perch on the bench in the arena next to the other contestants. It's fucking freezing in here today and my pebbled nipples shine through the material of my new jumpsuit I found in the wardrobe. I had desperately not wanted to change in this place, but I had managed to fuck myself so hard last night that I tore a hole in my jumpsuit, so I didn't have much choice.

That has never happened to me before. I have never had a wet dream in my life, nonetheless over a fucking evil creature.

In my dream, he had tied me down and tortured me with his long, forked tongue until I came over and over for him. What is even more terrifying, I had *begged* him to sink his fangs into me. I had pleaded for him to inflict pain on me and then kiss it all better with his rough lips. I never thought I'd ever enjoy sex, let alone rough cruel sex, but perhaps that's what happens when it's all you know—

No. Death is different to my husband and his family. Death will torture me and make me suffer but will make sure there is a perverted smile on my face as I bleed and cum for him.

What the fuck?

I scold my dirty mind before I can even continue that trail of thought. *What the fuck am I doing lusting over this incredible evil power?* I should be terrified of him, not desperate to submit to him. And yet that throb between my legs screams the truth. I'm crazy and I want the God of Death to fuck me into submission.

"Good morning, Monsters and Monstresses!" Misery cries out her welcome to the empty audience seats as she waves her arms around dramatically. My stomach twists when I stare up at the Hellish family. It churns even more when those dark eyes are locked firmly on me. His eyes are intense, challenging me to look away. Then, his nose twitches and an evil smile creeps on his lips as though he knows something I don't. The intensity of his gaze has my cheeks burning and I look away from him as if I continue looking he might hear my desperate fantasies.

"I do hope you survive these trials, little mortal. I'll be very disappointed if I don't get to fuck your pretty little brains out before your soul dies."

Fuck him and fuck his dirty words that haven't left my mind since he growled them to me. The throbbing between my legs won't die either. *Maybe I need to just wank myself off after this trial? Maybe that will stop the desperation for him?*

"Today's trial," Misery's voice echoes around the arena loudly, "will be a great test to see whether you'll last in the depths of Hell." She peers around excitedly, soaking up the attention. "Today will also be a competition between two teams who will be fighting one another."

I stiffen at the mention of teams, bile rising in my throat. I listen to each word eagerly, searching for what horrific things will be thrown at me today.

Misery turns to face us. "You will be faced with wicked creatures and caught in a hell maze. There are no rules, and you have twenty minutes to survive. There are two ways to pass this trial. Either the team with the most alive members at the end wins or the team of whichever person manages to find the golden skull which is hidden in the depths of the maze."

My heart lurches in my chest in shock. I hear the other contestants wail in horror, but I can't find myself feeling anything but anger towards the Hellish family and this sick and twisted game.

Misery spins around in her stunning yellow dress with black skulls creeping up it. It ricochets outwards and flutters in the most mesmerising way. "Team one is Prey One, Six and Ten. Team two is Prey Two, Three, Seven."

Prey Three's head snaps at me and I can't help but look at him too. Wide-eyed, he stares at me in disbelief and then back at Misery. He tried to hide it, but I saw it loud and clear: *distress.* His leg starts anxiously jumping up and down at the thought of competing against me and even my palms start to feel clammy.

"There are no rules," Misery booms with a wicked smile, repeating the phrase again. I frown as I try to decipher what the hell she is trying to hint at but before we can, the glass arena around us begins to fog up and change.
The glass windows around me are immediately dull, and black tar seeps from the ceiling, obscuring my view of my fellow contestants and the Hellish family. The floor shakes as it descends into the pits of Hell, and I struggle to hold on to prevent being tossed around like a ragdoll.

It feels like an eternity before the descent finally screeches to a halt. And then abruptly, the floor tilts and forces each contestant apart. I leap towards my group but suddenly, two large stone walls trap me alone and slowly start to enclose around me.

Horror strikes me and without hesitation, I begin running through the maze. As I do so, something drips down on me from the sky. *Blood.* It coats my skin, the heavy dark stuff drowning my body.

In the distance, I can hear the shrieks of the other contestant members all yelling out to one another, trying to find the group again. The path curves around to the left and I follow it, however, as soon as I lurch around, the shriek of an animal has me stumbling to a halt.

Suddenly, I am face to face with a wicked-looking monster, drooling as it spots me. It has a decaying bird's head, wolf's teeth, a tail resembling a snake, and front legs like those of a large dog. It rears its ugly head in my direction and scratches at the floor as though it's winding itself up to attack.

Slowly, I start to back away, but the monster leaps forward and without hesitation, I'm sprinting away from the yapping beast.

The whole ground trembles and shakes as its huge body smashes into the floor behind me. I hear the sound of chains rattle and crack, dragging on the cold hard floor. Everything within me screams that I'm not fast enough as the beast howls and the sound comes from above me. My lungs heave, my thighs ache and the bile shoots to my throat. I don't ever risk taking a look behind me.

I shoot left, further down the path before I see the shadow of jaws above me.

With all my might, I throw myself as far away from the huge talons and at the same time, the sound of metal cracking shrieks around the maze. I tumble as I roll around, and my vision is instantly distorted. The pain rocks through me but I jump straight back to my feet, just in time to throw myself right away from the jaws which still pursue me. The saliva drops down, creating puddles of slime, and the stench is horrific. Above me, the world rains more blood down on us, as though God himself is mourning his creation's pending death.

A terrifying howl rings through the maze as the creature stalks closer to me, backing me up against the stone walls. I will my body to run away but it's almost no use. The huge creature blocks off my only exit and unless I can scramble out from underneath him or sprint left faster than him, I'm done for.

Its beady eyes lock on me and the low snarls almost force me off my feet. It rears its ugly head back and flashes the disgustingly long fangs.

Everything happens so fast. One minute, it's stalking and enjoying the slow threat, and the next, the creature pounces and snaps its teeth in front of me. I shriek as the chomping jaws reach inches from my face.

Confused, the monster leaps forward and tries to sink his teeth into me again, but something is stopping him. The collar around his neck seems to be attached to some indestructible rope, chaining him back to where I found him.

I waste no time sliding past the jaws and sprinting left up a different fork in the maze. Behind me, I hear the monster try to charge but he is stuck, and he howls out his frustration.

I never stop, pushing in fear that he might break free. The maze seems alive now with shrieks and hollers from all types of creatures and mortals being destroyed. One particularly loud cry rings out a couple of metres away from me on the left but there is no way to get to it because of the large solid wall that keeps the humans away from one another.

My heart races in my ears as I stumble around the maze, forcing me forward to the next deadly creature. However, just as I come to a fork in the maze, a female shriek rings past my ears.

"Tom! Tom, no!" Prey Six's voice cracks as she pleads for her life. All instinct tells me to run in a different direction but something within me breaks as I hear her beg.

Unwillingly, I find my body charging towards the desperate cries and what I find almost winds me. Tom throws his girlfriend to the floor and holds a knife to her throat. She scrambles and fights and cries but it's no use, he's much bigger and stronger than she is.

"Sorry, baby, it's kill or be killed," he screams in her face, grabbing her head and smashing it into the ground. Her head is bloody, and she lies in a pool of blood, her matted blonde hair turning scarlet. *Just like Leonardo's hair after a fresh kill.*

The comparison has me stumbling forward.

"Get away from her!" I cry out before I can stop myself. His ugly head snaps in my direction and delight almost swarms his eyes. "Oh, I was really hoping I'd find you after she dies."

Then, he presses the knife to his girlfriend's neck and slashes it.

"No!" I scream before charging at him. Common sense tells me to run away. He's armed and I'm not. But the fury streams through my veins as I tackle him onto the floor. He slices the weapon at me over and over, barely missing me each time. I try to move faster, desperate to anticipate his next move.

"You little bitch!" His large hand snaps around my wrist and he bends it until I fall off. He easily manoeuvres us, so he sits on my stomach, forcing me to the ground. I buckle around desperately. He slams the weapon into my head but at the last minute, I throw my leg around his waist and send him flying backwards.

We both scramble for the knife but luck is on my side. I grab the weapon and plunge it straight into his cheek. I feel the way his teeth pop out of place on impact. He shrieks and cries and I *should* flinch.

Pure survival instinct takes over as I pull the dagger from him and plunge it into his chest. He weakly tries to grab at me as I stare over at his mutilated girlfriend with cold, glossed-over eyes and no pulse. Any plans I had for him to bleed to death alone fly out the window as the injustice swarms through me.

Violently, I kick him onto his back, and he falls like a sack of potatoes. His eyes are wide, fear and pain intermingling in one.

"You fucker! You fucking dick! You killed her!" I stab him repeatedly in his body, a cry of frustration escaping my lips. "You didn't have to steal her chances like that—"

"Prey Ten!" I hear another voice echo around the maze. My head snaps up as my furious gaze lands on Prey Three. His torn-up face from the fire is stained with blood from the sky and he stumbles towards me.

"Go! Go! The Goblin is coming!" he races past me, trying to grab me by the arm.

"Goblin?"

And then I see the huge fucking beast from my first trial. It's slow as it moves around the maze, trying to listen out for prey. As soon as my eyes lock on the beast, I feel my sanity slip.

It's the same cunt that escaped my death.

"No, don't—" Prey Three tries to grab my arm again but I shake him off.

"Run or I swear to God your next!" It's an empty threat. He is perhaps the only mortal I have no plans on killing but if he gets in the way of my fury, then I'll be left with no choice. His eyes widen as he stumbles backwards. Absolute terror pulls through him, and soon, he's sprinting away like his life depends on it.

Slowly, I rise to my feet as the Goblin creeps closer. I toss the weapon between my fingers.

"Don't you fucking dare," the sudden gruff voice of Death rings through my head. Horrified, I stare around, desperately searching for him. But he's not here. *"Run, little mortal. Do not fight him."*

"He's mine," I growl under my breath.

"He will destroy you in a maze. You had luck and distance on your side in the first trial. You will not get such a blessing here. Run!"

I can even feel his scowl and rough grip around my body, pushing me away but I shake it off. It takes everything within me to ignore his demands but eventually, I zone back into the fight as the Goblin is within fifty metres of me. He hasn't heard me yet, so moves with ease, glaring over the walls of the maze, rearing its gills in every direction to listen out for sound.

I toss the weapon between my fingers again, quickly adapting to its lightness, before I start towards the beast. I see red as I hold the weapon high, ready to plunge it into his groin area where my previous marks are. However, just as I get within striking distance, another howl shrieks through the maze and a second Goblin joins the tight gaps in the walls.

Oh, fuck!

I skid to a halt as the sudden realisation of two against one isn't looking too good, but it's too late. The sound of pebbles tumbling underneath the first Goblin has him spinning around dramatically, flailing his arms around, searching for me.

"Get the fuck out of there!" Death hollers in my mind, making me flinch. It makes me lose focus and I fall off balance, slipping to the floor. The ground next to me explodes as the Goblin's huge hand pounds into the floor, sending shock waves all up the maze. It cracks the floor in half, but I manage to spring back up before I fall to wherever the fuck lower goes.

"Little mortal, run!"

"You think!" I cry out in the heat of the moment, completely forgetting about the Goblin's one good sense. The second beast charges towards me, flailing its huge arms around and within the last second, I manage to tumble out of the way of the bludgeon.

My weapon flies out and I catch his arm, causing the evillest howl to escape its lips. And then, suddenly, the most terrifying sight happens. The creature raises its huge arm with disgusting green slime oozing out of its talons. It swipes frantically, only just missing me.

The first Goblin joins in the fight, and they both tower over me, waving their arms around. They end up smacking against each other, and all hell breaks loose. The two, in their ginormous states, roar and attack one another until the floor trembles so hard I can't escape.

"Thirty seconds left, little mortal. You can do it. Don't let the green

stuff touch you." Death finally gives me some encouraging news, and this almost replenishes my energy. I throw myself left as one Goblin stumbles into where I was just standing.

The floor cracks underneath its huge weight and I must dodge yet another hole in the ground. Shadows leer over me until I'm almost in complete darkness, the beasts hiding me from the light of the sky. It takes extra caution to avoid the gaps as well as ensuring I'm not in the fighting beasts' way.

Hope brims in my chest as I see an opening between one of the beast's legs. I take my chance and race towards it, however, just as I do so, my ankle slips off a crack and I tumble. Fear shoots through me as my fingers grip the edge of the cliff.

Thankfully, I muffle the scream into my arm as I scramble back up out of the boiling hole which beckons me to the fiery depths. The stones tumble down from me disrupting the fight momentarily. Horror sweeps through me as one taloned claw swipes down and throws me across the maze. It feels as though I'm flying for ages before I crash into the stone wall, tumbling to the floor. Agony shoots through my back but the real pain screams in my thigh. Terrified, I grip my thigh with the awful green sludge staining a gaping wound. A pained whimper leaves my lips.

Fuck! Fuck! What the fuck is that?

"Shit, little mortal!" Death hisses and from the crack in his deep voice, I know that whatever is burning into my skin, is not going to be good. The pain only seems to grow worse and worse until it feels as though my whole leg is on fire. Pathetically, I roll to my stomach to try and get the energy to continue running from the beasts, but it's too late, both Goblins hear the cry of injured prey, and they bound over. I bounce against the floor like a fucking ball as they crack holes in the ground.

However, just before they can reach me, the most deafening claxon rings around the sky, signalling that the trial is over. At the same time, the world around me erupts into chaos.

CHAPTER TWENTY

The fury bubbles through me as I tear the door open to my little mortal's room. I don't give her a second to process what is happening before snatching at her arm and yanking her towards me. She stumbles, momentarily startled and scared.

"Where am I?" she hasn't had a single second to process where I flashed her, so her confusion is understandable, but my rage refuses to answer stupid questions.

"What is wrong with you? Are you trying to get yourself killed? What was that all about?"

"I'm still here, aren't I?" Even in her dazed state, she fights back.

Fuck, she is sinful.

"You were reckless and stupid trying to take on two Goblins."

"I was not!" She juts her finger into my chest. "If it weren't for you, I'd have gotten out of there much fucking faster. You distracted me!"

As soon as the words leave her lips, the room turns frosty cold. Behind us, the door slams shut, and the noise is deafening. Black mist seeps from my skin, displaying my rage for her to see. I expect her to flinch, but she shows me no reaction, only spurring the furious beast inside of me.

She yanks her arm away from me and crosses her arms with a

displeased look. "Is that supposed to scare me?"

I start for her, and she finally flinches but suddenly snaps in half, grabbing her thigh in agony. Unwillingly, I feel my fangs sharpen as the anger consumes me. I replay her stupid act in my head repeatedly.

"You're injured."

"I'm fine! Get out!" She pathetically straightens her posture and juts her chin up. It's fucking futile I can smell the blood wafting around the room.

"You're bleeding and I can smell the tears pricking in your eyes."

"I don't cry."

Defiant little bitch.

My hand snaps to her throat and I squeeze tightly until she splutters. She might not show her fear, but I hear every goosebump on her skin jump to attention. That slightly sweaty smell of nerves taunts my nostrils too.

Baring my fangs, I drag her close to me. "You need to clean it, little mortal. It will keep burning and causing more damage until you do."

"I'm fine!" She shoves me in the chest. Within the blink of an eye, I flash us out of the room and into the bathroom. She shrieks in fear and pummels me harder than before when she sees where we are. I stiffen.

"Clean it."

"Get out! Leave me alone!"

Pure panic vibrates through her and I can smell the fear in the air. Something in my chest roars at the strange reaction.

"Little mortal, the flesh-eating bacteria will continue eating at your leg until there is nothing left. What part of that do you not understand?"

"Fuck off! Just fuck off!" She's wild as she thrashes in my arms, not caring about ripping the wound in her thigh. I release her only because she is causing more harm to herself.

I try to seem as uninterested as possible despite the burning within my chest. "Clean. It. I don't give a shit about you or what happens to your leg, but I find you must be more attractive writhing from the pain I give to you, not some other creature. Got it?"

Her fingers tremble as they hover over the open wound before shakily pressing down. The blood gushes between her fingers, staining that pretty pale colour red. The sight makes my cock stir and her whimpers do not help. Within me, the beast roars in anticipation.

"It hurts," she whines quietly. Her eyes flutter closed as she forces herself to take deep regulating breaths. When they reopen, tears prick in her eyes, but she frantically blinks them away. Her fingers shake as she tries to touch the wound again. This time, she sinks her teeth into her bottom lip to muffle the moan.

'Make her stop hiding from us!' The beast is furious, but I keep him caged. I push past her and force the shower on before impatiently waiting for her.

"Water will help soothe it."

"I will not shower in front of you!"

"I'm here to make sure you keep your leg, not fuck your mortal pussy."

I hold my breath and wait for her to strip, but instead, she shoves her leg under the tap and turns it on. She winces and hisses as the ice-cold water smacks down on her sensitive skin.

"Fuck," she cries out before her cheeks stain red. Her eyes widen in shock as if she didn't mean to say the word audibly, but I heard it loud and clear. My cock stirs and the darkness in my eyes flashes forward.

I take a shallow breath to try and calm myself down. "Get in the shower. And you're not cleaning anything if you leave the jumpsuit touching the wound. It's muddy and sweaty and has the bacteria on it too."

"I'm not stripping," she snaps out of her dirty thoughts and the terror returns.

"I'm not asking you to strip, little mortal. When I see you naked for the first time, I want your legs spread open and that pretty pussy on display for me before I feast. I don't want the first time to be watching you shiver in the shower, all weak and blubbering."

"Fuck you. I will never get naked for you."

I close the gap quickly before she has a chance to react and tear the jumpsuit. I make the hole big enough to stop the bacteria-infested clothing from touching the wound but nothing more, as though I'm respecting her wishes.

What the fuck is wrong with us?

Just as I tear at the material, something odd jumps out at me. Not only has she got the awful wound from my creature, but there are old scars staining her skin. Horrified, she screams and smacks at my hand, but I barely react. The red lines are deep and sore, tugging her skin together in a jagged way.

Who the fuck has marked her?

"Get out!" her hollers become more frantic and desperate. She stumbles backwards and hides the wound with her fingers. However, I'm much faster. I move her into the cold shower before she can do anything else. "No! Death! Don't!"

Ignoring her, I clean her wound with the shower hose. Bits of mud and green pixels slowly fall away from her wound. She tries to push at me but I'm an immoveable force against a little mortal. Her small whines ripple through my body. My jaw tightens.

"I can do it myself! Leave!" She hits me again, and this time, I snap.

"Do you really think you can tell me what to do?"

Her eyes are wide, panicked, when I grab her little wrists in mine. The terror still flickers around her expression and that ridiculous jealous feeling pangs in my heart. *What in the actual fuck is she more scared of than Death?*

I open my lips to spit some awful remark at her, but at the same time, the beginning scents of an infection waft up my nose. Angrily, I stare down at the wound with the flesh-eating particles still chewing away at her thigh. She tries her best to ignore the pain but her bottom lip trembles.

"I'm going to have to remove the more stubborn particles," I grumble as the only option presents itself.

"No! That will hurt! Please don't!"

"Little mortal, I have no choice. You can do it if you'd like but the bacteria will eat through your fingers as well as your thigh. Which option do you choose?" I bark, losing my patience as I smell more and more flesh decay.

She sinks her teeth into her lower lip and shakes her head. She looks so innocent here, a stark contrast to her furious demeanour as she fought my creatures. In a desperate attempt to control my racy thoughts, I grind my teeth together.

"Bite down," I pull my shirt off and shove it between her lips, but I instantly regret it. She obeys me so quickly. Now, her mouth is full, and her eyes are full of fear.

'Fucking Hell, Death, I don't think I can hold off for much longer.'

She is momentarily taken aback as she stares down at my naked torso. She eyes me up appreciatively, though tries to be subtle about it.

'She wants it. Fuck her. Fuck her hard and faster and ruthlessly and —'

"I'm going to start now," I force the dirty thoughts from my beast out of my head but as I sink to my knees to get to thigh height, I realise how doomed I am. I'm level with her dirty little pussy that came so well for me last night. My cock springs into action.

Even the way she tilts her thigh slightly for me to get a better angle makes me lust more violently for her. I fist the shower hose and bring it back on her thigh before I do anything I might regret. Above me, her knuckles turn white as she grips the shower door and braces herself.

I press the jets back up to the wound and gently start picking off the particles from her thigh. She screams into my shirt, agony racing through her. I smell the tears prick back to the surface of her eyes and I hear the way her breathing becomes more irregular. She holds her breath as if that will stop the pain.

"You must breathe through it," I tell her whilst never taking my eyes off the wound. Something within me twists. I have longed to see her writhing and crying from pain since the moment I saw her and yet the only thing that runs through my veins right now is concern. *And fucking jealousy.*

The beast roars furiously. *'I am going to tear those beasts limb from limb, rip their eyeballs from their sockets, and play their nerves like an instrument for ever hurting what is mine to hurt.'*

"Breathe, little mortal." I snap when her breathing still doesn't regulate. She gasps and inhales a load of air through her nostrils, it sounds breathless and frantic, but at least she's drawing oxygen back into her system. And then I feel her fingers on my shoulder, and I startle.

Furiously, my eyes dart up to her and I realise she's tried to touch one of my swimming tattoos. Her eyes plead an apology but the way her fingers curl as if to touch me again shows me she isn't really sorry.

'She wants us, Death. Force her clit against the tattoos and make her cum from all the unsorted bad souls.'

"Don't fucking touch me," I feel my eyes bleed their familiar darkness and I look away before she can see the effect she has on my body. I'm in two minds. On the one hand, it would be so delicious to rip through her jumpsuit and fuck her mortal pussy. On the other, she's a distraction. And a damn fucking good one too.

I force the lump in my throat down and return to cleaning. She moans when I scratch at a particularly deep particle.

'That's it. I can't deal with any more of her struggling sounds—'

"Each tattoo is a soul which needs to be sorted into the correct punishment realm," I hear myself spit an answer to a question she never asked. Perhaps it's to take my mind off things, perhaps it's to distract her pain. I don't fucking know. But the words have started spilling from my lips and my body won't stop fucking disobeying me. "Right now, there are quite a few since I'm held up watching these trials and saving your pretty little soul over and over again."

She's quiet for a moment as she listens intently. It's ruined when I bring the jets closer to her wound and remove a bloody bit of mud from inside her thigh. She moans and I hear the tears slip from her eyes. Just as I go to watch her cry, she wipes them away with the back of her arm.

'Damn it.'

My jaw hardens and I refocus myself. "They move faster when I have heightened emotions." I can sense her frowning even without looking at her. I pluck another particle out and dispose again. "You know, anger, sadness, *horniess.*"

Again, I can't resist trying to catch her reaction. She is frozen, her cheeks are bright red while trying to avoid eye contact. And then I smell the start of her desire: a sweet and alluring scent, like fly to honey.

'The dirty little bitch. She wants this. She wants us—'

"Almost done," I grind out. She whimpers and her leg buckles when I grab another particularly deep one. Just as quickly as she falls, I have a hand under her ass, pushing her back to her feet.

'Wrong move, Death. Let me the fuck out. Her ass is so fucking soft and fuckable—'

She shoots upwards as soon as I get a handful of her ass and her squeal only sets the beast off more. But she doesn't move far enough to remove the contact, only bouncing on my hand as she falls back down again. She releases the t-shirt from between her lips and I don't miss the way she has stained it with her tears and spit.

Holy fuck.

Without warning, I feel my eyes bleed down my face and the beast springs free for a nanosecond before I throw myself halfway across the room. My heart races erratically in my chest as I frantically cage him back up before he can do any damage.

'Let me at her! Fuck, Death, I need her so fucking badly!'

My whole body turns cold as the adrenaline storms through me. The beast almost escaped. *Again. What the fuck? How did he do that? How the fuck is he growing so strong—*

"Is it done?" She looks petrified as she stares between the wound and me. The words refuse to come to the surface, so I instead nod tightly.

She releases a shaky breath. "It feels so much better already."

"It'll be fully healed by the morning." The lump in my throat makes my tone deeper than I intended it to be. I grind my jaw together and look everywhere but at her to distract my racing thoughts and sinful fantasies. "The bacteria live a very short life. It relies on quick multiplication to eat its victim. Now that it's all gone, you should heal as though you've just scraped your thigh.'

"Thank you," she whispers.

"I didn't do it for you, I did it for me. I don't want to fuck a girl who can't stand properly." I destroy whichever sweet moment she longs for. It works. Her rage flickers through her in a delicious wave of fury.

"Excuse me? I was just being polite! How dare you? You will not fuck me, Death. We kissed once, that's it."

Oh, if only you knew how much we've done together, little mortal.

"And as for that trial, it was a fluke mistake, and it won't happen again. I *will* fucking kill the next beast that attacks me."

"Did you not learn your lesson?"

Her nostrils flare in anger. For a moment, she is silent as angry thoughts flood around her brain. She opens her lips to say something, before deciding better and storming past me. I don't miss her little limp as she does so. My cock stirs.

"And where do you think you're going?"

"To my room," she hisses.

"Oh no," I grab her by the waist, "you don't get to take without giving."

I audibly hear her gulp. "Let me pass, Death."

"Why?"

"I don't want this. I want to go back to my room."

"You don't want what?" I force her to say the lie.

Lie to me, little mortal, let me fucking ruin you as punishment for your untruths.

"You. I don't want you—"

"Liar," I cut her off coldly and grip tighter on her waist. She trembles underneath, only spurring me on. "I can smell your desire, little mortal. I can hear you moaning my name at night. I can see the glistening in your eyes screaming to be fucked by the evil God who will own you as a pet."

"Fuck you," her voice is small. *Break for me, flower. Let me see how in control I am of you.* "I'm injured, I need to rest."

The sweetness of her desire intensifies in the room, and I groan. "You need to cum more."

"Let me leave."

"No, you've lied to me, and now you must be punished." I bare my fangs as I smirk down at her. Her scared little eyes cloud over with desire, but she tries to hide it. She plays the part of unwilling submissive so fucking well.

"You can pretend to *hate* the way your body responds so deliciously to me. You can fight me and scream that you do not want it as you climax over and over again for me and obey my commands. I don't mind you lying then, because at least you acknowledge that you *enjoy* being forced by me. But I will not allow you to stand there and deny that you want it in the first place when your body is begging to be touched." I force her flush against my chest. "You were stupid in that trial today, little mortal. Do you want to die for someone else? You're not allowed to. Your death is fucking mine. Let me fuck you, dead girl, and I will show you who you belong to."

"Death!" she gasps as she tries to push me away.

Within seconds, I force my lips against hers. She tries to resist at first but then, like me, her addiction to sinful desire takes over and she kisses back with just as much passion. A whimper falls through her as I wrap her legs around my waist. I take caution not to hurt her wound. *But why?* I want her pain and her tears. And yet, I don't want it like this. I want to be the one to inflict the pain on her, not some other creature.

My erection leaps out and presses her through the material of her jumpsuit. She cries out as I force her body to grind against it. With the hand that's not holding her body, I grab her breasts and push them together. Nothing I do is gentle or kind. I want her to feel the hatred as I fuck her small body. I want her to scream as she cums over her enemy's fingers and cock.

"Oh God," she gasps in shock when my fingers snap around her left nipple. I pull and play with them until she's a trembling, whimpering mess.

"Leave him out of it."

I grab my talons and rip through the material between her legs, and she squeals.

'Fuck the living hell out of her, Death, let's show her how delicious sinning can be.'

Her hands are all over my body too as if she cannot decide where she wants them to remain, and her soft little touch feels so fucking good. When I bring my finger to her clit, her nails sink into my skin. The beast inside of me growls as she torments him.

"You're fucking soaked already, dead girl." My voice is deep and dark, and it's clear the beast is slowly taking over. I force myself to remain in control. She is mortal and I am most definitely not.

'Let me out, Death! Let me fuck the pretty girl!'

'No.' I fight back in my mind. *'You'll kill her soul. Keep her alive a little longer. Let us play with the mortal whilst her heart still beats'.*

The beast howls in frustration but settles slightly enough that the pixels stop burning in my fingers. Her whimpers grow more frantic as I circle her little pleasure spot. I pull back to watch her contorting face, scrunching up as the pleasure swarms through her. She bucks her hips desperately and her eyes are tightly squeezed shut. I stop playing with her clit and run my fingers down to her tight little hole, but I pause.

"No fucking way, dead girl. Your eyes need to be open. You need to watch me make you cum. You will not think of anything other than your worst nightmare forcing your body to feel so fucking good. Got it?"

"Death," it's barely more than a whimper but the word vibrates over and over in my mind.

'Our name on her lips is so fucking delicious. Make her scream it! Make her cry our name out!'

Suddenly, I slam my fingers inside of her, losing control as her sweet scent swarms through my mind. Her gasp is replaced by a scream as I curl my fingers on the perfect spot. Before she has a second to react, I throw her thighs over my shoulders and force her against the wall. Her legs instinctively wrap around my head out of fear of falling from this height. I can't even pause to admire her sweet little mortal pussy before my snake tongue leaps out and attaches itself to her clit.

"Oh fuck!" she cries out as I devour her as though I'm starved. All the while, I ram two digits inside her tight pussy until it convulses around me. Suddenly, she falls over the edge, crying out her sweet release. I feel her fingers tug at my hair when she finishes riding the high, but I don't stop eating her.

"Death, please— I can't!"

I pull away momentarily. "You can and you will."

Then, I throw my face back between her legs and force her to another orgasm. Her entire body shakes as it wracks through her and this time something like a pained scream leaves her lips. Her thighs grip my head so tightly that I almost miss the sound of her release.

'Fuck, Death, Again! I want her writhing and crying for mercy as her body forces the sin through her again.'

I pull my fingers out of her tight pussy and force them between her lips. "Taste yourself, dead girl. Clean up the mess you made on my fingers."

Without hesitation, her tongue shoots out and she gets to work on sucking my fingers. I feel the way her cheeks suck in around my fingers and how her tongue darts around, not missing any part. She even moans as she does so.

What a fucking little whore for us.

Then, her cheeks stain bright red. She desperately tries to avoid eye contact as she hides her breathless pants. My fingers itch to strike her across her face.

"Never be ashamed of your whorish desires, little Mortal, because I will never apologise for forcing you to act them out."

I free my aching cock and fist it a couple of times. It's painfully hard. And then, without hesitation, I flip the little mortal so that she is upside down. She screams and grabs my thighs as though I'm going to drop her. My rough grip sinks into her thighs and I hold her effortlessly, ensuring her pussy is still inches from my face.

I breathe in her sweet, sticky taste and my cock bobs. "Suck my cock, dead girl," I demand.

"I can't! It's too big!"

"You'll have to adjust then, won't you?"

She hesitates until my forked tongue leaps out and attacks her overly sensitive clit. She squeals before pushing her head forward and kissing the tip of my cock sheepishly to hide her moans. And then something fucking wicked happens, her tongue darts out and she tastes my precum. It's nervous at first but as though the taste is addictive, she is quickly back for more, running her soft tongue up my bulging cock.

'Fuck, the dirty whore knows exactly how to suck our cock.'

I throw my face between her legs, increasing the speed of my tongue on her sensitive area to show her the pace we are playing at. Her fingernails sink into my thighs and the pain only spurs me on. When she opens her pretty little lips to take my cock in, I lose control and thrust fully into her mouth. She coughs and splutters from surprise but takes it very fucking well. She lets me fuck her face hard and squeezes her cheeks together to make it tighter. My balls tighten.

"Fuck, little mortal." I hiss into her folds. I then force my long tongue inside of her tight hole and wriggle around the forked end until she's screaming on my cock. I feel her whole body shake and hear her choke on her moans when she tumbles off the edge. Before she can calm down, I shove my thumb in her asshole and curl it. Her tight, puckered hole tries to refuse me, but I easily push through.

'Mine. Mine. Mine.'

I feel her grow frantic, wriggling around and scratching at my thighs as they grow too sensitive, but I can't stop now. My high is so fucking close. I fuck her little face harder and faster until my balls clench together and my release shoots out of me. Thick ropes of cum smack into the back of her throat. I groan as the dirty little mortal bobs her head back and forth, gulping down everything I give her. She lets me ride out my high and even whimpers in pleasure as she licks up any leftover cum that she didn't swallow.

I reluctantly pull my face away from her pussy and inspect the swollen, sticky mess. It's red raw from my beard and I can see it pulsating as it desperately comes down from her high. The churning in my stomach and my balls tightening has me wanting to force her over the edge again.

'Ain't no rest for the wicked, Death. Do it.'

It takes all of my restraint to flip her back around. When her feet land on the floor, she instantly stumbles and drops to her knees. Her bright red face stares up at me with a dazed and hazy look in her eyes. Tears stain her cheeks and there is a bit of my cum dribbling down her chin. Her beautifully fatigued look twists into something like anger. My cock bobs at the sight of it.

Even if she is furious, she says nothing. Those large round eyes challenge me, and I pray for her to spit something.

'Go on, little mortal. Give me a reason to pounce again. I can go all night. I can force you to go all night too.'

But, disappointingly enough, she slowly raises to her feet, trying her best not to wobble. Then, she twists on her feet and storms out of the room but there is no mistaking the tremble in her legs as she does so. She's like a newborn deer trying to escape the hungry lion, and unfortunately for her, that story never ends

well for the prey.

CHAPTER TWENTY-ONE

What the actual fuck just happened to me last night? He was so fucking awful, taking complete control over my body and forcing it to respond to him so deliciously. *Why the fuck did I enjoy it so much?*

I really want to hate him. It's nothing short of sexual assault and yet my pussy is still soaked for him, the next morning. Everything within me begs for him to continue making me feel so good in the worst way possible.

Am I broken? Why do I want him to force me again?

I've spent my whole life running from men who force themselves upon my body and yet with Death, it's different. I must be fucking insane. I know full well that Death intends far worse things on me than any mortal man ever did. And I'm not stupid— this isn't some fairytale situation where he would stop if I told him to. There is no safe word. There is no escape from him. And yet this thought fills me with too much excitement.

Peeling the material of my jumpsuit from my skin, the usual flash of fear and anxiety of somebody seeing me naked isn't as prominent as before. Perhaps it's from the exhaustion clouding my mind and body. Or maybe Death has fucked the common sense out of me.

I feel alert the entire time my skin is on display, and that deep throbbing of panic from revealing my scars to the world. My eyes remain tightly shut, refusing to watch myself.

My stomach growls in hunger, forcing me out of the safety of my room and into the communal area. I pray to be left alone. Lord knows I need it after the week I've had and the sinful things Death has done to my body, but I guess the big guy doesn't grant wishes to murderers.

"Oh, hey!" Prey Three spots me as soon as I slip out of the room. He peers up from his tinned food in his lap and gives me his best smile, but it is not as prominent as before. Something has snapped within his demeanour since starting these trials. Not that I can blame him.

"Hi," I respond quietly before heading over to my cabinet and grabbing the spam-looking tin out of it. I fish around for a fork before taking a seat on the chair opposite him. Even though I want to retreat to my room and be alone, something in his face tells me he needs a conversation. At least there's somebody to talk to in these God-forsaken trials.

"How is your leg?"

I grit my teeth and run my fingers around the wound. I refused to look at it whilst changing but it wasn't agonising pulling a new jumpsuit over it so that must count for something.

"Fine, I guess. How are you feeling?"

"Shattered," a dry laugh falls from his lips. He then points his head at the furthest door. "Have you heard from Prey One yet? I haven't seen him since the last trial."

I shake my head.

Shuffling around in his seat, Prey Three shoves another mouthful of food in his mouth before looking at me. "He looked fucked. I wouldn't be surprised if he didn't make it through the night."

"You think?"

"Yeah," he sighs. Then, his demeanour suddenly changes. "What do you think that means for us?"

"What do you mean?"

"Like what do you think is next? Will we have to fight each other or something because I don't think I'll be able to do that—"

"If we have to fight one another, you fight." I give him a stern look. "Take no mercy on me."

"I *can't*, you just remind me so much of—"

"Carolina?" the lump in my throat burns.

His whole face twists sadly. "Both of you are distant like you're always away in a different world."

Nausea rises in my chest, and I choke on my breath. "Prey Three —"

"It's Harley. Don't call me Prey Three. If I'm going to die soon, I want at least one more person to know me for *me,* not my awful crimes or my shitty situation after death."

"Harley," I test the name out quietly. The room feels tense with suspense and uncertainty. I almost don't break the silence but that nagging sensation within me forces me to speak before I can stop myself. "My name is Scarlet."

"Scarlet." A small smile teases his lips. "It's a beautiful name."

Scarlet, named after the colour of blood. The colour stained my skin in front of my husband and his friends.

"Thanks."

"So, Scarlet, any fighting tips you want to teach me or—" He chuckles darkly.

"Yeah, aim for the heart." It wasn't meant to be funny, but he laughs anyway.

"I guess I can be grateful that you didn't keep that knife in the end, right?" he continues using humour as a mechanism to hide his anxiety and I let him. I offer him a lopsided smile, almost revelling in his lightening of the mood.

He runs his hands through his hair and sighs. "These games are bullshit, aren't they? I've only just realised that even if I die, I'm still staying in Hell. My soul is too stained to go anywhere else."

I ponder on this thought for a while. "I guess but we were going to Hell no matter what so we might as well get a deal out of it too."

He chews on his bottom lip anxiously. It only just hits me that I don't know what he wants to do with his win. "What is your deal going to be?"

He pauses. A long silence drifts around the room before he looks back at me with sorrowful eyes. "I want to apologise to my family."

I frown. "For what?"

"I should have gone down in the cave with them. You know, the one from my trial—" he takes a shaky breath and loses himself in the memory. "We missed our original spot at taking the tour of Dad's work because I was throwing a tantrum. Didn't want to go down, did I? Just wanted to go to the park with my friends across the road but Dad was insistent that we see where he worked. If I didn't throw that tantrum, they wouldn't have gone down at the same time it blew up—" He chokes up on his breath and stares off into the distance. A slight tremble takes hold of his body and his bottom lip wobbles. Just before any tears can fall, he looks at me and inhales sharply. "Just one apology, that's all I want, then I'll die happy."

"Harley—" the words are snatched from my lips. *How can I console him when I'm actively competing against him?* I'm the reason that he will not get his apology. There is nothing I can do or say which will make this situation better. So, I stay quiet, and the guilt gnaws at me.

"But don't worry about me, Scarlet." He forces himself to be strong. "I never thought I'd be able to win these trials. I guess I agreed to join just to punish myself for all the wrong I've done before."

"It wasn't your fault. The cave, I mean. You didn't know and—"

He shakes his head. "You don't have to do that. Be kind, I mean. I've spent ten years trying to convince myself of that same fact, but it doesn't work. Guilt is larger than words, I guess. First, I killed my family, then I killed innocent people when I selfishly tried to end myself. Guess I'm just made to murder people."

It takes everything within me not to look horrified. "Nobody is made to mur—"

I can't even finish the sentence. Unwillingly, I think back to Leonardo and Maximo. They were most definitely born evil and only got worse. But Harley's different. There's something good in his badness, something pure in his mistakes. *Is evilness always so clear-cut?*

"I am not a monster, Scarlet, please remember that. I lied when I told you I killed a flat full of people because he evicted me. I tried to sound scary and intimidating in case anyone wanted to pick a fight with me—" he chokes as he spills the truth. "I was a coward. I killed myself. Self-immolated, to be precise, I wanted to die the same way my family did. But I was fucking dumb. I thought my fire would be contained in a bathtub. It's stupid, looking back. I drenched all the towels, lined the door frame and windows, and flooded the room to try and contain the fire. I wish I just hung myself in the woods now. Either way, suicide is a sin so I would have come here anyways, it's just a shame that I took four people with me on the way out."

The lump in my throat doubles and it chokes me up. "I killed a whole bus of people accidentally trying to shoot one man. I guess we are not so different."

He lifts his tinned food and offers me a small smile. It's full of pain. I find myself gently hitting the tin against his until there is a ringing around the room.

"To deserving our punishment," he says.

I swallow down my guilt. "To deserving our punishment."

His eyes twinkle when he smiles and brings another mouthful of food to his lips. However, just as he goes to say something, the room suddenly becomes hotter and hotter until the sweat licks off my skin.

My stomach twists and that anxious feeling bubbles up in my chest. And then I feel it— *all-consuming anger.* Tears prick in my eyes and my fingers curl into fists. My breath falls short, and I spring to my feet, readying for the fight. Finally, the awful beast reveals himself.

Rage leers over me, eyes burning with flames and fangs shooting out. His large hand grabs me by the arm, and he squeezes tightly. I try to shake him off, but he doesn't flinch.

"Prey Ten," he growls before those terrifying eyes shoot back to Harley, "And Prey Three."

"What the fuck? Let go of her!" Harley starts for Rage, but he easily throws him across the room. I feel the anger bubble up in my chest until I'm choking on the adrenaline. Harley smacks the wall with a hideous thud before tumbling to the floor. I turn my attention back to Rage and I swipe him across the face as hard as I can, but he barely flinches.

"Show me your anger, little mortal. Oh yes, there it is!" he's delighted as my whole body snaps in half and I try to escape his wicked touch. "It's *so* nice to finally meet you both."

He twists back to Harley and shoots his hand out. Dark pixels fly out, wrapping around his foot and then he tugs until Harley is flying back across the room. Rage secures his gaze on Harley and yanks him to his feet, steadying him when he stumbles. His eyes glare at both of us deeply and then they begin to bleed.

A horrifying shriek leaves my lips as images of Leonardo and Maximo flash across my mind. All the awful torture they inflict on me and the overwhelming emotions that follow. Tears flood down my eyes and my lips turn into a snarl. The anger is blinding, and it takes everything with me not to strike out. And then, suddenly, Maximo appears in the room with me.

Horrifyingly, I see his ugly rearing head in my direction and that cocky grin. His eyes twinkle with some mischievous plan and he reaches out for me. Reason shrieks that it's not *really* him, but the rage floods through my veins until I'm fully shaking. My teeth grind together and the vein pops in the side of my forehead.

Fucking kill him. He's right there! Take what is rightfully yours!

Fury takes full control of me, and I throw myself at my evil husband. He tries to grab me by the arms to stop my fist from connecting with him, but I am far too fast and furious to be held back. I drive my fist into him over and over again until the groans and shrieks of horror flood through my eyes. Blood pours out of his crooked nose, coating my skin in the sticky redness. I beat the evil bastard until my body aches, and everything hurts. A nagging feeling in the back of my mind screams for me to stop, but the anger forces me to keep going. And then, suddenly, Harley is next to me too.

What the fuck?

He beats the living shit out of Maximo too but with the most pained cry as though he is experiencing something different. The whole situation confuses me but I'm only seeing red. My fingers curl around Maximo's neck and I squeeze tighter and tighter. Then the most horrifying idea of ripping his throat out springs to mind.

Do it. Rip his vocal cords from his throat. Push your hand so far through his fucking neck that you grab his spinal cord. Snap his fucking body in half the way he desires to do the same to you—

However, just as I can yank on the sensitive flesh, I find myself smashing into something hard. Suddenly, I'm flying through the air before I can process it, everything makes me feel dizzy and sick. Large arms secure themselves around my waist and stop me from attacking. Then I smell the familiar musky scent that makes my head swim.

"Calm down, little mortal," Death's deep voice. "Snap out of it."

Red. I see red.

"Let go of me!"

Over his shoulder, I can see Maximo lying on the floor, head snapped to the side. Harley drives his fist into my husband repeatedly and the anger flies through me. "He's mine! Let me go!"

I use every inch of strength to fight against Death but suddenly, the absolute fury vanishes. Rage's cry of horror rings through the room and I hear him thud to his knees. Only then does Death relent his grip on me. I push past him, and the horror sinks in.

Prey One is completely and utterly mutilated on our living room floor. His blood and gore seep out into the cold cracks in the floor, his head exploding against the tiles and the stench of his ruined body harasses me.

Petrified, a scream escapes my lips and I stumble backwards until I stumble into Death. "Oh my God!" The tears sting my eyes. "Oh my God!"

I feel Death's tight grip on my arm. "Stop saying that name here, little mortal."

"We killed him!" I cry out in horror. "Fuck! We killed him!"

Harley suddenly snaps out of his trance and the terror sinks into him too. His head snaps between the mess oozing into his jumpsuit and at me. A horrified noise escapes him, and he frantically scrambles away. The blood stains his hands and face as he covers his mouth in shock.

"No! That was—"

"He tricked you." Misery's voice suddenly rings out and only now do I see her in the corner of the room, hand outstretched in Rage's direction. He's on his knees, clutching at his throat, gargling, and choking as something imagery seems to strangle him. The sound is so strangled and horrifying that I want to look away, but the fear forces me to watch this huge beast get punished. However, Rage doesn't remain on the floor for too long because Death's mighty fist collides with his chest. He fires dark pixels into the room at his brother, scalding and burning him.

"Death, no!" Misery hisses, releasing Rage from whichever trance she had him in. "Not here, Death, please!"

Rage snaps back into consciousness but cries out in pain as the pixels burn into his skin. Death moves so fucking fast that it's all a blur. All I can see is Rage's body smashing into different parts of the room, utterly destroying everything in its wake. He tries to fight back but Death is much faster.

My eyes catch the glimmer of a weapon slashing around, followed by trails of blood on the floor.

"Death!" Suddenly, two more people flash into the room. The Devil zaps just as quickly as the other two men and pushes Death away from him. Rage collapses on the floor, beaten, bruised and utterly disembowelled, but somehow still with a smile on his face. *Is he fucking insane?*

"Just as I expected," Rage cackles.

"Shut your fucking mouth, you dirty little cunt. How did you get in here without us knowing? What the fuck are you playing at?" Death is *huge* and leering over him in his ghastly state. He looks nothing like the man who throws my body around and pleases me. But now, the black mist stains the atmosphere and makes it hard to breathe, and his body bursts through his armour. His back is to me so I can't see his face and I'm almost glad. "You deserve another death for that!"

Just as Death strikes, Longing is in front of him. She grabs her son's face and holds him tightly before glancing back at Misery in fear. "Do it, Mis. Stop him—"

Suddenly, Longing is flying across the room as Death strikes her away as if she weighs nothing. And then the most terrifying roar rips from his body, knocking me over onto my ass. When he rears around to face us, the man who haunts my wet dreams has completely transformed.

For the first time in these godforsaken trials, I can truly say that the tremendous beast in front of me completely and utterly horrifies all other versions of fear I thought I'd ever had before.

CHAPTER TWENTY-TWO

The beast escapes. Completely and utterly fucking escapes.

I thought I had a handle on that terrifying creature but seeing my brother near *my* little mortal forced instinct to take over. *Him touching yet another thing that's mine...*

The familiar throbbing of my tattoos racing around my body, my bones and muscles expanding painfully comes to life, until I'm towering over everybody in the room, and that stinging sensation in my eyes which indicates they're pitch black and bleeding down my face. My fangs shoot out *through* my lips, and I bare them at my family wickedly.

'Fucking destroy them.'

Everything happens so quickly. My father charges for me but my talons sink into his hair, and I smash his face against my thigh until it explodes in blood and popped blood vessels.

On my left, my sister tries to restrain my arm but I'm much faster and I snap her arm in half, enjoying the shrieks of torment. I feel multiple forms of energy leap into my brain, but the beast has his protective shield up and completely blocks out any magic.

The room suddenly drains as I steal more and more energy. I move ridiculously fast, smashing into anybody who tries to stop me from getting to my younger brother who frantically tries to escape. He tries to flash out of the room but one fist on his armour has me yanking him back. A terrified noise escapes him as I thrash into him with my talons and claws until the blood stains my face. My tongue darts out and tastes it.

Wrong move.

Any minuscule slither of control I had vanishes. The room explodes as dark grey smoke bursts out, coating everyone in my death particles. Shrieks of horror and pain ring around the room as my particles destroy any Being close to me. In the depths of the agony, one noise rings louder around my mind.

My mortal.

'Fuck her, kill everyone in the room. They fucking deserve it, Death! Torture! Destroy! Ruin!'

The pain bursts through my own body as my family sends bolts of fire and energy into my skin. I struggle to dodge them as that completely animalistic part controls me. Any thoughts of defending myself vanish, and I work on torturing my younger brother, pushing all of my hatred onto him.

Behind me, another frightened noise tears through my little mortal. It's panicked, strangled and completely takes me by surprise. I find myself leering towards her and that's when I see it. True fear stains her face. Her eyes are wide, tearful, and bloodshot, mouth agape as the noise rips through her.

Horrified, she stumbles backwards until her back hits the wall with a thud. I smell the sweat clinging to her body, feel her heartbeat increase in her chest, and her breathing becomes frantic and stressed. Even her lifeline suddenly stops as her heart misses a beat in shock. She scratches at her throat as though she's being strangled. Her face is purple, her lips a dark shade of blue and I feel her lifeline suddenly drop. She fights, *still fucking fights,* even as her soul is being murdered. Even as I slowly murder everybody in the room.

"Death, stop!" my sister howls, "You're killing us!"

Even as the beast pummels and tortures and destroys my family, something deep inside of us cracks. It feels as though somebody is smashing through a wall of ice with a pickaxe. At first, it's a nagging feeling but it grows and grows until I'm suffocating.

"Harley!" My little mortal cries out as he drops to the floor in a pile of bones. Even as she is being strangled, her niceness is focused on that fucker of a friend.

Suddenly, it dawns on me why she sounds so agonised.

He's dead.

The monster inside of me howls in celebration as I feel his soul suddenly zap into the sorting circle of Hell. But the jealousy of his name being the last word on her lips has the monster reeling too. Her energy drops more until she is dangerously close to exploding away.

'Fuck, beast, get her out of here. She's going to be taken from us! Sorted without our interference! She'll be sent away! Please! Ple—'

"Death, stop this!" my mother cries out. It's pained and strangled but I can't look over to her to see her torture. My black eyes are firmly fixed on the little creature writhing around in uncontrolled agony on the floor. She splutters and gasps as the oxygen starves her little body.

Everything happens so quickly. When I blink again, the little mortal is pressed against my chest, tightly in my grip and I suddenly flash out of the room. I kidnap the small thing and force her into my Realm. A place no soul has ever survived and yet, the beast lets her live. It gives her a way around the curse.

As soon as we land, the strength returns to me. I drain all the energy from the tortured souls in my chamber and lock the creature back up in the depths of my mind. In my arms, my mortal suddenly snatches a sharp breath and I feel her lifeline return strongly.

'*Steal it again*,' the beast howls out. It self-sabotages, reason never seeping into his black mind.

"Death!" The tears flow down her face. She fights me with all her might fear still laced on her small body. Only this time, I let her go. She throws herself to the floor and scrambles away, eyes locked on me. Even though I'm back in the recognisable form, I can feel the terrifying image burnt into her brain. She whimpers and cries but not in a good way.

For a moment, the way she responds has me seriously doubting whether she'll want me again. It's such a fucked-up perverted and strange thought, but it flashes across my mind, nonetheless.

"You killed him!" Her voice cracks as she screams at me. "You fucking killed him! You stole his chances of winning—"

"Why do you care, dead girl? He was your competition!"

"And my friend!"

"Friend?" the word spits from my lips disgustedly.

"You awful fucking creature! You—"

Suddenly, I'm across the room, leering over her. "Careful now, dead girl. Don't say anything you'll regret."

"I hate you! I hate you! Take me back! I don't want this; I don't want to win!"

I bristle. "You don't mean that."

"I do!" she howls. The snot and tears stain her face as she blubbers away. Her whole body cowers from me. I want to feel some sort of pride and joy in her fear. Hell, I've been after this reaction since I first laid eyes on the little creature, and yet, this isn't the fear I want. I don't want her pure hatred; I want her sin.

"Take me back!"

Despite my regret, selfishness consumes me. She might hate me, but she will not leave me. Whether she likes it or not, she is mine. "You're mine."

"I'll never be yours!"

"You're Death's New Pet. You survived the trials."

"I break the deal! I don't care! I don't want to be here! Near you!"

Her words actually do something to me. I flinch. "You're just saying that."

"What must I do to prove to you that I don't want this?"

Suddenly, all resolve cracks. I *know* that I must go about this gently. The little mortal under my feet is writhing and terrified, and her heart is screaming that it's going to give up if she takes any more fear. But that has never been my nature. No matter how much I try, I cannot let her leave.

"Nobody can get into my Realm without starting to die," I snarl. "Nobody is coming to save you and I am sure as Hell not going to let you leave so you better get used to it, dead girl."

"You are evil! He didn't deserve to die so unheroically!"

"Stop talking about him." I feel the dark mist seep from my body as jealousy consumes me.

"No! He was my only friend and you slaughtered him!"

My jaw tenses. "You don't need friends in Hell."

She shrieks in frustration, but the noise turns to a whimper as I grab her arm and yank her to her feet. Immediately, she tries to fight me, but I don't let her escape this time.

"I won't apologise for killing anyone, ever, little mortal. Now that he's dead, you're mine."

Her arms wrap around her body protectively in a self-soothing manner. My lips curl as the little mortal desperately searches for some warmth.

We have no warmth to give to her.

"You want a hug, little mortal? Let my fingers cuddle your neck."

She gasps as I wrap my hand around her throat and squeeze slightly. She's horrified, absolutely terrified, but her anger, as usual, reigns. Her defiant little eyes twinkle angrily and she tries to peel me from her body.

There is that fight that I fucking love.

"Let go of me!"

The burning of the tattoos on my body grows too much as more unsorted souls pour into Hell. Everything within me longs to bring her close and turn her anger into pleasure. How delicious it would be to have her writhing underneath me, cumming repeatedly and hating herself for enjoying my sin so much. But duty calls.

"Fine," I release her, and she scrambles backwards but I smell that momentary reaction of regret and surprise. She rubs at her neck in a huge display. "Hate me, little girl, but you belong here, as my pet."

I twist on my feet and drain all the dark smoke from the room so she can fully come to grips with her surroundings. I sense her breathing catch in her throat as she stares around my throne room with the large stage in front of the solitary chair.

Without another look at her, I slump in my chair and summon my beast with a whistle. I hear her breathing grow irregular as the ugly creature sluggishly crawls out of the depths of Hell. He turns to me, dips his head in the lowest bow, and groans.

"Little mortal, come here." I click my fingers to irritate her. She hesitates, and for a second, she almost disobeys. At the last moment, she stumbles forward next to my chair.

"Sit on the floor."

"Fuck you," she spits. With a wave of my hand, I force her to her knees. She cries out in shock as her body is forced to respond to me. "Let me go!"

"No. You're going to learn what I spend the majority of my days doing. *Torturing.*"

"Evil beast!"

I ignore her insult even though my fingers throb to punish her. Instead, I turn to my beast. "Bring the first unsorted soul."

Dutifully, my beast warps in a young man with tan skin and bushy eyebrows. As usual, the fear is palpable, and I feed off of the energy. My beast drives a horn through the human's chest and the red pixels explode everywhere. The man cries out in a mixture of horror and pain. I lick my lips and soak up his sin.

"This one is being punished for assault and battery on an elderly person after a home invasion went wrong," I find myself explaining the situation to my little mortal without realising. Out of the corner of my eye, she watches quietly, her bottom lip between her teeth. Her eyes are wide and startled but she soaks up everything happening on the stage.

"What are you doing to him?"

"My creature is punishing him until all of his sins are expressed. Then, I will sort him into the realm he deserves."

Her eyebrows burrow together, and she never takes her eyes off the screaming man in the middle of the stage. His guts pour onto the floor and his shrieks grow louder and louder with every attack. She barely flinches.

That's my good girl.

After a couple of moments, the familiar throbbing pulls through the room. I flick my fingers out and the man explodes into particles. Then, with a headbutt from the monster, he disappears into the sorted realm.

"Where did he go?" She appears almost disappointed that the torture has stopped but I know it's my perverse mind changing her tone of voice.

Inhaling sharply to stop the dirty thoughts in my mind, I

manage to ground the desire. "I sorted him. He will do three thousand years in the worst psychological Hell loop before becoming food for my beasts."

"Three thousand years?" she startles. "But I only did a couple hours and—"

"He deserved it, little mortal. Don't try to tell me how to run my Realm."

Her lips slam shut, and she turns back to the stage. She still hates me and tries to give me the silent treatment. I almost laugh. I sense her frustration and it's fucking delicious but it's short-lived as my monster pulls another soul onto the stage.

This one is younger but reeks of poison as though it's stained his soul. My beast quickly gets to work destroying the soul until its cries are nothing but a melody in my ears. Again, I want my little mortal to react and cuss me out more, but instead, she watches quietly, her eyes never disappearing from the stage.

"What's his crime?"

"Multiple accounts of rape and petty theft." I sigh and lift my fingers but before I can send him anywhere, my little mortal speaks again.

"What is his punishment?"

"Four and a half thousand years in a Hell loop and then he will be forced to work the mazes."

"Make it six thousand." My little mortal decides to hand out punishments. I should be fucking furious that she dares tells me what to do and yet my cock springs to attention. I physically readjust myself in my chair and she must sense it too.

Her pretty little eyes dart over to me. "I'm not kidding, Death." She says sternly.

"I know you're not."

"Make it six thousand years."

A small smile creeps to my lips. "Come here."

"No,"

I pout at her, mockingly. "Are you still sad that I killed your *friend*?"

"How dare you!"

"Relax," I roll my eyes. "He is in one of the maze's. If you behave, you might be able to visit him soon."

She visibly startles. "Are you lying?"

"Why would I lie about that?"

"Because—"

I wait for her to come up with a good response but there is nothing. Without another word, I pat my lips. She hesitates.

"Join me or you'll never see him again."

Shakily, she rises and follows my hand gesture until she is standing in front of me. My hand snatches out and I quickly move her onto my lap. She cries out in shock, only spurring me on more. I force her to sit in my lap, to feel the hardness of my cock against her back. A gasp tumbles from her lips.

"Death—"

"Little mortal wants to make the demands?" I growl into her ear. Her whole body responds to my warm breath, and I audibly hear every hair stand up on the edge of her skin. She slowly trembles under my touch.

"Make them, then. Show me how ruthless and evil you are whilst you still have your human soul, little mortal."

I lift her body so that my hard cock rubs against her pussy. Her fingers jump to my wrists, and she tries to free herself from me but it's all for show. I can smell the wetness already soaking the thin material. She whimpers and I almost lose control.

"Do you like feeling my cock against your greedy mortal pussy?"

"Oh God—"

My fangs sharpen and scratch against her neck, drawing blood. She cries out in pain. Fury consumes me. "What did I tell you about using that name down here?"

CHAPTER TWENTY-THREE

"The only name you should be moaning is mine. Got it, dead girl?" His voice is dark and malicious. I can't see his eyes, but I know for a fact they're black as sin, raking up my body until he owns every inch of my skin.

"I'm sorry," it's the first time I've ever apologised to him, and I don't know why I say it. I long to moan the name again, to make him angry. It's fucking ridiculous since my body hasn't stopped shaking since I saw him in his true form. The monstrous beast they describe him to be.

"Don't apologise to me, little mortal. Apologise to yourself. You've just signed your death warrant."

What? My whole body tenses up and my fight or flight panics. I squirm against him, but it only puts more pressure on my throbbing clit. *What the fuck is wrong with me? I'm terrified of him but also desperate for him to make me feel good again!*

"You smell so fucking delicious," he growls as his hand slowly runs down my body. I fall forward when he releases me, and I'm forced to hold onto his knees to stop me from falling off him. He grabs my tits viciously and pulls at my nipples until I'm panting.

"Beast, continue!" He suddenly barks out an order. The hideous creature in front of us dips his head before bringing another soul to torture. My eyes slam shut as I try to focus on not feeling the pleasure that he brings to my body.

I focus on the horrified cries of the next victim but at the same time, his fingers find my clit and I jolt. However, as I do so, I bounce off his cock and it presses deeper into me, straining against the material of my jumpsuit. Pleasure instantly hits me.

"Fuck!" I cry out involuntarily as he forces me close to the edge.

"I knew you'd like this, you dirty whore. You're getting off to the sound of bad people being tortured. You were made to be my little pet, weren't you?"

"Yes!" I answer him quickly and I instantly scold myself for being so desperate for him. He grinds into me, and my head rolls back. Then, I feel something slither around my neck and get tighter. I instantly panic and pull at the thick rope which slowly cuts off my oxygen.

"You ever heard the saying enough rope to hang yourself?" His warm breath burns the sensitive part of my neck. The hairs jump to attention, desperate to feel his lips against me. I whimper and nod my head, only tightening in. My head feels fuzzy, but all the blood rushing makes my pleasure increase.

"That's what you have, little mortal. I'll give you enough freedom to decide the torture on each bad soul but if you ask too much of me, then you'll suffer. Got it?"

"Yes!"

"Fuck you're desperate. Look at the way you're grinding your hips, desperately trying to cum on my dead cock." He growls. Then, he increases the pressure on my clit and nipples. I'm a panting mess, desperate for him.

"Tell me what his punishment should be."

My head is completely gone.

"Speak, little mortal. You wanted power and now you have it." He mocks me as he nips at my ear. A long whine falls from my lip as the pleasure grows too much.

"Please!"

"You are not allowed to cum until you sort him."

"Fine! Make him food for the beasts or something!" I become frantic.

I can almost feel him cocking an eyebrow up at me. "Nothing else?"

"And lock him in the hell maze!"

He groans in pleasure. "Now we are talking, little mortal."

"Please, I did it, now fuck me!"

"No," he suddenly growls in my ear and my whole body tenses up. "The next time I fuck you, your mortal soul will be gone. Only then I will ravish you until you are nothing but stained with sin, dead girl. For now, cum over my fingers and enjoy your last mortal orgasm."

He doesn't even finish his sentence before my orgasm rocks through my body. The rope strains at my throat, cutting off my oxygen as the waves crash into me repeatedly. A pleasured scream falls from my lips at the same time as the pained one falls from the tortured soul on stage. Death never stops circling my clit and tugging on my nipples, forcing me to continue riding my high.

"Keep going, little mortal," he barks before pushing me off the cliff again. A wave of heat passes through my body and my toes curl. The pleasure smashes into me again making my whole body feel like jelly. I cry out his name again, my eyes shutting together, desperately trying to ground myself. After what feels like centuries, I come down from my high. He spins me around so that I'm forced to face him, and I see that wicked look in his eye. My body moves automatically for his cock to return the favour, but he stops me.

"I want to cum on your naked body, cover you in my semen to mark you as my own." He growls. I instantly freeze up.

"Naked?"

"Did I stutter, little mortal?"

"I won't—" My breathing hurts and it feels as though my whole body is seizing up. Death's eyes grow large and round as he frantically tries to figure out what's wrong.

Naked. He will see your scars, your wounds, your insecurities. Or what's even worse, I'll have to face the truth of being a scarred creature for the rest of eternity.

"I can't—"

"Little mortal, what is happening?" his hands run all over my body as if to try and soothe me, but the thought has already plagued my mind. I choke on a breath. His talons sink into my skin and the sharp pain forces me to take oxygen into my lungs. It grounds me slightly and I feel more in control.

"What happened to you on Earth?" His jaw is tense, but concern is laced in his voice. "What are you so afraid of?"

"I'm ugly."

A snort falls past his lips. "You're afraid of being ugly?"

"Not *being* ugly, I am ugly. You haven't seen my skin—"

His fingers leap to my jumpsuit, and he readies himself to rip at it. A squeal falls past my lips and I latch onto his hands. "No! Please!"

"Listen very fucking carefully, little mortal," he growls. "You will never be ugly to me, got it? Your sweet, sinful and feisty attitude have my cock bobbing but that pretty little face and your curvy fucking body—" he groans as though trying to contain himself. "You are so fucking gorgeous it hurts. Show me your skin, dead girl. Show me what you are trying to hide because I promise you it will not bother me."

"Death, I can't—"

"You can and you will." He tears slightly at the jumpsuit. My hands jump to cover it from his eyes. His whole body trembles and I can feel the anger seeping from him but he does his best to hide it from me.

For the first time, when he reaches for my smaller hands, his touch is gentle and oddly comforting. I sink my teeth into my bottom lip. Hesitation consumes me and the self-loathing has me shaking my head 'no'.

His Adam's apple jumps out as he swallows hard. "Let me in, little mortal."

Everything forces me to keep my hands hiding my skin, but his gentle touch slowly peels my fingers away and I let him. His eyes remain firmly locked on mine and I hold my breath.

Slowly, he rips down my jumpsuit and helps me step out of it. The cold has my nipples instantly jumping to attention and the hairs on my body leaping outwards. He never lets his eyes drop from my face until I take a shaky breath.

"I am going to look at you now, okay?" It's the first time I've ever heard him ask for permission and it has my body responding to him in a way I really wish it wouldn't.

Patiently, he waits for me to dip my head before his eyes roam down my body. He inhales sharply and I slam my eyes shut.

"Open them." His voice is hard and authoritative. I hesitate but when I feel his fingers curl into the softness of my hips, I obey him. Cold, furious eyes stare back at me.

"Who did this to you, little mortal? Give me a name so we can torture the fucking shit out of them."

"More than one person," it's little more than a whimper and I feel so fucking pathetic. A tremble takes hold of my body. I refuse to look down at myself, ashamed of what I might find. I stopped tending to wounds a couple of years ago when I no longer recognised my body in the mirror. I fear what I might find if I do check.

His cold touch seems to soothe me as much as I try to convince myself otherwise. He trails his fingers up and down my skin, following along scars and skimming across burn marks. A whoosh of air flushes past me and I feel Death behind me, inspecting my whole body. I hold my breath. Then, suddenly, a large, twisted mirror appears in front of me. I squeak and turn around, but Death forces me back to face it.

My eyes remain firmly shut. "Please, I can't—"

"Listen to my voice, little mortal," he whispers as his hands trail around my body. I feel him against my body and to my surprise, his huge cock twitches against my back. My hands reach back in shock, and I feel his hard, stony body, completely naked. Startled, I pull away quickly.

"We're both scarred, and we're both naked," he tells me in a dark voice. The lump in my throat throbs as I will the tears away.

"I can't look at myself, Death."

"Then look at me instead."

His touch against me has me melting. I desperately want to see what he looks like without clothes and that primal part of me has my eyes slowly opening. A flash of my pale skin, stained with dark red lines, comes into view but I force myself to look at him behind me, towering over me. His dark tattoos swim fast around his body, smashing into one another. It looks painful but his face never reveals any unease. Instead, he stares straight at me, scanning me for a reaction. His muscles ripple when he moves his arms around my body to embrace me, and my tongue darts out to coat my bottom lip. I look so small in his arms.

When he pulls me flush against him, I feel something tickle my back. "Do you feel that?" he whispers. "You can feel the souls leaping from my body."

Wide-eyed, I jolt against him, but he forces me back against him. The way they move massages my skin beautifully and reluctantly, and images of them against my nipples flash to my mind. He must sense my instant desire because those eyes darken.

"Look at yourself in the mirror and then I promise you will have whatever dirty thoughts you're thinking of."

"Death—"

"I'm not going to tell you again. I tried to be kind, little mortal, but we both know it's not in my nature. So, you're either going to look at the beautiful woman in the mirror or I will punish you."

His words have me instantly doing what I'm told. My nakedness jumps to attention, and I scan down my scarred skin, stained with imperfections. As if to ground me, Death's hands still roam up and down my body. I watch quietly as he lightly traces every single scar.

His breathing becomes unsteady, and I can sense his fury, but desire controls him. His cock twitches against my back repeatedly until he pushes it down between my legs. I whimper out as it slides against my slick wetness. He slowly moves my hips until I'm grinding on him. My legs threaten to give out, but I know he will catch me if I fall.

"You are so fucking stunning, little mortal." He growls. "And looking at your scars only makes me want you more. I love broken little toys."

"Other men did this to me. You're okay with that?"

His eyes darken and bleed. "Fuck no. But I know that we'll get our revenge, little mortal. They've broken my mortal canvas, but you haven't died yet. Your soul is clinging to the ruined mortal body. When I kill you, your imperfections will disappear and then I can ruin you myself."

CHAPTER TWENTY-FOUR

"Give me their names, little mortal. Let us torture those who hurt you and then destroy any evidence of them on your beautiful body. Let's get you your revenge."

I'm such a cunt for even mentioning that what I want to do to her is worse. *Isn't the human way full of compassion and empathy?*

'We are not human, and we will never pretend to be. She knows exactly what we are and she will have to learn to love it.'

"I've got my revenge against most of the others that hurt me, and I killed Leonardo on the bus, but it doesn't feel enough."

"He's already dead?" I'm stunned by this realisation. "What's his last name? What does he look like?"

"Leonardo Gownes. He was an ugly man; tall I guess and stocky but the thing that distinguishes him from the rest is—" She hesitates as though remembering it brings her pain. "His hair. He was completely bald except for this blonde mohawk—"

A blonde mohawk? Why does that sound familiar?

"But in killing him I killed myself so I could never get revenge on the man who deserves it most."

"Wait, you died on the same day as him?" I say quickly as the dots slowly connect. I distinctly remember the burning in my hand whilst trapped in the office, being scolded by my father. I remember returning to sort the troublesome soul, only to be interrupted by my mother and I sent him to a random hell loop so I could sort him at a later date.

"Yes. Have you seen him?"

"Yes," the wicked smile that coats my lips is wicked. "And what is far better news, my little mortal, is that he hasn't been sorted yet. That pleasure can be all yours."

Her face twists into something inscrutable. I can't tell if she's excited or terrified at this opportunity. Then, her eyes dart down at her naked body, and she hides herself instantly, the thoughts horrifying her.

I click my fingers and suddenly my beautiful little mortal wears the most stunning dress of nails, shimmering in different shades of black and grey. The nail heads rest against her soft skin to not pierce her skin, but they stick out threateningly. I long to yank her against my naked body and cause myself pain but I know that I won't be able to control myself after that.

"Death, this is beautiful!" It completely takes her by surprise and thankfully distracts her self-loathing thoughts.

Within the blink of an eye, I redress myself before clicking my fingers. Beside me, a stunning, scarlet-coloured seat emerges from the depths of hell. It has deep cracks in it and is severely broken but that's exactly what I want. *A broken throne for my broken queen.*

"Take a seat, little mortal," I smirk, offering a hand to help her sit. She takes it quickly with a newfound confidence. I purposely created a design that was both beautiful and threatening but also showed off her perky breasts and long slender arms.

I can't wait to see her coated in blood.

"Leonardo Gownes, monster!" I bark out the demand before

reaching over to my little mortal. I mean to pat the throne, but her smaller hand quickly slips into mine. I bristle. Suddenly, I snatch my hand away from her.

"Listen here, little mortal, the only time I'll ever hold your hand is to get the angle right when I fuck you." Even as I spit the spiteful words, I almost don't mean them. Her open fingers remain in the same position as when they were wrapped around my larger hand. I eye them up angrily. "I won't hold your hand, but you can squeeze mine. Give me your pain, dead girl."

She instantly grabs at me. I feel my fingers click as she clamps down. It takes everything within my evil nature not to pull her towards me and fuck the anger out of us both.

Before I can do anything, the atmosphere changes as a body is dragged out from the hole in the floor, kicking and screaming. The soul looks worse for wear with various shades of black and blue staining his skin. What's even better, he's completely naked, bearing all to us. Beside me, my little mortal stiffens. I can't tell if she wants to cry or attack.

'Hopefully both,' the beast coos.

"Please! Let me go! Please! I'll do anything—" he blubbers as my monster leans over him, demon claw at the ready. However, just as my monster can disembowel Leonardo, Scarlet shoots out of her chair.

"Wait!" she cries out. Both the monster and Leonardo's head snaps in her direction. It brings me *so* much pleasure to hear the way Leonardo's stomach drops in his stomach and the fear suddenly increases.

"Sc—Scarlet?" He is fucking mortified.

She slowly saunters closer to the stage, and I can't take my eyes away from the way her hips sway beautifully in that dress.

"Scarlet! What the fuck is happening? What are you doing here?"

She says nothing as she takes the steps one by one. Her eyes are glued to the scene, but her face remains inscrutable.

"Let me in, little mortal. Give me your deliciously sinful thoughts." I tell her telepathically, but she doesn't respond. Instead, she sticks her hand out and snatches the demon bone from my creature. He bobs his head and gives her distance, recognising what ought to be done. My little mortal circles the whimpering man in the middle of the stage. She throws the weapon into each hand to familiarise herself with it.

"Scarlet!" he shrieks. "Scarlet! No!"

Suddenly, he scrambles away but my beautiful little predator is much faster. She sinks the weapon deeply into his thigh until his cries ripple through the room. His blood squirts out and coats her bare feet. I quickly flash a bottle of whisky into the room with me and gulp at it, fascinated by the show.

"You," she spits poison at him. "I killed your body and now I will kill your soul."

She pulls the weapon from his thigh, and he snaps in half in agony as the jagged weapon causes him suffering. However, she plunges it straight back into his hand which clutches the wound. A howl escapes his lips.

He flails around in fear. "Please, have mercy! I never did this to you!"

"You *did* torture me, Leonardo. Don't lie to a woman with a weapon." Again, she strikes him in the flesh until there is a pool of blood around them. She works with such ease and such precision; it is as though she was made for this life.

With one stab to the stomach, she drops the weapon and uses her fingers to pry the flesh apart. Leonardo shrieks in agony and desperately tries to fight her off but he is quickly drained of energy as he pours out onto my marble floor. He cannot die a bodily death like before, so he is forced to endure constant suffering until she decides to sort him. This thought makes me fully erect.

How long will you torture him, little mortal? What wicked things do you have in store for this sinner?

She forces her hand into his stomach and yanks out his intestines. Then, she wraps it around his neck and chokes him. Her creativity of torture has me falling forward in my seat. I can't even remember the last time I blinked, nor do I want to. My only focus is on the wicked woman on the stage.

"Choke," she smiles as she says the word. "Feel what I endured for twenty-two years straight and know that even once I'm done with you and I move onto Maximo, you will suffer for eternity, and I will not."

"Please!" he hollers and it's like music to her ears. For a second, her eyes flutter shut, and she soaks up the experience.

Fucking Hell, she is perfect.

When her eyes reopen, they are dark and full of anger. She scoops up the blood on the floor and pours it over Leonardo's face. On top of choking on his intestines tightly wrapped around his neck, he is now waterboarded with his own blood. She rips at his mohawk as she stains the blonde hair red.

"*This* is what I'm used to looking at." She loses herself in some memory and it takes everything in me to stay seated. What I really want to do is flash over to her and remind her of where she is, and who she's with. That she is safe by my side because nobody will ever lay another fucking finger on her again.

"Does that hurt, Leonardo?" her words ooze sarcasm. "Do you want me to stop? To give you mercy?"

The most beautiful laugh tumbles from her lips. My knuckles turn white as I grip my bottle of alcohol. I want to fist my cock and cum as she plunges her weapon into her abuser's heart.

"Do it, little mortal." I find myself hollering like an excited audience member and not the overseer of the punishment. Her head snaps towards me and when that hatred is directed at me, my body is alive.

'Come over here and use the demon claw on me, little mortal.'

But just as quickly as she looks at me, her attention snaps back to the writhing man in her fingers. She continues to punish him until his shrieks have her wincing and clutching her pounding head. Only then, does she fall back onto the floor and smile. Blood coats her toes and splatters up her body and she looks fucking delicious. I long to fuck her over her abuser's dying body.

"Send him to a Hell loop that has me torturing him for eternity," she says without ever looking at me. My cock bobs in my trousers and I find myself eagerly responding. "Yes, ma'am."

Then, she plunges the claw into his heart and his soul leaps from his mutilated body. It bursts into pixels with a roar of agony before vanishing before her eyes. Even though his soul has been sorted, the mangled body remains behind, much to her delight. She slowly rises to her feet. She doesn't even fucking shake when she turns to face me.

"Can you bring alive people down to Hell?"

Speechless, I shake my head no. She ponders on this thought for a second. "Okay, am I able to return to Earth to drag them back to Hell?"

Fucking Hell, you devious and delicious woman.

My lips curve into a twisted grimace. "I thought you'd never ask."

CHAPTER TWENTY-FIVE

My breathing hitches in my throat as I feel the hard ground beneath my feet and smell that familiar tinge of bleach wafting from my prison opposite me. It feels as though my heart has finally given up as I stare numbly at the house. This is the first time in my life that anger replaces fear in the face of my trauma. Death appears next to me and as soon as he appears, the world turns several shades darker. A cold chill sweeps across the forest, making the trees howl in fear. Below him, the green grass withers away.

His eyebrow cocks up as he watches the world around him slowly decay. "It's been a while since I've been to Earth." He says out loud but it's not clear whether he is talking to me or himself.

The lump in my throat bobs as I advance closer to the house. Death is hot on my heels but slightly behind me, as though to let me lead. I feel the world around us darken and shrivel away and there is an immense sense of power running through my veins.

"I want to burn this place to the ground," I hiss.

Death chuckles darkly behind me. "Your wish is my command."

Suddenly, he creates a fireball in the palm of his hand. It burns bright blue and flickers of scarlet spit from the flames. I feel the warmth up against my body.

"Come here," he instructs before holding his hand out to me. Nervously, I obey him.

"Touch the flames."

"What? It'll burn me."

He bares his teeth at me. It's a silent display of his authority. "Don't make me repeat myself, little mortal."

My heart races in my chest as I slowly reach forward. The flames lick my skin and I feel the heat singe the hairs on the back of my fingers. I flinch and pull away.

A low growl escapes his lips. "Now, little mortal."

"Okay! I thrust my hand into the flame, squeezing my eyes shut, anticipating the pain which is about to burn through me. However, no pain arrives. A warm sensation coats my hand like it being dipped into water. Wide-eyed, I stare down at my mortal hand burning in the flames of Death's fireball.

"What? How?"

"It will not burn you," he grits his teeth as he stares down at the flames. It licks at his skin, slowly peeling away at his body until it's red raw. I gasp.

"It's burning you!"

"Well, of course, little mortal. I kill everything, including myself." His poignant words have me tripping over my thoughts.

I kill everything, including myself, but not you. Not just yet. My mind seems to add to his sentence and my stomach twists deliciously.

"Now that you know it won't burn you," he grabs the burning hand and clasps my fingers around his wrist. It seems to burn him, and his jaw tightens. "Throw my hand at the house. Set that prison alight and let's dance in the flames."

His eyes twinkle maliciously, matching my own. Any inkling of doubt instantly disappears as the devious hunger grows in my chest. With a deep breath, I turn to face my prison and a smile licks my lips.

"Goodbye, prison." It's barely a whisper, meant only for my ears, but I don't miss the way Death freezes up. He's so fucking tense beside me, and a dark mist seeps out of him again. I grab his wrist and do as I'm told, thrusting his hand forward.

Suddenly, the fireball hurls into my prison and the most deafening boom ripples through the world. The ground visibly trembles, and I stumble. Before I can fall over, Death's arms snap around me.

"You are only allowed to fall to your knees for me." His growl caresses my mind most sinfully. My stomach twists and the hairs on the back of my neck leap to attention. I feel his arms snake around my waist as he brings his fangs to my neck, scraping the sensitive skin.

"Go get your revenge, little mortal."

He releases me and I instantly spring into action. With a newfound hunger in my chest, I kick down the front door alight in flames. I step into the house, and I'm shocked by the ferocity of the fire. The paint has already peeled back, and wooden beams start to collapse in on themselves from the impact of the fireball.

Shrieks and cries from men in the rooms of the house fill my head like a sweet melody. I want to go and witness every single fiery death, but I'm here for one person in particular. The rest can meet me at the sorting stage.

My head rears left, up the stairs, and before I can hesitate, I find myself taking the stairs in two. Death is close behind me. It feels as though he's my shadow rather than this omnipotent presence which controls life and ruin.

The breath in my lungs hitches the closer I get to my husband. He's so close that I can feel the old tears burning in my mind. Horrific memories flash in the back of my mind, more violent and vicious than I could ever anticipate. I force myself to take a steady breath, but it doesn't seem to work. My whole body shakes, and the bile rises in the back of my throat.

No! You can't do this! Turn back! Run away! The self-doubt shrieks for me to escape again. Involuntarily, I stumble backwards but Death's hard body forces me to keep going.

One strangled, frightened shriek ripples through the hallway — or what's left of it anyways. It's like my predator senses have been alerted and I race towards the beautiful sound. However, the ceiling has partially collapsed and trapped him inside the room. Death's gentle touch strokes past my hip as he slides past to remove the damage for me. He lifts the whole thing with such ease before throwing it behind us. It creates a horrific crashing noise as the floor gives way below the weight of the broken ceiling.

We are trapped. There's no going back now.

Despite the anxious thoughts, my body does not shake in fear. I feel perfectly alert and aware of what's going to happen. An evilness soaks through me. I pull all the rage, fear, and agony that beast of a man inflicted on me in twenty-two years to the surface. Now it's my turn to be the monster.

Death holds his hand out and helps me jump across a missing part of the floorboards. My dress floats out stunningly, in all its violent glory as I land. As soon as I cross the threshold, I scan the room for the dead man walking. When I spot the cowering man in the corner of the room, trapped under the cupboard which has fallen from its position. It crushes his legs. I lick my lips.

The monster has found its injured prey.

"What? What the— who are?" he stumbles over his words, not able to make out the two shadows on the other side of the room. Behind me, I hear a large gust of wind as Death forces a hole through the roof of the building. The moon's gaze tears into the room, revealing my furious face to my infamous husband.

Horrified, he desperately tries to wriggle from under the cupboard to free himself. It's fucking pathetic and he barely moves an inch.

"Scarlet!" It's a gasp and a cry all in one. "What the fuck? What are you doing here? How are you—"

With a malicious grin, I stalk closer to him. "It's my turn to speak, *husband*."

"Get away from me!" Panic floods him. Again, he frantically smashes at the cupboard, but the solid oak has been untouched by the fire. I send a little smile over to Death who groans at my delight. I can't see him, hiding in the shadows, but I feel his hard gaze attached to my body. He soaks up every movement, every reaction, every utterance. I perform for him, and he fucking loves it.

"Oh, my dear," I hear the sarcasm laced in my voice as I snatch Maximo by the chin and tilt his face around. I soak up the anxiety in his ugly appearance and it brings me a ridiculous amount of joy. "If only that phrase actually worked. I would know, wouldn't I?"

"I'm sorry! I'm sorry! Just get away from me—" he must sense the newfound power oozing through my veins because he melts instantly. Twenty-two years of pure horror and agony in this man's hands, and he breaks like a fucking twig when confronted with *true* power.

Behind us, the fire roars louder and the shrieks of dying men plague my dirty thoughts. My fingernails sink into his chin until he winces but it's not enough.

Malicious instinct takes over and I pull two nails from my dress and bring them to his cheeks. He tries to scramble away from me, but I slam my foot down on the cupboard and the added weight has him howling in pain. I hear the way it snaps. His fists shoot out and he narrowly misses me. Even with all the adrenaline pacing through his body, the pain blinds his reaction times.

"You're right, torturing is fun," I chuckle darkly. My voice doesn't sound like my own. It feels like I'm living out some fucked up fantasy dream and yet I am totally grounded. With a glisten in my eyes, I press the nails into his cheeks violently until the skin splits open for me.

Maximo tries to shake his head to escape me, but it simply rips the flesh, causing much more damage. A delighted noise falls from my lips.

"Make that noise again!"

"You're fucking insane! Leave me alone! You fucking bitch!" He tries to swing for me again but I'm much faster and I dodge the attack.

I tut. "Now, now, be a good sport, husband."

Blood drips down his face, and I'm momentarily infatuated by the oozing scarlet colour. A real sense of completion fills me. I almost want to cry at the realisation that I'm finally doing what I promised I'd do for twenty-two years. My fingers itch to scoop it from his cheek and taste it. I'm not sure what type of animalistic instinct consumes me but it's very fucking powerful.

Suddenly, a whoosh of air knocks me to the side and without warning, Death appears in front of me. His fists clamp around Maximo's fist which tried to strike me. Instantly, the bones explode, and mangled nerves and tendons leap out of the bundle of mush. Maximo howls in agony and he desperately tries to pull away from the *death* grip but it's no use.

"You dare touch what is mine?" Black mist oozes from him more freely now. Under the moonlight, I can see the way his tattoos swim faster than they ever have before. I resist the temptation to reach out and feel their anger.

"What the fuck are you? Ah—fuck! It hurts! Let go! Fuck—"

"Apologise to her," Death growls. "You better fucking plead for forgiveness and maybe, just maybe, we will go easy on you."

The breath catches in my throat when Maximo's eyes jump to me. They turn wide, and pleading and a long string of begs fall from his lips. "Scarlet! I am *so* sorry! I'm a vicious, wicked man and I should never have hurt you or kidnapped you or Hell, I shouldn't have done anything to you! I am so sorry!"

His head snaps back to Death almost expectantly. The dribbling snot mixes with his streaming tears. He has never looked so fucking pathetic and weak in his life. "Please! Go easy on me!"

"I lied. We will never go easy on scum like you," Death growls before his fist slams into Maximo's chest. The word *'we'* rings around my mind beautifully until I feel my heart swell with some unknown feeling. *Love?* Most definitely not. *Pride?* Perhaps. *Anticipation?* Abso-fucking-lutely.

Death breaks every rib, shattering the cage which protects his vital organs. When he turns back to me, I can see the beast threaten to escape like it did before. His eyes bleed down his face and I can see his muscles threatening to burst through the armour. It flexes unnaturally as his body tries to force through.

I expect the fear to shake through my body, but it never comes. Instead, absolute admiration and awe consume me. I want to beg him to torture my ex-husband in front of me. I want to see Maximo squirm under the touch of a more powerful being. Everything within my broken soul *needs* the beast to be unleashed, and yet, Death holds onto his sanity.

He gently offers me a hand and pulls me closer to my ex-husband.

"Do it," his voice is hard and cold, no slither of sympathy laced in the tone. "Fucking ruin him before I do."

It fills me with such excitement. Without hesitation, I leap onto Maximo, and I plunge my hand into his broken ribcage. He howls and shrieks, trying to strike me but Death effortlessly holds his wrists in a single fist.

My sharp fingernails find his heart and I squeeze hard. The muscle contracts in my fingers, fighting back. However, with a single tug, it frees itself from his body, and my husband cries out for the last time. His breathing is snatched from his body, and he instantly dies under my fingers.

However, I don't move. The muscle burns in my fingers and it feels so fucking heavy. A lifetime of constant suffering, over in a single moment.

"How does it feel?" Death's voice startles me. It's full of lust and desire. I feel his arms snake around my waist, and I know I should shy away from him. I should be on the floor, screaming in anger and misery. The last thing I need is to be near someone so malicious. I shouldn't be in the arms of yet another dominant, controlling man. And yet, my body throbs when my back presses against him.

"Tell me,"

"Good," the single word is breathless.

"Only good?"

A sharp breath slips from my lips as the realisation slowly settles. "I'm free."

"Not quite," I feel him smile against my neck after he pushes my hair to the slide. "Do you know how sexy you look, drenched in blood and in a dress which pierces skin?"

My whole body is alight with desire from a single question. Around us, the house falls apart and the fire roars louder and louder. It's almost hard to hear him, but each word pierces through my mind deliciously. His hands roam all over my body until I'm trembling for him.

"Now that you got your end of the deal, little mortal." he growls. "It's my turn to claim my new Pet."

CHAPTER TWENTY-SIX

I have been waiting for this moment since I laid eyes on the sinful little mortal. It's not every day you meet a mortal so full of hatred and sin mixed with pride and confidence. She didn't shake for me back then, but she learnt who's really to be feared. And now she is here, trembling below my body. Her breathing is erratic, I can smell her desire and her anxiety.

She's stained in another man's blood but that only makes my cock stir. She is too pretty to be free from that scarlet colour.

"It's my turn to claim my new Pet," I nip her ear as I finish my sentence. She whimpers and it almost sets me off. Everything she does is so fucking delicious and perfect. I want to bend her over and fuck her senseless until her soul explodes and is stained as part of mine. Once I'm finished with her, she will be just another dead girl trapped in my Realm of Hell.

Mine for all eternity.

"Will it hurt?" she's uncertain but it's too fucking bad. A deal is a deal and there is nothing in this universe that could stop me from taking what is rightfully mine.

"Yes,"

She gulps but the timid thing doesn't run away from me. She must be insane because she leans back into me, rubbing her ass against my erect cock. My balls tighten and I force myself to take a deep breath to regulate myself.

"I'll make it hurt less." I run my forked tongue up and down the sensitive part of her skin behind her ears. She shivers and I smell another wave of desire flood through her.

'She responds so fucking well for us.'

"What do I need to do?"

'And she's fucking eager.'

"Take it, like a good little mortal," I tell her with a nasty grin. "By the time you come down from your high, you will be dead and mine forever."

She gulps again. I hear the way her eyes flutter shut, and she presses against me, putting her full trust in an evil God who has only ever wanted her demise. It's so fucking attractive. My fingers find the zip on the back of her dress, and I pull it down. Her hands shoot up instinctively to hide her naked body from the world.

Anger radiates through me. "You will never hide yourself from me again. Got it? I own you, dead girl. You are mine and I will always have access to what is mine."

"Death—"

Without warning, I rip the dress from her body. She squeals but the good girl knows not to disobey me. Instead, she keeps her arms tightly by her side as my eyes rake up her toned back and round ass.

My hand strikes out and I spank her sensitive skin. She yelps but takes it so fucking well. I free my cock from its restraints, and it excitedly bounces against her back. I position it against her little slit.

"You're fucking soaked already. Does your greedy pussy gush

when you kill?" Her hips buck at my dirty words, and it only spurs the beast on more. "Will you beg for your orgasm after you've murdered a bad man?"

"Death—"

"Tell me. Do you fantasise about being ruthlessly fucked over a dead body?"

"Yes, fuck Death, yes!" she cries out so beautifully. Any restraint I had snaps and I plunge my huge cock into her pussy. She screams and her fingernails shoot out into my wrists as she tries to steady herself. I don't give her a second to adjust before I start fucking her hard.

Her screams match those in agony being burnt alive, and it makes my balls tighten so deliciously. My hand snakes around and I play with her little bundle of nerves until she's a panting mess. It doesn't take long until she's whimpering and frantically meeting my thrusts.

"Oh Death!" she cries out as I force her first orgasm through her. Her pussy walls clamp deliciously around me until my cock hurts from being squeezed. Nonetheless, I continue pummelling her in front of her dead husband. She falls forward and grabs the burning wall. I force her thighs in the air to get a better angle. She hollers as I smash her G-spot over and over again, not giving her time to come down from her high.

"I know you can give me another one," I growl before snatching at her hair. Her head shoots backwards and like a good girl, her lips fall open. Before I can stop myself, I spit in her mouth and she obediently swallows.

'Oh fuck, Death, I don't think we can hold on much longer—'

"You love being fucked like a dirty little slut, don't you?"

"Oh, my—" my fingers jump to her throat, and I squeeze before she can say the next word. As soon as the pain hits her, my beautiful little mortal squirts everywhere. The orgasm slams into her, wave after wave until my name on her lips echoes down the burning house. I feel her shake from the aftermath. The hairs on her body stand to attention as if to try and push me from her.

I pull my cock from her pussy and run it back to her asshole.

"Wait—"

"Mine," I hiss before plunging inside of her. Her wetness makes it too easy to slide in and she's instantly screaming in pleasure. Her head falls back against me when I force two fingers inside her pussy at the same time.

"I'm so full!"

"Take it, little mortal, take my dead cock in your living asshole," I growl into her ear. She shivers as I force her neck to the side. My fangs throb in anticipation and I can smell the sweetness of her soul. It begs me to claim her life, to fucking ruin any chances of her going to Heaven. I scrape it against her skin to increase her anxiety. When her heart rate spikes, I know that I'm done for. There is no going back now.

"Remember to breathe through it," I give her one last bit of advice before plunging my fangs into her neck. She cries out in agony and her whole body seizes up. Her sinful blood instantly swarms my tastebuds and makes me feel dizzy. It's the most delicious fucking drink I've had in ages. I feel her lifeline deplete as I continue to fuck her. Her nails draw blood around my wrist. Her screams turn to whimpers as she grows weaker and weaker. I flick her clit repeatedly until her pain turns to absolute pleasure. My name stains her lips over and over.

"Good girl, die for me. Let me ruin you," I pant in her ear as I sense her orgasm close. My balls tighten and I feel the tension build up inside of me.

I plunge my fangs back into her as our orgasms rip through us. I roar out my high as I empty my cum into her dying body. She is frantic as the pleasure becomes too much for her. Then, suddenly, I feel her go limp in my body as complete exhaustion forces its way through her.

She squeezes around my cock one last time before I steal her life from her. I completely and utterly ruin the sweet little mortal and force her into an eternal death. And I do not have a single bit of remorse.

CHAPTER TWENTY-SEVEN

The agony is fucking blinding. It feels as though I am completely destroyed, on fire and drenched in ice at the same time. Every nerve snaps and rebuilds, and I can feel my skin peeling back from my body only to reform again. At the same time, the pleasure attacks me. His name falls out of my lips repeatedly and I desperately try to fight the overwhelming sensation forcing its way through my body. But it's too late. My mortal soul explodes into a million pieces, never to reform again.

When the blinding light stops burning my eyes, I find myself back in the sorting room, on my knees. I immediately feel Death behind me. He leers over me, desperately scanning me as though I might break any second now.

His cold touch presses against my naked shoulder as if to give me strength. "Welcome to eternal death," he gently helps me to my feet as his warm breath caresses my neck. He turns me around before his dark eyes begin bleeding. They roam down my body appreciatively and a groan slips from his lips.

"A blank canvas for me to ruin," he growls under his breath, but I hear every word. It sends bolts of electricity through my body and just when I thought I couldn't want him anymore, my body becomes alight again.

"I have a surprise for you, dead girl," his hot breath caresses the skin on the back of my neck. I'm instantly alive to the sound of Death's dark promise.

Without missing another beat, the room around us fades into nothing. The once dark crimson walls dripping with blood and gore transform into a dark, starless night. A sudden chill coupled with a gloomy cloud lurking around them pulls the new atmosphere and I stumble closer to Death absentmindedly.

"Look around, dead girl."

Breathless, I stare around at what appears to be a graveyard, coated with a thick layer of smoke. If I stepped away from Death, I knew I would lose him in the grey cloud, but I could still make out little bits of rock sticking out of the uncut lawn, each with a scribbled inscription, screaming out the deceased person's life. I feel it in my chest — all the lives claimed and snatched from the cemetery, leaving nothing but a wasteland for humans to mourn over.

"Gravestones?"

His hard fingers curve around my hips and he forcefully moves me a couple of metres into the graveyard.

"*Your* gravestone."

The breath is snatched from my chest. "What?"

Without another word, he guides me further into the smoke until I feel it clogging up my lungs. Only when my legs feel as though they are going to give out does he forcefully stop me and make me look at a huge, towering gravestone.

This one is far different from the others. The grass has been cut, and the soil has been patted down neatly, starkly contrasting the untamed, uncared-for stones around us. The gravestone itself is blood red and has dark black cracks running through the marble, twisting and turning throughout. Some cracks sprout into the most beautifully deranged flowers I've ever seen, curling in at the name in the centre of the stone.

"Scarlet Mortal?" I feel sick as I speak the name out loud.

"Yes, because I was never going to let you take another man's last name to the afterlife now, was I? It's 'til death do us part, and you are both dead, my pretty mortal. You're mine now. And yet I wanted to be reminded of how perfectly mortal you were when I first ravaged you. My little mortal turned dead girl."

"Death. How did you know my name—"

"This isn't sentimental, dead girl," his voice is suddenly harsh, full of grief and hatred. "This isn't some wicked display of love and happiness. You still belong to the God of Death. I gave you a gravestone and a new last name as a display of ownership. You are my little pet. You do as you are told."

My eyes slam shut as I lean up against his hard, cold body. Those viciously large arms snake around my neck and they force me close against him.

"So, listen carefully, Scarlet Mortal." He scrapes his fangs against the sensitive part of my neck, awakening every inch of my body. "You will run and hide amongst these gravestones, and if I catch you, I will fuck you back to Hell where you belong as Death's new pet."

I'm completely and utterly speechless, but he doesn't rely on consent. He never did, never will, and I will never ask that of him. Our bodies do all the talking when speech isn't good enough.

"Got it?"

I nod frantically. Even though I can't see him, I *feel* the way he smirks against my body. He squeezes me one last time and it hurts but I melt into the familiar pain. Then, he whispers against my cheek and the games begin.

"Run, dead girl. You can't escape death."

Without hesitation, I lurch forward and sprint like I've never sprinted before. The wicked fog only makes it harder to navigate as I bounce around the gravestones, desperately trying to hide. That odd, perverted part of me almost wants to make this easy for him. I want to run in circles and then lead him back to my gravestone, open my legs, and invite him in. And yet, reason, that stupid little voice, forces the fear through my veins, and the adrenaline forces me to run like I'm being hunted.

Because you are.

In the distance, I hear his low chuckle. It's deep, throaty and promises so much torture. And my body couldn't respond quicker.

My lungs heave and my legs ache as I throw myself left before narrowly dodging another gravestone. And then, suddenly, he appears in front of me. Just before I can collide with him, I take a sharp turn and dash away, but it's not long before he appears again. I escape but I'm met with the same fate. Only this time, he loses interest in pretending I can run away from him. His hand shoots out and snakes around my waist. Before I can process what's happening, he has me pressed against him, fangs sinking into my neck.

The pain pierces through me and I scream in pain as the bubbling sensation burns through my body. I feel it flood through me, again and again until my head is dizzy, and everything is heightened. Even my toes throb in agony as wave after wave I'm hit with torturous pain. Death doesn't give a shit though; he keeps sucking at my blood as though it's his lifeline.

"I will never stop doing this," he growls. Then, suddenly, the overwhelming pain turns into incredible pleasure. An orgasm smashes through me before I can stop it. My knees buckle but he refuses to let me move from against his body. He keeps sucking until I'm scratching at his chest, whimpering from the aftermath of my high.

Another one hits me just as unexpectedly, but this time, his fingers plunge inside of me, and I'm forced to ride out the high. His huge cock presses against my slit and he forces me to grind against it. All the while, his beady eyes roam every inch of me, desperately soaking up every reaction my body has to give to him.

"That's it, dead girl. Sin like a bad little mortal should," he growls before plunging into me. A shriek falls past my lips as he fucks me in the cemetery, taking no mercy on me. He plunges harder and faster, his rough grip on my hips bruising my skin. I feel my tongue fall out of my mouth and he latches onto it. I feel drunk on his kiss as he consumes me. Everything is alight, the mix of pain and pleasure deliciously blending into one.

"Death—" I cry out as his fingers twist at my nipples. "Death, I'm going to—"

"Do it, cum all over my dead cock."

Suddenly, the orgasm plunges through me for the third time in five minutes. I slump onto his chest, breathless and dizzy. He pulls his cock from my pussy and twists me around. Then, he plunges into my asshole, and it feels like I'm tearing in two. The pain is unbearable but the position he hits has me screaming in pleasure. A low growl erupts from him. It's the most fucking delicious thing I've ever heard in my life.

"Take it, dead girl. Feel my hot cum fill up your dirty, dead womb."

My eyes slam shut as the pleasure consumes me. He fucks me harder and faster until a grunt falls from his lips. I feel him tense up against me before ropes of hot liquid squirt into me. His erratic breathing echoes through my body and his thrusts become lazy.

His arms seem to tighten around me, forcing me still. I tell myself it's because he's not done fucking me. He hasn't finished getting his pleasure out of his little pet, and yet, the way his head rests in the cross of my neck, and I feel his lips caress the softness of my skin, something has shifted.

It feels less like him using me as he comes down from his high, and more like a twisted embrace. The best possible hug a Being forged from sin and stained with death could possibly offer a little mortal like me. It's not much. It's awkward, the position hurts and I'm nauseous from my multiple orgasms, but I relish in the twisted pleasure only he can give to me.

"Death's new pet," he nips at the sensitive skin on my neck and a whimper slips from my lips. I feel the way his talons caress my soft skin, and it could easily be mistaken for some sort of affection. But, in reality, I know that he is carving light scratches into my skin from the slight burn.

Still inside of me, I feel his hard cock grow as he teases himself. My walls clamp around him deliciously. Then, he forces me back around, so my legs are wrapped around him, and he presses his huge erection against the entrance of my pussy. However, he doesn't push forward.

"Do you feel what you do to the God of Death, little mortal?"

"Yes," it's little more than a whimper but with my lips parted, he consumes me in his kiss. Every inch of my skin, every thought in my mind, every memory stained into my soul… he steals everything from me and replaces it with unimaginable pleasure. A kiss of Death with the God of Death. I feel my body spark alive despite having just died.

For the first time, he smiles. *Like actually fucking smiles.* His lips tip up against mine, and I feel some sort of happiness seep from him in the most perverse way. I feel drunk on his sin.

"Mine to own for the rest of eternity." He whispers. "Mine to torture. To please. To ruin. To kill over and over again."

EPILOGUE

Three days later.

"There she is," I hear a familiar voice ring through the room.

I tense up before rearing my head around the large back of my chair opposite the sorting stage. I didn't think I could be distracted today. I have a particularly long list of rapists to torture and punish, much to my delight. But that single sentence has me breathless.

"Harley!" I scramble off the chair ungracefully with a squeak. My long, blood-red dress that Death designed for me catches on the skulls protruding from the marble floor as I desperately race across the dark room. I must look like a baby deer on new legs as I stumble towards blackness, searching for that familiar voice. However, before I can get much further, a pair of open arms pull me into a warm embrace. That smoky smell wafts up into my lungs as soon as I'm close to him and it fills me with an immediate sense of relief.

"Oh gosh! You're okay!"

"Well, not really," he chuckles, never letting me go. "I am dead."

Frantically, I pull away from him to get a better look but it's futile. I'm no longer under the blaring spotlight hitting the stage and we are secluded by shadows. With a light tug, I yank him towards the stage, but something stops him from getting any closer. As though I've pulled him into a wall, he grunts and falls flat against something invisible.

I squeak. "What?"

"Death said I can't enter his Realm. There is a curse to keep creatures out, including me." I hear Harley sigh and it makes my heart constrict. Before the despair can sink in any further, he continues talking. "But he did mention loopholes. I can be on *this* side of the room to visit you. It's one of the borders between Realms."

"I can't see you though!"

As though hearing my complaints, the room suddenly explodes bright red, casting a torch over us, and Harley is instantly revealed.

"Oh fuck!" I cry out in shock. I fall backwards and land on my ass ungracefully.

The man in front of me is *nothing* like before. The man I once knew had his whole body stained with red-raw burns and scars, but now, his tan skin is smooth and without any imperfections. He holds himself more confidently too, head high, chin jutted out, and his smile actually curls the way it should. What takes my breath away, however, is the paleness of his fluffy hair. It falls into his face, and he must keep blowing at it to be able to see, revealing the bluest eyes I've ever seen.

I can't help but see the resemblance now to Carolina in his psychological trial and my heart constricts painfully at his boyish charm that was snatched by fire and suicide. He goes to reach out to help me up but some invisible forcefield pushes him gently away. If he's offended by my complete overreaction, he doesn't show it.

"It's all gone," he says proudly, twisting around to give me a better look. "I look just how I did before my *first* death."

I am utterly speechless as he yet again makes light of a dark situation. Even in a new physical form, his dry humour stands firm.

"Go on," his cheeky smile returns, "tell me how handsome I am."

A short pause sifts between us, but he taps his foot against the ground impatiently to fill the void. "I'm waiting."

His lightness seems to snap me out of my shock, and I push myself onto my feet with a smirk. "Can't. It's a sin to lie!"

He snorts unattractively. "You're in Hell. I think you're allowed to sin."

I can't help the smile that tugs my lips at the playful banter. I've never been quick-witted or one for humour, so I do what I do best and send a cheeky jab into his ribs. He tries to fight back, but I quickly move.

"And here I thought you'd get faster once you hit immortality." I mock him, jumping back into his side of the room to give him more of a chance. I poke him again in the stomach. Pathetically, he holds it with a pout.

"Ow! Not my belly fat. That's not kind."

"What? You're still afraid to fight me?" I tease him. "Afraid you'll lose *again?*"

He grabs his chest and feigns that he's taken offence. "Not my fault your owner killed me!"

"Survival of the fittest, I guess."

It's fucking insane how our dark humour keeps our sanity intact, but I wouldn't have it any other way.

"Tell me, Death's New Pet," his smile turns twisted. "Did you get your revenge?"

The dark shimmer in my eyes does all the talking for me.

Harley smiles brighter. "Fantastic."

Before I can say anything else, I feel another presence flash into the room with us. Death doesn't waste a moment before pulling my body into his large embrace. I instantly melt into his touch and get drunk off his musky scent.

"*There.* We are even now." He says the words as though he has delivered on a burden, but the tone of his voice screams an ulterior motive.

"Thank you," I whisper. I feel Death's hot breath against my cheek, and I nuzzle into him. A slight rumble slips from his lips as though he is groaning in approval. It makes my body burn deliciously.

"I would also like to thank you," Harley speaks up. My head snaps in his direction and I frown. Death seizes up behind me.

"Don't—" he starts but Harley doesn't back down.

"I am really grateful that you let me say goodbye to my family before I was sorted. That's all I've ever wanted. Just that one last conversation to apologise."

He quickly dismisses the act of kindness. "Whatever. It was just to stop you both bitching."

My heart lurches from my chest. I try to turn back around to face Death, but his claws lock onto my hips and he forces me forward. He refuses to let me see the blush which most likely stains his cheeks. He will never let me see him do anything nice or kind or sweet for anybody.

Of course not. And I'm almost thrilled to play ignorant.

We are creatures of the night; banished to the darkest Realm of Hell for all of eternity; bound together by a fucked-up deal with the Devil.

There is no such thing as goodness down here.

But maybe, *just maybe*, there might be something called love. If love includes the deranged, fucked-up promises we carve into each other's souls.

CHAPTER ONE OF DELPHI DECEIVED

(This is set wayyyyy before Death's New Pet).

THREE WEEKS IN THE FUTURE

My body threatens to give away as I force it to charge faster and faster down the hallway. The darkness consumes my surroundings, but I have meticulously remembered every single twist and turn in this wicked house. A banging sound echoes around me, though I am not sure if it's the monster's footsteps behind me or the pounding of my heart.

I lurch around the corner with lightning precision. The rough carpeted floor sinks its teeth into my bare feet, making me wince, but I don't give it another thought. I cannot afford to give it another thought.

Faster. Further. I continue my escape.

Eventually, a towering room with a golden staircase greets me, dimly lit up by the floating lamps. The stench of bleach fills my nose, slithering up my nostrils like tiny snakes, suffocating me. My lungs burn fiercely and my eyes stream at the pain. But it's better than the metallic twang of blood that usually swarms around the mansion. *His* home. *My* prison.

I thrust my hand out into the centre of the room and the scarlet-coloured pixels shoot out of my palm. Like fire licking my fingers, the pixels burn me, turning my pale skin red. I wince at the uncomfortable feeling but force more pixels out. I must escape! I must escape— no matter the cost!

Hope starts to brim in my stomach as they form a circle and race around like cars on a track. Faster and faster, but not fast enough! They should be creating a portal to get me out of here, but instead, the sparkles now lamely fall to the floor.

I throw my other hand out to try again. *Nothing.*

With a grunt, I hoist up my weighted dress and continue running. I rub the sweat out of my eyes with my elbow. It's not safe for me to remain still for long, he's close behind. I can feel him. I can smell him: warm, musky, and furious.

"Great Goddess of the world," I pant as I charge up the stairs. Despite the majority of the dress being bundled into my arms, the length still catches me up. I stumble and fall. My hands shoot out, narrowly saving myself from face-planting the oak stairs. My now bruised knees and palms scream out instead.

"Of Heaven and Earth, and everything in between. Of life, death, and purgatory. Of the past, present, and future," I chant my curse as I scramble to my feet to continue my ascent. A nagging feeling in the back of my mind begs me to look back to see if he is catching me. But I know better than that. Never look back. Never give the Predator the satisfaction of seeing the fear in your eyes.

"Of…"

My foggy mind thumps in my head as I desperately try to

remember the words. It has been over nine hundred centuries since I last had to speak my magic into existence. Usually, my fingers remember the wicked dance of a curse. But they have snatched my magic from me; they have made my body weak and magicless. I am defenceless against the monster hunting me. It's all their fucking fault!

"Of something and something else." I grunt, "Life and death? No, fuck, I've said that already!"

I skid to a halt and tear my gaze to the three metal doors in front of me. A deafening boom rips out from behind me as the monster advances closer and closer. The door doesn't budge as I yank on the handle. I try the other two quickly, but my fate is the same. All three doors are locked. They all bend to his wishes… to keep me captured. Cornered. Helpless.

"Delphi!" The beast's roar echoes around the room, sending shivers through my body. The sound is like no other. Everything shakes and for a moment it feels as though the walls and ceilings might give way. At least that would be a quick death. Much quicker than the one he has in store for me.

"Delphi!" he hollers again. This time, a strangled cry of frustration leaves my lips and I yank on the handle again, pleading for it to open. But it's no use. I can now feel him in the room with me. Frightened, I spin around and peer down the stairs. If I can just maintain this distance between us, perhaps I'll be safe. Maybe I can escape?

All thoughts of hope escape from me when those black eyes sink into mine. His body heaves as he pants, and his suit threatens to explode from the assault of his expanding muscles. Raven-coloured hair tumbles into his eyes but it doesn't matter, I can feel those dark orbs trailing up my body, taking in every inch of me. Those fucking eyes never miss a single spot.

His lip twitches upward as he growls. "What is the next line, darling?"

My heart leaps in my chest. Desperately, I throw my palms out in the hope of my magic returning. Now more than ever I need protection. Again, the pixels miserably tumble to the ground. Shit!

"Stay away from me!" I shriek, and my voice cracks. It's a pathetic sound, like the noise a baby deer makes before the lion closes its teeth around its neck. His head cocks to the side and if possible, his expression darkens.

"I mean it!" I try again weakly but I stumble to a halt before I can spit out any insult or threat. What can I really do to protect myself from the God of Power? He controls everything, and soon he'll control me.

"Don't make me repeat myself, witch!" he snaps. Suddenly, he is no longer standing still at the bottom of the stairs, silently seething. Now, he is taking the stairs in twos.

The cry leaves my lips before I can stop myself, "No! No! Get away!"

He ignores it and quickly ascends closer to me. Mortified, I stumble backwards until my back is firmly pressed up against the middle door. The coldness seeps through the thin mesh material of my dress and I shiver. My mind races as I silently pray for it to swallow me up, to save me from the monster's advances.

"What's the..."

"I- I don't know!" I half whimper, half yell before he can finish. Amused by my reaction, his lip twitches. It isn't a smile, but it isn't a frown either. The only thing I can liken it to is a lion's mouth twitching as it readies itself for the kill.

With a huff, I lurch left to jump around him, but he is much faster.

Suddenly, his mighty grip fastens my wrists together and he slams me up against the door. I flinch as the sound almost deafens me. A hungry look courses through his eyes. His tongue shoots out and he licks his lips, desperately trying to taste my fear in the air between us. I can't tear my gaze away from the fangs which slightly protrude now.

"Let go! Let go! For fuck sake, Power, please let me go!" I beg, but it's no use. If I have learnt anything about Power, it's that once he sets his mind on something, he does it. My anxious thoughts do nothing to calm me down. He's going to kill me. He's going to eat me alive. After all, he is Power incarnate and I'm his lowly Priestess. His Prisoner. His sacrifice.

"Luckily, I do," he says smugly. I feel his hot, teasing breath taunt the skin between my neck and ear. A shiver takes hold of me. The sensation promises so much pain.

"Oh, high Priestess, of pain and…" he begins. The colour drains from my face. I know the next line. "Go on," he nudges me, "Tell me, what is the next word?"

The whimper is small and desperate as it falls from my lips, "Submission."

"Exactly," he bares his fangs in a wicked smirk. "And that's why you won't be leaving. I own you. And you *will* be my sacrifice."

I frantically try to think of the next line of my curse, to call my magic back, but the lyrics are like granules of sand racing through my fingers. I can't seem to grasp the slippery fuckers! He wraps those malicious arms around me and yanks me flush against his body. Then, I feel his sharp fangs scrape against my neck.

"Ah, so close to escaping, sweet Delphi," he grunts. The sound is tense and almost desperate like he can't tell whether he wants to fuck or kill me. That malicious smile spreads across his face when I gulp.

Much to my fear, he continues his sentence, "So close and yet *so far*."

EXCITING NEWS

'lOVE AFTER LIFE' SERIES WILL CONTINUE!

This is a set of twisted, erotic, fantasy, stand-alone novels focusing on obsessive & unhinged dark romances.

You've read:

Death's New Pet

Next in the series:

Delphi Deceived. (Out Jan 2024.)

BOOKS BY THIS AUTHOR

We Shouldn't

A dark, erotic reverse Harem romance novel.

Rebecca:

I just needed to be alone and write my new romance novel—two simple, achievable tasks— until my dad's hot best friend, Brandon, shows up in my life again. Promising to help me research for my new book, he introduces me to his sex club, but that's where I meet his two irresistible brothers: Dags and Vixen. I soon realise that Dags is an insane murderer and Vixen is my obsessive stalker. Yet I can't help but spread my legs for them whenever they command it.
And then the pact is made: play with each brother for a week, and by the end of it, I must decide which brother gets to fuck me first.

Sounds simple enough on paper but a death sentence for sinful desires. Must I really choose just one brother, or can I have them all?

Please Don't Make Me Kill Him

I fell in love with the man I was supposed to kill, and the man who wants to kill me. Both relationships are forbidden, but I've always craved sin. Must I choose only one, or can I have both?

Isla
Being a killer is scorched into my DNA. I infiltrate my target's lives to gain information about them before I make my fatal hit, all in the name of profit. For twenty years, I never made an error. And then Lucius's name appeared on my hit list. I never anticipated that he would teach me that life without sin is incredibly delicious. And now I must choose between his love and my mission.

Titan
Isla Morris is as good as dead. One day, I will crush that pretty little monster, and I will give my murdered family the justice they deserve. She will regret the day she ever missed my name from her hit list. But first, I want to play with her as much as she played with my family. Her dark love is tasty, but I hunger for her ruin even more.

Mr Anderson

It is scandalous. It is forbidden. And yet it feels so right!

When Willow is forced to return to University after a tragic incident, the school assigns her a tutor to get her back on track. This tutor, Mr. Anderson, is everything Willow tries so desperately to avoid: dangerous, unpredictable and completely irresistible.
Despite the risks, Willow finds herself head over heels for the gorgeous man with the mysterious past, and very quickly learns that nothing is as it seems.
As she battles her intense attraction for her tutor and the chaotic life events unravelling around her, she is forced to solve the one question she cannot answer no matter how hard she tries: who really is Mr. Anderson?

Illegal Activities

After Maya is freed from the Russian Mafia prison, she falls into the arms of another Mafia boss- Alessio Morisso. She swore that she would never become a prisoner again, but after stirring up a war with her feisty and sarcastic attitude, she is no longer safe to return home. The only way to ensure her survival is to marry Alessio.

However, beautiful and bold Maya will not be an obedient little housewife. On the contrary, she wishes for control and to escape. But when the lines blur between wanting to escape and desiring her new husband, Maya finds herself doubting everything she knew about herself.
Could she really resist his charms or must she join forces with him to take revenge against the Russians?

Made in United States
Troutdale, OR
12/02/2023

15237945R00136